She knew Holly had been murdered, but now she was in danger too...

There was a knock at the door and Kenya yanked it open, thinking it was the maid service. A strange woman was standing there and something about her spelled trouble. "Miss Shekenya West?"

"Yes, that's me."

"I'm here to collect my niece's remains."

It took a frozen second to react. The woman slid inside the open door and stood there like a monument to hard living, her face a map of wrinkles and scars, crossing over each other like conflicting road signs. "That your boy you were talking to? Bet he's as good-looking as his daddy. And you, too. You turned out mighty fine-looking. Real pretty."

Something about the woman put Kenya on guard. "How do I know you're Holly's aunt? I never heard her mention you and she and I were close. Close as sisters. Why are you just now showing up?"

The woman opened her purse and took out a picture. A very young woman was holding a plump, laughing baby. "That's Holly's first birthday. She was a real cute little thing. That's me, would you believe?"

"That doesn't prove anything. Look, Mrs..."

"Willis, Hannah Willis."

"Mrs. Willis, I'm in kind of a hurry to get on the road. I've got to get back to work, okay? Can we have this talk some other time?"

"How about, like, now?" A sleazy little man, pretending to be unlocking the next unit, turned back and pulled a gun out of his jacket pocket. He backed her into the room, followed by the woman who shut the door with a bang. Kenya backed up until her knees hit the couch and she sat down hard.

The Mama Tree lives in the Thicket, a place so wild it hides all kinds of creatures who don't want to be seen. Prayer bundles and gris-gris bags dangle from its matronly branches like ornaments on a mother goddess. It has hidden Kenya and her disfigured face until, healed by the loving care of her grandmother, she emerges again, morphed into Chantal West, the sexy R&B Princess of Memphis. Her triumph is shattered when the body of her childhood friend Holly Simpson is found in a dumpster. Could the fresh tattoo on the body possibly be a caricature of her killer? Kenya has hit many bumps on the road of life, and even some ditches, but there are no air bags for this one. Detective Grover Moss knows in one millisecond that this crazy, beautiful woman is the love he is looking for and, in the next millisecond, that she will be the cartoon killer's next victim unless Moss finds him first.

KUDOS for *The Mama Tree*

In *The Mama Tree* by Trisha O'Keefe, we go back to Julia Springs, Georgia, with Kenya Jones, all grown up now and singing for a living. In fact, she is now Chantel West, the current R and B princess of the South, singing up and down the East Coast and even out in Las Vegas. But Kenya's life turns upside down when her friend Holly is murdered and Kenya's own life is threatened. She finds a protector in Memphis Detective, Grover Moss, who follows her down to Georgia and even to Switzerland, attempting to keep her safe from a maniacal killer, who's trying to kill everyone she cares about. O'Keefe's character development is superb, her plot strong, and the tension builds with every page. This is a good book for when you can't sleep, as you won't want to put it down until you get to the end. ~ *Taylor Jones, Reviewer*

The Mama Tree by Trisha O'Keefe is her second book about Julia Springs, Georgia; the swamp called the Thicket; and the strange characters who reside there. In this episode, Kenya Jones, who was fourteen in the last book and killed her pedophilia stepfather in self-defense, has grown into a lovely young woman with a voice like an angel, becoming Chantel West, a rhythm-and-blues diva. Her friend Holly Simpson calls her right before a performance asking for money or someone is going to kill her. Kenya knows that Holly wants the money for alcohol or drugs, so she tells her to call her tomorrow and hangs up to go and perform. But the next morning she finds out that Holly's body was discovered in a dumpster, and the guilt Kenya feels is outrageous. She vows to find out who killed Holly and make them pay. But when she gets a call threatening her life and that of her six-year-old son, she panics, and calls the detective who had informed her of Holly's death, Grover Moss. He takes his vacation time and drives south to Georgia, both because he doesn't want anything to happen to her or her son, and because he can't get her out of his mind. What follows is a hilarious, harrowing, suspenseful escapade that will make you laugh, make you cry, and make you chew your fingernails. A wonderfully entertaining read. ~ *Regan Murphy, Reviewer*

ACKNOWLEDGEMENTS

To my immediate family, who just about made this book impossible, and to my extended family my cheering section, especially my cousin Jack and his wife Janet, cousins Pam and Kim. To Lara, my long-suffering editor who proves that two pair of eyes are better than one tired pair.

The
MAMA
Tree

Trisha O'Keefe

A Black Opal Books Publication

GENRE: PARANORMAL THRILLER/WOMEN'S FICTION/SUSPENSE

THE MAMA TREE
Copyright © 2016 by Trisha O'Keefe
Cover Design by Jackson Cover Designs
All cover art copyright © Trisha O'Keefe
All Rights Reserved
Print ISBN: 978-1-626944-71-8

First Publication: JUNE 2016

Published by Black Opal Books **http://www.blackopalbooks.com**

The
MAMA
Tree

Chapter 1

S
even minutes, Miss Chantal."

"I hear you, Jimmy."

In her dressing room at the hotel two blocks from the Mississippi, Kenya was spinning a cocoon round her fragile ego. When she emerged from its nurturing threads, she would be Chantal West, The R & B Princess of Song.

It was a ritual she had gone through nightly for ten years, morphing into someone else until she almost believed the hype her agent put out in almost every form of media imaginable. Her face had even appeared on the little cocktail napkins and coasters in the hotel bar where she performed until Kenya herself had put a stop to it.

"I'm not a parking place for some drunk's drink," Kenya had told her agent. "Or a place to wipe his mouth."

To make sure the name, like the face in the mirror, belonged to Chantal West, she studied her reflection for any clue the plastic surgeons had left behind. The R & B Princess sounded like she was some kind of royalty, not a girl who had helped kill a man and bury him in quicklime. A girl so disfigured that pregnant women used to make a cross with their fingers and spit as she passed.

Not a girl who had been beaten, burned, and then turned out of the house by her own mother.

Just like in the old horror movies where ordinary people turned into werewolves and vampires, Kenya Jones morphed nightly into Chantal West. It was so ridiculous—no, her life was so ridiculous, Kenya burst out laughing. *Ridiculous, but awesome.* Somebody, a lover or a friend, had said it and she owned it—everything that went with being Chantal West.

"Hello, baaaby…" Her alarm snapped her back to her showbiz self. Five minutes until show time. No time to feel sorry for the little girl she used to be. She was billed as the hottest act in town. And with Memphis being the town, that was some kind of hot.

With a steady hand, Kenya added another coat to the eyelashes of Chantal West, The R&B Princess. To make sure her eyes didn't crinkle at the corners, she showed her perfect teeth in a wide smile. Sexy, sultry, provocative— the adjectives used to describe her skittered through her mind like dry leaves across ruts in a dirt road.

Despite the hype and the perfect smile, she thought of her mind as looking like an empty house—the echoes of children's laughter lurking in the dark corners of rooms with gaping closets No life inside, no fire.

'*Listen!*' A familiar voice rumbled like thunder inside her head. '*And be warned, baby girl.*'

Despite the urgency of the moment, Kenya froze, mascara brush in midair, practiced smile frozen. In the mirror, her own image was being replaced by tall, ghostly ferns, arching up from a forest floor where a tree cast a shadow as big as God's hand. A tree where, across decades, people hung their prayer bundles or the gri-gri bags, curing them, dangling from its matronly branches like ornaments adorning a mother goddess.

She knew that tree very well. The Mama Tree embodied all that was natural and sane—the tree and Root Woman, her Aya. The Mama Tree lived in the Thicket, a place so wild, it hid all kinds of creatures who didn't want to be seen, even herself as a child.

The Mama Tree had soothed her wounds and sheltered her until Aya had found her, cradled in its roots, thick as arms. Aya told her all the smaller trees around were The Mama Tree's children because they had sprung from her seeds. Like a good mother, The Mama Tree protected them with her branches until they grew up and got sassy. Then they were on their own. But since she was strong with years and wisdom, the kids didn't roam very far away. They always came back to be family again—and so the forest grew.

Kenya really had to smile at the thought. Aya was big on family, especially put-together families like hers. They made the world go round, families did. That's what her Aya, the Root Woman used to say. She was a healer whose medicine was found in the natural world of South Georgia. A hoo-doo priestess who mixed Christianity and paganism with the same care that she mixed poultices and potions, knowing the individuals they were meant for.

Early on, sometime after the Great War, Aya had wandered from the coast inland, from village to hamlet, until she had settled not far from Julia Springs in a remote place called the Thicket. The Mama Tree was already there, presiding over her extended brood. Aya knew right away that's where she wanted to build her church, sheltered by The Mama Tree.

Kenya sensed Aya was watching her from afar, wherever that was. '*Is that you, Aya? What you want? What's going to happen?*'

The familiar voice said, '*You never know what life's going to bring.*'

Her cellphone played a riff from *Blueberry Hill*,

shattering the vision. Kenya put down the mascara brush and shook off the presence of Aya before pushing the speaker button. She already knew by the ringtone it was Holly. Holly always meant trouble.

"Hey, girl, you'll never guess what I heard today."

No matter how far from the Thicket she came, even here in Memphis, Kenya had always dragged the past with her—in memory *and* the person of Holly Simpson. Holly was one of those remnants of the past Kenya had tried to cover just as she did her own scars.

Slightly dazed, she fumbled among the jars and bottles, not wanting to deal with the mess Holly inevitably brought when she called—drugs, always money, her probation officer, pimps—not now, when she was getting psyched to go on.

With a sigh, she pressed the speaker button. "I never will so tell me, but make it fast. I got to go on in a minute." She had to sound too busy to deal with her friend's messes. But Holly qualified as family, so that meant Kenya had to take time for family, especially when Holly was about all there was beside Freddy and Sheldon.

"You remember back home? Where your grandma used to live? The Thicket they used to call it. They're going to make it a shopping center. Put an All-4-A-Dollar store in there and everything. Can you see that? All those little yellow plastic bags they got floating all over the place? Your grandma would have a fit. She'd slap a curse on them so fast, they wouldn't know what was what."

Kenya felt like somebody had grabbed her by the throat and was choking the air out of her. *That is sacred ground, only yards from The Mama Tree.* "You mean in the Thicket?" Her voice sailed up a few octaves. She wanted to tell Holly what she had just seen in the mirror, but there wasn't time. "They can't do that. That's swamp ground, girl, an All-4-A-Dollar store'll just disappear overnight. Sink into the mud." She emphasized by snapping her fingers with their painted fingernails. "Gone!"

"Not going to be swamp any more. They're going to drain it and pave it over. Some ol' crazy developer!" Holly was high. That wasn't news. Holly usually was.

"Three minutes, Miss Chantal." Her grip stuck his head in the door and closed it like a cuckoo on a German clock.

"Who's that? Chantal, who?"

Kenya picked up the phone. Taking the speaker off, she said urgently. "My grip. Listen, I've got to go pee. Later. Call me tomorrow not too early, okay? I got a late night tonight."

"I heard him say Chantal. That what you call yourself now? Chantal?" She could tell Holly was playing with her, holding out the approval she knew Kenya yearned for. "Mmmm, yeah. I like it. Kinda got sizzle to it."

Kenya rolled her eyes. "They called me that a long time now, Holly." Why didn't the girl take the hint? "Yeah, listen, I got to go on. Call me, ya hear?"

Here it comes, the touch. Every conversation with Holly ended with hitting her up for fifty dollars here, two hundred dollars there, then a thousand. Now, the desperation in Holly's voice told her it was going to be more. "Kenya, baby, I need to borrow some money real bad. I swear I'll pay you back. Maybe I can sing backup like we used to, remember those days? When we first started out with Reverend Jeremiah?" Her voice skittered upward like joint smoke toward the ceiling. "'Member how we did 'Wading in the Water'? Got us a couple of gigs."

"We did that. I remember. But you got so you didn't show up. You still got the habit, Holly. I know that's why you called. You need money. We'll talk tomorrow. I got to go now. Call me tomorrow, okay?"

The wheedling grew to a whine."But I need the money right now, Kenya. A whole lot of money or they'll kill me."

Kenya sighed with growing impatience. With Holly, it was always life or death. That was the world she lived in. "I've got to go, Holly. We'll talk tomorrow, okay/"

Clinging to the phone call like it was a rope and she was drowning, Holly asked. "How's Sheldon?"

"Growing like a weed, eating like a horse. Bye, Holly."

The voice on the other end grew plaintive. "Kiss him for his Auntie Holly, ya hear?"

"We'll talk later," Kenya said, knowing already what she was going to say. *You need help, Holly No amount of money's going to save you.*

She heard the Shades of Grey warming up with "Lullaby of Birdland," and she was out the door before she realized she still had the phone in her hand. Rick, the owner of the Jazz Club, was saying. "Please welcome the glamorous Miss Chantal West and the Shades of Grey." She threw the phone to a stage hand and walked on under the spotlights, half Kenya Jones, half Chantal West. The morph had been interrupted by Holly's phone call, reminding her what reality was about.

The spots from the disco ball danced over her lithe body, her blue sequined dress clinging to her, poured on as a second skin. But behind the whistles and admiring eyes, she felt the threats of a well-known predator. Man. She knew him well—in her dreams, her nightmares, invading the sanctuary of her body, choking the life out of her.

Chantal West could face them boldly, with fierce eyes, a sultry voice, and words sharp enough to draw blood. She showed them lots of leg, deep cleavage, drooping blue-shadowed eyelids, *everything* but her scars, now papered-over by layers of her inner thigh and makeup to hide the difference in skin tone.

Miss Chantal could do it all, even give encores, receiving notes with hundred dollar bills tucked in bouquets of roses with suggestive questions: Would she spend a few hours with an admirer? How about a whole night? Chantal West scribbled "Go to hell!" on each card and sent them back. It was all the same to her if they never received it, and the stagehand split the hundred with the doorman, dumping all those roses in the trash can.

ʚ৲ঌেৎ

The stagehand had put the phone back in her dressing room, but Kenya had gone home without it, thinking it was in her purse where she usually kept it. That was why she didn't find it until late the next afternoon when she went in for rehearsal.

When she located it, there was a call from Holly, and also a one from another number, a strange number. So she called that one first, thinking someone at the school might be calling about Sheldon's afterschool program, where he stayed until Mrs. Bradley picked him up. Knowing Sheldon, he was probably in trouble for something.

Instead, a man answered. "Moss here."

"You called me? Name's Chantal West."

There was a pause while he fumbled through some papers. Finally, he said. "Miss West, do you know somebody named Holly Simpson?"

"Why? Who wants to know?"

There was a tired sigh at the other end. "Miss West, I'm a detective with the Memphis Police Department. I'm calling regarding a one Holly Simpson. You know her or not?"

"Is she in trouble again?" It was the usual story: Holly was in jail and a detective was calling, which usually meant a felony. Already, Kenya's mind was mentally thumbing through the pages of attorneys she knew.

"I'm afraid she's dead."

Detective Moss had just dropped a bomb on the world of Miss Chantal, the R&B Princess. She listened as Moss read off the grim details from the police report. Holly had been found in a dumpster by the river, her throat cut. Her hands tied with wire, her mouth gagged with a bloody rag. She had been beaten so badly about the face and head that it was only by the rest of her that Kenya identified the friend who loved her like a sister.

There was a childish tattoo on her upper right arm— a crude heart with H.S. loves K.J. done with an ink pen and needle long ago. Kenya knew it well. She had it put there when they were on the road with Reverend Jeremiah's Gospel Choir. As she listened, Kenya Jones rubbed her own upper arm as it tingled in sympathy with her friend's pain.

Detective Moss droned on as if he was reading a car manual on how to change a spark plug. "The body was covered in needle tracks," he said, "and an artful tattoo of a shark riding in something with wheels—a skateboard or a scooter." Detective Moss didn't recognize the tattoo artist. He was familiar with most of them, but it was fresh. He put out the word at all the tattoo parlors in Memphis to find out who did it. He knew some guys, he assured her. Everything he said sounded like the TV news from another room, just noise. All Kenya could see was her friend's golden arm, the one she had felt around her at the worst times in her life, sticking out from beneath a sheet as if it were detached.

"She had a habit, I take it," he said, jolting her back to reality.

"Sorry, what's that?"

Moss repeated the question. He sounded tired, as if he'd been up all night the night before and every night before that.

'*Don't speak ill of the dead. They been through a lot just living.*' Kenya ignored the warning. "She had a lot of bad habits. You name it, Holly did it. She had so much to give, so much love, but she just wasted it, just threw it away. Alcohol, pills, mainlining, Holly did it all."

In the end, reluctantly because it was the last thing on earth that she thought she would ever have to do, Kenya agreed to identify Holly Simpson so they could get on with their investigation.

When Kenya walked into the Memphis Central Law Enforcement Center, heads turned in her direction, heads that usually didn't turn unless somebody was holding a weapon or throwing something.

The young woman in uniform behind the front desk fumbled for a pen, her face lighting with a wide smile. "You're Chantal West, aren't you? Me and my boyfriend caught your act at the Hilton the other night and thought you were really awesome. Can I have your autograph?" She pushed a notepad and pen through the window in the bulletproof glass.

Detective Moss looked just like he sounded, big and tired, and there were bags under his eyes, as if he hadn't slept more than three hours consecutively for years. And he was wedge-shaped, like he had been breaking down doors on nights when he should have been grabbing Z's.

Something happened in his eyes when he saw her. It was as though, just for that moment, he saw her standing in his doorway in a floaty, yellow dress. Grover Moss was aware of winter turning to spring in the drab city around him. "Miss West, I'm Detective Moss. Come in and sit a minute. I know this is a hard time for you."

She sat down because, all at once, she didn't want to be there, and if she remained standing, she would run out the door. Somewhere in the back of her mind, Kenya had always been afraid Holly would end up the way she had, murdered, her body thrown in a dumpster. But dealing with it was something else entirely.

She sat on the hard edge of her chair, holding onto the purse in her lap as if it were going to take flight. Detective Moss's deep voice kept coming from far away, as if she was drowning and he was trying to throw her a rope. But she kept slipping farther and farther down inside her mind, seeing Holly's face, hearing the funny way she used to talk, telling jokes, laughing…

When she snapped out of it, Moss was there in front of her, lighting a cigarette and giving it to her.

"I don't smo—" she started to say and then took a drag. "Thank you. When can we go? Identify her, I mean." She couldn't even say the word "body."

"I'm sorry I had to ask you to come down here, Miss West. I know it's hard, but I found your picture in her purse. You'd signed the back of it."

He fished in a manila envelope and brought out a wallet-sized photo of her taken during the time they were in Reverend Jeremiah's Gospel Choir. Her hair looked awful—kind of a fro with bangs. It was just after her first plastic surgery to fix the damage to her eye, and she thought at the time that she looked beautiful. Holly must have, too. Fifteen years ago. Sweet Holly had still kept that picture instead of all the glamorous publicity shots Kenya had given her. It was as if someone had handed Kenya back her teenage years.

Moss droned on, unaware of the memories the picture had resurrected. "There was nothing else in it. They took everything valuable, I'm afraid, phone, wallet, but I found this one scrap of paper with your number on it. It was tucked in a zipper pocket with the picture. Funny how the thieves didn't even bother taking it. The things that are most precious to us are not the things they steal."

With numb fingers, Kenya took the crumpled scrap of paper from him. It was from her kitchen notepad. She had scribbled her private cell phone number, available only to the school and a select few. Holly had been one of them. Kenya wiped tears away quickly, afraid there were more she couldn't stop. "She called me last night, just before I was to go on. Wanted money."

"She say what for?"

"Didn't say exactly what for. Usually drugs or bail. But she sounded scared, said they were going to kill her. Could I please have a drink of water?"

"I've got something better." Detective Moss went around to his desk and came back with a small bottle of vodka. "Do you mind if I don't have ice?"

She felt better after a long drink from a Styrofoam cup. "I believe that will do me 'til I get home. Thanks for the drink, Sergeant Moss"

"It's Detective. Did she say who was going to kill her? Who she was going to pay? A dealer, her pimp, maybe?"

That was the first time she knew Holly was into prostitution. Kenya stood up, then sat down again. "No, she didn't mention names. Kind of crowd she hung around with doesn't go by names. If they have names, I don't want to know. Can we go get it over with now?"

It was bad, so bad that, even though they kept Holly's face covered with a sheet, Kenya retched up her lunch in the morgue drain. The only way she could identify her childhood friend was by the pen and ink tattoo on her upper arm, H.S. Loves K. J.

"Can I drive you home or get somebody to give you a lift? Your husband? Boyfriend?"

Is he hitting on me? "No, thank you, Detective." She hoped the ice in her voice would put him off, but not too far off. Kenya knew then she needed Detective Moss more than she had ever needed anyone in her life

Kenya, aka Chantal, had hit many bumps on the road of life, and some ditches. There were no air bags for this one. It was as if part of herself had ended up in that dumpster, part of her life.

The detective whose name was Grover, first or last she couldn't remember, said she could have the body when the coroner was finished with it. It sounded like she was having her car repaired.

"I'll be wanting to ask you some questions, but not now." He was making an effort to be kind—she sensed that. Her body felt rigid, hardened like the shell of a turtle. Inside was the silent scream of a living creature without a voice. "We'll find whoever did this and make him pay."

"Yeah, right," she burst out, wanting to hurt him, the man who had delivered this blow to her life. Like the many men before him who had inflicted so much pain. "Like you give a rat's ass about somebody like her. Well, let me tell you something about Holly you never knew, okay? She was a good person and she loved my son and me. She loved us. Her daddy was a rolling stone, you know what I mean? Her mother was a druggie, usually in prison for dealing. What kind of chance would you stand with a druggie for a mother, huh? She never had a chance, never."

Spring changed back to winter in Detective Moss's eyes. A winter night, in fact. "I know. I see way too many of them. Way too many. But it's also nice to see someone who's made a success of her life. Like you, Miss West. I've heard you sing around town. Nice to meet you at last. Sorry it had to be under unpleasant circumstances."

Moss winced, knowing he had said the wrong thing by the look on Kenya's face.

She got up, a slender beautiful lily in her yellow dress, which she would go home and burn in her marble fireplace. "I'll see myself out. Goodbye, Mr. Moss."

Moss could have kicked himself for always saying the wrong thing to pretty women. He had compared the dead girl and Chantal West as if they were equals. Chantal had everything going for her—beauty, talent, charisma, dedication.

Her friend obviously had little in the way of resources, a fact the unapproachable Miss West had pointed out herself.

Still, he stood in the doorway to his office, watching her go, thinking some lucky man was going to comfort her tonight.

Kenya managed to drive herself home, burning the dress while belting lime-flavored vodka, then crawled up the stairs to Sheldon's room. She awoke to find him snuggled beside her in his narrow bed, smelling of soap and barbeque chips.

Her son stroked her cheek with little-boy fingers. "You sick, Mommy?"

"Your mama's just sad, baby."

"Why? Why you sad?"

"'Cause your mama gotta go home, my baby. Just 'cause she's gotta go home now, and she hates to leave you, is why."

"But *surprise*! You *are* home now. You're home, so sing me a lullaby, okay?"

"Okay." She sang with tears running down her cheeks as she cradled the child that had become hers tonight.

Chapter 2

When the autopsy was over, the coroner's office released Holly's body to Kenya since no one else came forward. She made arrangements with a funeral home to have Holly cremated and they gave her the remains in a biodegradable carton that said Simpson on it neatly printed on a label. It was a weird sensation, holding her friend in her hands.

Holly, who had been part of a chosen family—mother to her son, surrogate sister—was now reduced to a pile of gray ashes. Aya, the venerable Root Woman, had always told her that people were just made of dirt and they would eventually return to dirt, but Kenya hadn't really believed that was possible until now.

To give her death some dignity, Kenya bought a fancy urn at a shop run by a Chinese man. He had said it was carved soapstone, pale green with an intricate design. She asked the funeral home attendant—he called himself a funereal consultant—if he would transfer the ashes to the urn. He was a little miffed and said something about they usually didn't do that.

That's when Kenya lost it.

"Well, you damned well better do it now, or I'll sue

the pants off you, you little pissass!" The words weren't even out of her mouth before she realized "Miss Chantal" was only a disguise, a fancy name for Kenya Jones whose step-father raped her over and over until finally Aya had bashed his skull in with a shovel. She apologized to "Pissass" who looked like he had smelled something bad. "Oh, I'm sorry! Just the strain of losing my friend, you know what I'm saying?"

But it seemed that the pissass consultant knew all about her, the whole story. His eyes said he knew she was a fraud from the start, no matter how hard she tried to be genteel. "No problem, miss. I'll be right back in a jiffy."

With the manager, she thought.

But she refused to give in to tears, her mascara would run and that would confirm Pissass's suspicions that she was a fraud. Instead, she sat down, crossed her long legs, and adjusted the veil on her smart hat. She and Holly were going home to Julia Springs, Georgia, riding in style in Kenya's Escalade all the way from Memphis. She would leave Sheldon with the housekeeper. He was doing so well in school she hated him to miss even a couple of days.

Besides, she was afraid they would run into Holly's mother, Marquisa. Above all else, she didn't want Marquisa to know she had the boy. Marquisa sullied everything she touched with her drug habit and her nasty pimps. She'd done hard time for prostitution and drugs, but the state had let her and thousands more like her out early on probation.

Like mud running downhill, Kenya was afraid Holly's mother would somehow learn of her daughter's death and, smelling money, gravitate back to Julia Springs. Knowing Kenya would be back for the funeral, she would try to hit her daughter's rich friend up for anything she could get her hands on.

❧❧❧

It happened just exactly the way Kenya hoped it wouldn't. Marquisa showed up at the Glory Road Church where the green translucent urn sat in state on the gold draped altar.

As if she had been invited, she plunked herself right down next to Kenya in the first row along with all Holly's cousins, uncles and aunts. They were good Baptists who had only darkened the doorway of the Glory Road Church to pay their respects and get a good take-out meal.

None of them looked at Marquisa, ignoring her the way they had ignored Holly and her troubles during her lifetime. Immune to families being torn apart by a disinterested bureaucracy, they gloried in their cohesiveness, their middle-class aspirations and, above all, the purity of the forgiven.

Marquisa whispered to Kenya, so close Kenya could smell the whiskey on her breath. "Hello, missy, you're looking mighty sharp these days. Must be rolling in the green by the looks of that outfit. I hear you've got some gig going in Memphis. We'll have to get together when I'm out that way."

The new priestess was about to speak or Kenya would have gotten up and moved somewhere else. She was forced to listen to the sermon with Holly's mother's whining little whisper in her ear like a persistent mosquito.

"What a life," Marquisa whispered. "I wish I was up there in that urn instead of Holly, people saying good things about me, singing over me, praying over me. Instead, here I am being stiffed by my own family, treated like shit. Holly was killed probably by some sadist John. What a goddam sorry life, and mine is the sorriest."

"Amen to that," somebody in the row behind them said.

The priestess in the stately crimson and saffron robes that Root Woman passed down to her came up to the altar. Placing her hands on the urn, she prayed and a hush fell on the wailing, gossiping congregation. Even the babies stopped fussing. The priestess turned around and looked straight at Kenya.

"Your friend Holly says not to blame yourself for what happened to her. She says she so happy she free and clean, she can't tell you how good it is. She says you've got a life to live and you go live it, and don't cry for her, not even one single tear. Because she's free and happy and feeling all the light come through her heart again. The cleansing light."

Even Marquisa joined the guests in a loud amen.

Leaving the altar, the priestess approached Kenya stretching out her hands. Without hesitating, Kenya gripped hers, knowing what was coming because her grandmother often did the same thing when she was feeling bad, hating herself for being the cast-off object that she was. The priestess placed her hands on Kenya's forehead. At once, all the pain and worry streamed through those brown fingers as if they were tubes of light while the woman swayed and prayed in Geechee-Gullah.

The scratchy voice of Marquisa broke the spell."S'cuse me, aren't you going to bless me? I'm the mother of the deceased." A ripple of outrage went through the assembled guests, but the priestess didn't hesitate. She moved her hands over to Marquisa's weaved head.

"Your daughter says all is forgiven. Go in peace."

Marquisa turned around to the people behind her. "Hear that? My daughter's forgiven me. That means you high and mighty folks ought to, too."

When it was over, the people all filed out to eat the banquet church members had prepared—ham, fried chicken, and fish, mac and cheese, slaw and cornbread, and as many desserts as filled the cookbooks of their grandmothers, enough to furnish a small army. Unapologetically the "small army" marched out, each with several to-go boxes stacked for those "who couldn't attend."

Kenya remained behind, frozen in her expensive black silk dress. She picked up the green urn on the altar, then sat on the steps, cradling what was left of Holly. "I'm sorry I let you down. I will always miss you, but I'm glad you're in a better place, and I swear I'm going to kill the bastard who did it to you." She sat like that long after the service was over, cuddling the green urn, so still that people thought she was asleep.

"We fixed you a plate," they whispered, one by one, approaching where she sat on the step. The women were a composite of the benevolent mother she never had. "Come and eat. You're as thin as a rail." Getting no response, they left her food on the warmer for her.

The priestess knew Kenya was her predecessor's granddaughter. "Leave her here with me. She has to make her own peace with her friend. It may take all night. Just go home and pray for both of them."

So the women of the Glory Road Church went home and prayed for one of their own who was dead, then added a prayer for one of their own who had returned.

Chapter 3

Faun Walker was a winner, everybody in Julia Springs said so. Not only was she beautiful, a trait which defined a winner in the eyes of the old timers, but Faun was also brilliant. An academic star. A winner of the Young Scientist Award three years in a row given by the Phillips Foundation for innovations in science, she was head of her own startup company begun in her sophomore year in college, mapping genes that identified flaws in the way brain tissues developed.

A biotech company had offered to buy her out and keep her on at a mega-salary, but Faun wanted more. She wanted the excitement that comes with discovery and the power to take her company in the direction she chose, not where some board of directors wanted which was inevitably to line their pockets and sell out to a conglomerate. Faun hated the huge conglomerate pharmaceutical companies who controlled the prices of drugs the world over and vowed to protect her fledgling from their predatory CEOs.

Her live-in boyfriend/roommate, Chuck, thought she was crazy for turning down all that money on mere principle and told her so, even when they were making love.

"Baby, you better start mapping your own genetic code to find out whether insanity runs in your family," he whispered.

The next morning on returning from classes, he found his books, blankets, clothes, and miscellaneous stuff on the landing. There was a note clipped to the tee shirt on top of the pile. It said, "Sorry, when it's just too much work to work out, it isn't worth working out. Hope you find someone who keeps you focused without bothering with principles. Faun."

He joined a growing list of ex-boyfriends/roommates.

All her friends and ex-lovers agreed, Faun had a mysterious side. Conversations with Faun Walker either centered on work or love affairs, but usually work. She rarely mentioned her family except her younger brother, Rudy, who they knew played football and had a steady girlfriend every month.

That's why they were surprised to meet her parents when they visited the university one homecoming weekend. Her mother was as beautiful as Faun, but very shy, hardly having anything to say, just nodding and smiling a lot. Her father was a towering monolith as befit a police chief.

The Walkers took everybody out to dinner at fancy places that didn't fit the student budget and sat there glowing with pride but silent, as their daughter and her friends conversed in science-speak. The Walkers approved of all them—the FFs as they referred to themselves or Faun's Friends—with one exception.

The girl called Angela who rarely looked anyone in the eye, but darted glances at everyone, especially at them.

When Isis asked Faun about Angela, her daughter brushed the subject away as if people were too trivial to analyze. "Angela has issues, that's all. She's a great mathematician, though. End of story."

When Faun suddenly left the week of finals to attend a funeral, the buzz around the FFs was that a close relative had died.

"She just said she'd be back and to keep things going at the lab. Whatever." Steve, the lab assistant shrugged. "I got my end covered. I worked out shifts for everybody like she said. You know Faun. She'll be calling to check every five seconds, anyway."

But Faun didn't.

That was the trouble—nobody knew the girl really well enough. They would have been amazed and more than a little bewildered to see her sitting beside her mother and grandmother Lois in the pews of the Glory Road Church. Quade Walker was outside directing traffic and, by his presence, heading off trouble that might erupt between the conservatives and the Roaders as they were known locally.

Since Root Woman's death, the church had taken on even more Christianized aspects as though embarrassed by its African roots. Even the Episcopal priest Father Andrews had preached there once. The congregation nodded in approval as he characterized the tenants of their faith as an alternative to mainstream Christianity—a religion that incorporated ancestor worship with old African practices of hoo-doo. Nevertheless, the locals referred to it as the voo-doo church and the old rumors still had life: making strange potions, killing babies, planting curses for money, and worst of all, the dreaded Evil Eye.

After the singing and wailing was over, the guests made the rounds of the three tables set up in the Fellowship Hall, sampling the vast array of dishes, eating little but taking home a lot, as if eating in a more sanctified setting made the food more palatable.

Seeing her mother and Lois caught in conversation, Faun went back into the chapel where Kenya was slumped at the altar. She slipped into a pew and waited for Kenya to move, but the graceful woman in black seemed to have been caught in some unseen firestorm— turned to stone by the ashes in her hands.

At last, Faun couldn't stand the climate of pain, that threatened to burst through the roof of the small wooden church and shatter the stars. Going up to the altar, she sat down and held out her arms to the grieving woman.

At first, Kenya stared dumbfounded at the blonde girl, but Faun resembled her mother so much, it was hard to distinguish between the two in the dim lights. Remembering nothing but kindness radiating from that face, Kenya slumped against the cascade of golden hair and burst into sobs.

"That's it. Let it go, let it go," Faun whispered. "Tomorrow we're going to take her to The Mama Tree and leave your tears there. That's where she wanted to go. She wanted us to do that for her."

છાલ

The next morning when Faun grabbed a quick cup of coffee in the kitchen and announced that she was off to bury Holly under The Mama Tree, her father announced it was against the city's health code to bury someone or even spread their ashes on city property.

"Since when is it city land? I thought the Thicket was outside Julia Springs. Health codes and all that stuff don't apply there."

Quade had a soft spot when it came to his children, especially his daughter who resembled his beloved wife. But the resemblance ended on the outside. Inside, Faun was the polar opposite of her mother, Isis, except for her heart. *Small wonder she excelled at gene research*, he thought as he watched his daughter's eyes light up with determination. *That comes from her mother's side. The determination to make things right, regardless of the law.* Trouble was, he, as police chief, was caught squarely in the middle.

"Look, baby—"

"Oh, Dad, don't call me that. I run my own company now. Well, almost. I just need a rest, you know? All this stuff is happening too fast and I just want to stop for a while, okay?"

Quade knew what it was to feel overwhelmed. He closed his daughter tight against his big chest and stroked her hair. "You're still my baby, understand? Now, don't start with me. I don't make the laws, I just enforce them."

Faun slipped from his arms as if he had been holding a dream. "You keep saying that,, Dad, but this is Holly, for pete's sake. I mean, they just want to bury Holly there by The Mama Tree."

Quade knew his daughter well enough to tread lightly. "Who wants to, honey?"

" Freddy and Kenya, Papa. Mama and Grandma Lois ought to come, too. Make it a family thing."

He tried another tack. "Last I heard, her no-count mom wanted her buried in town at the AME Church in town."

"Marquisa was turned out by that congregation years ago." Isis who had been listening from the kitchen joined the conversation. "If Holly believed in anything, she believed in the Glory Road Church. That was Root Woman's doing, Kenya's grandmother. She wouldn't turn away anybody. I knew Holly better than most people. Because of her mother's addiction, she had drugs in her system from the day she was born. And Kenya no doubt feels responsible for putting her in harm's way—"

Faun shook her head impatiently. "What are you talking about, Mother? I'm sure Kenya never meant—"

"Let your mother finish, Faun," Quade said quietly. "You interrupted. Go on, honey," he said to his wife. "You mean when they took their singing act on the road with that bogus preacher."

"The Revered Jeremiah." The tone in her mother's voice was acidic, something Isis never resorted to.

Looking at her parents as if seeing them objectively, like middle-aged strangers in a restaurant, Faun saw that they were of one mind, as though the same thought occurred to them simultaneously, carrying all its implications and history with it.

"Back in the '90s, this man called the Reverend Jeremiah discovered both Holly and Kenya singing in the Glory Road Church choir. He took advantage of two young girls who had nobody to protect them because, by then, Root Woman was sick with the cancer that later killed her. In the end, he left them high and dry in some big city, and I guess got them both pregnant. That's how it all got started. Kenya was an instant hit in jazz circles and Holly...well, Holly went downhill fast. She just couldn't take all the temptations that kind of life has to offer. I never heard what happened to the baby."

"But Kenya's got a little boy, I heard. Is that Holly's child?"

Isis smiled and looked at Quade. "Who knows? And anyway, it looks like Kenya's doing well, judging from the clothes and the Cadillac."

"Mom, if you're trying to say why I haven't had a permanent relationship yet, I—"

Isis looked at her daughter, a mirror image of herself twenty years ago. "Faun, it's hard for you to believe, but it's not about you at all. Just let me finish, then you can take from it what you want."

"Oh, so this is a lesson, is it? A lecture thinly disguised as a story about two women who wanted something more out of life than you'd find in Julia Springs? Amazing!"

"Faun, that's enough!" Quade could stop a man from beating his wife by his presence alone, but it was just spitting in the wind to try to stop the women in his own family once they got locked into a battle. That made him the enemy.

"Enough what? Enough logic? Why won't the town let Kenya bury her friend where she wants to be buried? In the Thicket beneath The Mama Tree?" Faun was getting tears in her eyes. When passion overwhelmed her, she was close to a meltdown. "I don't get this whole thing. The past has nothing to do with what's happening now."

Quade sighed, thinking her brother was so much easier to deal with. If you said, "That's enough!" Rudy shut up. "That's because you don't listen, Faun. Just pay attention and listen to what your mother is telling you, okay?"

Frustrated, Isis got up and left the table. "No, she's got to experience the whole thing, Quade. She can't be told. She has to learn her way. That's how it is."

When Isis had retreated to the kitchen, Quade waited until the dust settled. "You happy, now? You've made your mother mad and that takes a lot from you. Since you and Rudy were born, she thinks the sun rises and sets in you kids. I do, too, but I know you've got faults. One of them is you think everybody else is dumber than you. Well, you're wrong, girl. Dead wrong. Everybody's got genius in them somewhere, 'cept maybe me. I know I'm a plodder, but it's the plodders of this world that get something done."

"Oh, Pop, that's not what I meant." Faun threw her arms around his neck as far as she could reach. "I'm sorry for sounding off. It's just that this town is so…so…ante-diluvian sometimes."

"I thought we were just antebellum or some damn thing." Quade chuckled at his own joke and kissed his daughter's bright hair, so like her mother's. He had never in his life thought he could love any other person except Isis, but she had given him two more chances to expand his shriveled heart to include his children. He thought sometimes his heart would burst from being so full. "Now, go see if you can make up to your mother like you got around me, little girl."

Faun faked an extravagant sigh. "Pop, I'm not a little girl but I guess that's an improvement over baby."

༐ࠏ༐ࠏ

Faun heard about Kenya, Holly, and Root Woman while peeling potatoes in her grandmother Lois's kitchen. Her grandmother was snapping pole beans and Isis was making fresh hummus, which her father had learned to love in the Middle East wars. That's where he got the scars on his face and body and in his mind, scars which in the early days made him wake up screaming. "Get out! Get out! It's going to blow!"

"So you wanted to know how Holly ended up the way she did?" Lois took over the conversation after see-ing Isis wasn't going to offer her daughter any opportuni-ties to become argumentative again. "Then I'll tell you, but only if you'll agree to keep your mouth shut until I'm finished and that'll be awhile so don't go getting antsy, hear me, missy."

That night Kenya was watching the motel TV when the phone rang. She sat up, reached for her cellphone, thinking it must be Sheldon calling because he had a bad dream or Grey Greyson wanting to make up and get her to come back to work. Instead, the voice on the other end was menacing a warning in every syllable.

"Don't go digging too deep, Miss Jones, or you just might fall in the same grave as your friend. Wouldn't that be cozy now?" Before she could get her breath, the caller rang off. When she pressed the Calls Received button, the number was blocked.

Kenya was wide awake, a thousand thoughts racing through her mind, none of them staying long enough for her to concentrate on. *Holly's pimp trying to scare her off cooperating with the police? Her drug connection afraid of the same thing? But which one? Holly had said herself she had several suppliers? A fearful John afraid she'd get him in trouble with his wife?*

Realizing she was alone with Holly's remains in the soapstone urn, she said aloud. "Who was that, Holly? Whoever it was knows my number and you must have given it to him. How could you do that, girl? They'll think I'm going to rat them out to the police, which is exactly what I'm going to do, if I just knew who they were. Show me something, some way that I can help you, honey. God knows, I would have given anything to keep you alive, even the drug money you asked me for, if I knew they were on your back like that."

Just then, her purse fell to the floor, spilling its contents, and as she picked it up, gathering the stuff off the sticky motel carpet, Detective Moss's card was the last thing she collected.

Squatting there beside the bed, her satin night gown pulled up as if she was peeing in a field, she dialed the number on the card.

A weary voice answered, "Moss speaking."

Kenya didn't care how crazy she sounded, she just knew one thing. She needed that big dumb detective between her little boy and whatever was out there waiting to snare them. "Can you come down to Julia Springs right away? I just had an unnerving experience."

There was a long pause at the other end. Then Moss said, "Are you aware it's quarter after one here in Memphis?"

"Oh, sweet Jesus, I'm sorry. You must think I'm crazy. I'm so scared, I'm not thinking straight. This is Chantal—I mean Kenya West."

There was a sound like a horse exhaling through its nostrils. "I figured. How can I help you, Miss West?"

"Like I said, by coming down here to Georgia and figuring out who is threatening to kill me."

Detective Moss cleared his throat, in case this ditzy, high-toned albeit sexy-as-hell girl didn't get the picture. "In case you have us confused with a bodyguard service, I can give you the names of some guys—"

Chantal West cut him off, putting on her best smoky voice to say, "Detective, you want the name of Holly's pimp and at least two drug dealers?"

Again, long pause. "You trying to work a deal on a cop, Miss West?"

"Maybe. Put it this way. If you want the lowdown on two kingpins in the heroin and coke trade, you'll get on down here. I'll throw in the pimp for sweeteners." She threw in a throaty laugh just to make him squirm.

"In exchange for?"

"Otherwise, I stay in Georgia and my information does, too. Somebody just threatened my life, and I'm going to find out who. Maybe I'll find Holly's killer while I'm at it—or maybe a hooker druggie doesn't mean that much to you. You know what I'm saying?"

Another big-man sigh came over the phone. "Look, I got some time off coming, although I was planning on spending it doing chores around the house, not in godforsaken Georgia. Where in hell is Julia Springs? And for your info, Miss West, you aren't the only one who's lost someone to heroin. Good night. And I wouldn't order room service if I were you."

*e*ɔ*e*ɔ

After a restless night, Kenya arose and took the soapstone urn and a shovel out to the Thicket. Blessed by the early spring rain, she easily dug a hole at the foot of the oldest tree in the dense woods, The Mama Tree. Its lowest branches spread some twenty feet in both directions. Mistletoe crowned its top hidden by the canopy of forest. It was the Queen of Trees, elegantly draped with Spanish moss and home to a myriad of small creatures.

Saying snatches of what Geechee-Gullah prayers she could remember, she put a handful of Holly's ashes in the creek that gave the swamp its name, the Hanahatchee. She did it so that Holly's body would return to the sea from whose depths all life was born. Next, she gave a handful to the morning breeze so that her friend's soul go to be with her ancestors who were waiting, no doubt, to scold her for wasting her life. Kenya had to smile, thinking of Holly's grandmother, Mrs. Simpson, a no-nonsense ex-schoolteacher with rulers for fingers. Even she couldn't control the adventurous girl, so full of life, so full of promise and laughter.

At last, Kenya buried the remaining ashes at the foot of The Mama Tree and poured good whiskey over the fresh dirt. That was a libation for the earth so it wouldn't turn her friend loose in case of a flash flood. She had a vision of some redneck snatching the soapstone urn from a leaky old rowboat and emptying it of Holly's remains, then giving to his girlfriend to put bubble bath or plastic flowers in.

Kenya then parked the shovel nearby and sat down in

the drizzle, heedless of her straightened hair that was starting to frizz, that there was mud on her pedicured toes and four-inch heels. Her designer outfit would go straight to the cleaners when she got back to Memphis. She didn't give a rat's ass about clothes for once in her life, or that the steady rain was running down her collar.

She sat there, absorbing the beauty of an early spring, the birdsong in the trees overhead, the playful ripple of the nearby creek, the perfume of a nearby crabapple tree.

"I thought you'd be here under The Mama Tree." It was Faun Walker, walking as though the sun was shining. Blue jeans rolled up and wearing a T-shirt with Einstein on it, she came through the underbrush barefoot, not even looking down but looking up. It had been a long time since Kenya had walked looking up, way too long.

Faun sat down beside Kenya among the elephantine roots of The Mama Tree. "Grandma sent these." From a wicker basket, she drew out bundles of dried herbs, sage, and ginseng root. "She said your grandmother would want Holly to have a proper send-off."

Kenya struggled to be gracious to this white girl who wasn't even born when she lived in the Thicket, whose father had helped put her through foster care. "That's kind of you all, but I don't have the faintest idea what to do with all that stuff. You take it...what's your name again? I'm so bad with names."

"It's Faun Walker, Isis's daughter." Faun smiled to herself, knowing full well it went unsaid that all white people looked alike.

"Your daddy the police chief? Quade Walker?" When Faun nodded, Kenya threw back her head and laughed, showing a perfect row of white teeth. Whole flocks of nesting birds rose up like whispered prayers and the woods came alive with deer taking cover. "Oh my god! I remember now. He was the one who put Holly in Juvie and wrote off my stepfather's death as an accident, even though I clobbered the bastard with a rock! I owe him my life and you're his daughter? Then you're something special, I know."

"My grandma says you're special, too."

"Well, that's not a sentiment generally shared by this community," Kenya said, suppressing a smile. "You notice you're the only one showed up this morning after that big service last night. Probably they all got indigestion from eatin' too much."

If Faun was startled by Kenya's revelations, she didn't show it. On the contrary, she countered Kenya's skepticism with options she may not have considered. "Maybe they thought it was you who wouldn't remember The Mama Tree. Or maybe they knew about the city granting a license to the developer of a strip mall to build over the Thicket." She didn't add the city had also passed a new ordinance about burying *anything*—deceased pets, mattresses, car batteries—in the Thicket.

Kenya figured that out for herself. "You mean, they're going to put it up right here? A strip mall? Holly said that, but I thought she was…" She hesitated a minute, then tears rolled down like silent mourners behind a hearse. "You know, that's the last thing Holly said to me, but I was just so damn busy being me that I didn't listen 'til now."

"I guess that is true of a lot of people." Faun looked up to where the sun was chasing away the clouds. "Looks like the rain is letting up. Want me to show you what to do with the stuff in the basket?"

"Go for it. Repatriate me to The Mama Tree tradition." As Kenya got up, her high heels sank in the mud, so she leaned on the girl while she slipped them off. The minute her feet touched the earth, she felt something shoot up her legs. It was a sensation so palpable, she checked to see whether fire ants had run up her silk blend pants.

"It's just earth's core," Faun said, with a smile. "I feel it, too, every time I go barefoot, pulling me down to ground-level earth every time I think I'm flying high."

"Ordinarily, I'd say that's what I was doing. But now that I'm down to earth, let's do it, sister."

Opening the basket, Faun took out a small bottle of wine. "Here, pour this on the ground and say 'I return this to earth that she may partake of her own fruits.'"

"I remember Root Woman doing that. She made some good stuff, too." Feeling awkward, Kenya did as she was instructed.

Next came the burning of the sage. The two of them circled the tree, chanting the prayers. Some words of the old language came back as if a memory plug had been pulled. She said them, then sang them. They were down to burying the ginseng when a cellphone rang.

"That's mine. Here," Faun said, dropping the small plastic trowel. "Go ahead. I'll be right back."

She left Kenya by the feet of the tree and hurried a short distance away. "Yeah, Steve, what's up?"

"I'm at the lab. Somebody's been in here."

Faun had a mental picture of Steve, running his dirty fingernails through greasy hair.

"Like...I don't know. It's a mess. We've been hacked as well. Our files have been fucking scrambled. Scrambled! You've got to get back here on the double. I don't know where to start."

"I'll be there sometime tonight. In the meantime, start by calling campus security."

"They're here now. I gotta go. Hurry up, will you? It's fucking bad."

Faun put her cell phone back in her jeans, feeling

suddenly cold. Kenya was digging away, planting the ginseng and now praying in Geechee-English. She looked around and caught the expression on Faun's face and stopped.

"What's wrong?"

"Don't stop! It breaks the spell. Here, I'll help." Faun squatted beside Kenya, finishing the chant and covering the hole with red earth. "There," she said, getting to her feet. "Now, I've got to go. Something has come up and I have to go back to school."

"Bad news? It is bad, isn't it?" Kenya fumbled in her handbag. "Here, take my card—and this is my private cellphone number. Call me on that and I'll answer anytime of the day or night. Only my son and his principal have that one—and Holly did. Don't forget now. You're family. I mean that."

The two women embraced as if they were survivors of some disaster, then Faun ran back through the path in the woods. She told her parents as much as she knew about the break-in and packed up the few things she had brought home.

"Take it easy, baby. Vandalism is common at schools nowadays." Quade leaned in the doorway, watching his daughter pack. "Probably after drugs. They think all labs contain meth or the stuff to make it with."

"You don't understand, Dad. Our research files have been hacked into. Everything's scrambled. Steve says it's a mess."

"Has anybody...I don't know...threatened you lately? Or maybe it was the kid you threw out the other day. You think?" He was like a smoking volcano, leaning in the doorway, quietly rumbling. *If anybody attempted to hurt my baby*—Quade didn't follow that thought because he knew where it would lead.

It was evident by the way Faun was walking around

with her cell phone glued to her ear that she wasn't into theoretical thinking. "Oh, Dad, I don't know right now, okay? Just let me get there and I'll call you."

"Quade, stop playing detective and let the girl get on the road," his wife said from the hall stairs. "We'll know more when she knows more."

"As usual, you're right. Can't blame me for trying, honey. Baby, you take care of yourself, first and fore-most, you hear." Quade kissed his daughter's free ear. "And hurry back. We always miss you when you're gone."

<center>~~~</center>

Faun drove straight through, stopping once for coffee and a muffin. On the way, she got a constant string of bad news from Steve and the rest of the crew. Someone had hacked into their files and corrupted them with malware, encrypting data and hijacking whole DNA records. What was worse, the actual DNA slides were gone. Someone knew the specific slides to look for and took them.

All lab techs said it had to be an inside job, but she checked the list of scheduled lab workers. There was no one she wouldn't trust with her life secrets, if she had any. The lab secrets were something else entirely. But no one knew all of them. She had deliberately planned it that way. No one but she did, and she kept the master file in her purse on a jump drive in a secure box in her room, and on Nebulous, a data parking site on the Net.

Faun glanced over the list again. "Wait a sec, who's this? Bjorn? Who's he?" she demanded of Steve who was scratching his head.

Steve bent over her shoulder and Faun drew back. "Him, he was the guy the tech department sent out to see what happened. He's okay, bonded and everything. Be-sides, he's a grad student here. What's wrong? Why are you looking at me like that? You think I have cooties? I'm telling you I have an allergy to soap. It makes my head itch something terrible."

Her reply was not meant to make him feel better. "I don't care if you have scorpions in your hair. It's that you let a total stranger fool around in our database. No telling what he stole or screwed-up."

"It was already screwed up before he got here, I'm telling you. That's why I put in the request, to see if somebody from Tech could salvage the remains and put a lock on them until you got back from Grandma's funeral or wherever." Steve turned and walked away, talking angrily to himself about dealing with temperamental bitches.

"Hey, I wasn't criticizing. I just wanted to know—"

"Yeah, yeah. Call Tech yourself if you want to know. I'm outta here."

The other lab workers looked at her over their computers. She knew what they were thinking, *There goes my F-ing funding for this job.*

"Things are not as bad as they look," she said. Usual Faun, usual confidence, but she was the only one who felt it. "I've made backup files for every bit of data we've collected. The thing is this: Is it just a random act of vandalism or are we a target for something bigger in the food chain? Anyway, time will tell."

"Somebody turned off the centrifuge. That batch of DNA is history." Misty Wong took her eyes off her microscope long enough to look at Faun. "Somebody had to know enough about what we were doing to do that."

"Then they should know we always try to duplicate the cells in case there's a power outage. There's a matching batch in the fridge, and its record is in my books, the hard copy."

"Good thing. That's one of the files that's scrambled

into code soup." Another lab assistant, Randy Sparks, looked at Susie and then at Faun. "I think they definitely knew what they were doing. This operation was only aimed at us. I asked around the different labs. This was the only one touched."

"Could someone be trying to sabotage your doctoral thesis, do you think? It's a common practice even among faculty," the biochemist major Emily McBride asked.

That was the question in all their eyes, knowing their grant funding hung in the balance.

"They won't derail us, guys. Onward and upward, that's where we're going. Come on, let's put Humpty Dumpty back together."

Her first call was to Dr. Murphy who supervised the grant from Biolabs. His answering machine played a punk rock riff from pre-millennium times before a fried-sounding voice demanded. "Leave a beeping message, okay?"

Faun left a brief explanation of what had happened, having seen him deleting a message before two words were spoken. Then she called the Tech department. It was closed. That's when she noticed the time on her phone. It was 11:30 at night.

She looked at the long line of computers. "What are you guys still doing here? Go on home."

A half dozen pair of red, puffy eyes looked up from what they were focused on.

"Go home, okay?" she repeated.

Angela Morris spoke for everybody. "We'll stay and try to clean up the mess."

"Correction, I'll stay. You have classes tomorrow, or you're teaching boneheads, whichever. See you tomorrow, same time same place."

They left reluctantly and headed for the local pub. It turned out they hadn't eaten, except Steve, who had kept a roll of bologna and a loaf of French bread in the closet. He'd passed out sandwiches nobody touched.

She felt it rather than heard it—through restless dreams of big trees. Kenya was saying, '*It's him! It's him!*' But *him* didn't have a face.

Faun snapped awake as the lab door opened and a flashlight danced around the walls. Her phone, never far from her hands, said 2:25. She sat up, grabbing her phone in the same movement.

"Okay, whoever you are and whatever you're doing, I'm calling 911 and campus security on a two-way call. So if you even try to get away, they'll—"

"Ask for my ID?"

"Oh, a smart one. I get it. Some kind of frat prank. Think you can bluff your way past campus security with a fake ID? Do you know what you've done by vandalizing my research? Maybe cancelled life for a lot of innocent kids, that's what! What's your name so I can tell them who's responsible for their slow death?"

She shone the beam of her cell's flashlight directly in the intruder's face. He was holding up a university ID that had a picture on it. Blond crewcut hair. Blue eyes. Height: six feet, two inches. Faun raised the beam about a foot. Sure enough, blue eyes stared back at her with just a hint of laughter in them.

"Chris Bjorn, Department of Technology, at your service, Miss Walker. I assume you are Miss Walker, hence the hostility. By the way, I don't belong to a fraternity. Never my thing, socially-speaking, and far too much money. I am officially a geek."

"Not so fast. Bjorn. You were here while I was away. How do I know you're not the one who infested my files with malware and tried to derail my whole project?" She was her father's daughter, after all. He could be as slick a con artist as a carnival coin toss operator and she'd still trip him up. "You could be working for the other side."

The tall blond man tried to hide a smile which made her even angrier. "I might give that option some thought, if they pay better than the university. Look. I'll just go quietly back to the lab and return in daylight, which is breaking in the East even as we speak. I just thought I might try and save some of your files with this anti-malware program I copied from the university stash at great risk to my person, I might add. But if you don't trust me or my credentials..." He backed toward the door. "In the meantime, I suggest you call Dr. Murphy about your break-in. But I wouldn't mention the other side if I were you. Graduate students have a tendency toward paranoia about their projects." Chris Bjorn shut the door behind him, leaving her in the dark.

Chapter 4

Kenya had the cellphone clutched between her shoulder and her ear as she went around the motel room gathering up her clothes.

"That's sooo good, baby! That's real smart."

Sheldon's voice sounded so little and far away. She could picture him gripping the house phone with both hands, telling her about the spelling contest he had just won. "I didn't actually win, Mama. I was runner-up, but if something happens to the winner, like she gets sick or something, I get to take her place in the citywide contest."

There was a knock at the door and Kenya yanked it open, thinking it was the maid service. A strange woman was standing there and something about her spelled trouble.

"Miss Shekenya West?"

"Hold on, Sheltie, baby," Kenya said, covering the phone so he couldn't hear. "Yes, that's me."

"I'm here to collect my niece's remains."

It took a frozen second to react. "Baby, I'll call you back tonight. Go to school. I love you. Kiss, kiss. Bye."

The woman slid inside the open door and stood there

like a monument to hard living, her face a map of wrinkles and scars, crossing over each other like conflicting road signs. "That your boy you were talking to? Bet he's as good-looking as his daddy. And you, too. You turned out mighty fine-looking. Real pretty."

Something about the woman put Kenya on guard. "How do I know your Holly's aunt? I never heard her mention you and she and I were close. Close as sisters. Why are you just now showing up?"

The woman opened her purse and took out a picture. A very young woman was holding a plump, laughing baby. "That's Holly's first birthday. She was a real cute little thing. That's me, would you believe?"

"That doesn't prove anything. Look, Mrs…"

"Willis, Hannah Willis."

"Mrs. Willis, I'm in kind of a hurry to get on the road. I've got to get back to work, okay? Can we have this talk some other time?"

"How about, like, now?" A sleazy little man, pretending to be unlocking the next unit, turned back and pulled a gun out of his jacket pocket. "No time like the present, Miss Chantal." He backed her into the room, followed by the woman who shut the door with a bang. Kenya backed up until her knees hit the couch and she sat down hard.

The rat-faced man leaned over her so close she could hear his chest wheeze. She had the distinct feeling he didn't care if he died in the next instant, so long as he was oblivious to his pain. She knew a hard addict when she saw one and Ratface was one for sure.

There was that nothing-to-lose look in his reptilian eyes that people had who would kill their own mothers for a fix and he was getting close to needing one. Too close to play games.

"Now, tell us what you know about Holly Simpson,

or you know what? Your little boy won't make it to school."

Kenya felt her blood turn to ice. "Oh, God! You wouldn't hurt a child! Oh, please, I'll tell you what you want to know, but please don't involve him. Please! He's only six years old!"

"That depends on you, Kenya, and whether you want to cooperate!"

"I do, I do! Ask me anything you want, I'll tell you." She looked from one to the other, knowing she had to play for time, knowing they were here to just make sure she hadn't let slip anything about Holly to anyone else. She prayed for a break, and then it came in the most unexpected way.

"Knock, knock! Maid service. Good Morning!"

The woman who said she was Holly's aunt lunged for the door, putting the chain lock in place as it opened to reveal two wide blue eyes.

"No, damn you! No!" shouted the fake aunt. "Go away!

But Kenya let out a scream. "Help! Get the police! They're going to—"

At this point she was knocked unconscious by Ratface with a blow from his pistol butt.

There was silence from the other side of the door and then. "Well, I never! These city people sure are strange."

ℰ৲ℰ৲

Grover Moss was weary and not disposed to put up with Jim Crowe laws or redneck disregard of the anti-discrimination laws or any of the shit Georgians are famous for. He was mildly disappointed he didn't run into anything but the courtesy Southerners are also famous for, even though they were probably faking it.

So when he pulled into the luxury inn Shekenya Jones, aka Chantal West, aka God knows what else, was staying at, he was surprised how warmly he was greeted by of all things, a black manager.

"I'm here on official business," he said, flashing his badge. "Staying one night. Miss Kenya Chantal West staying here?"

Why did the guy look like he was sitting on a hot poker? "Room. 119. Shall I ring, sir?"

"No, I'll go around." Moss put his badge away and as he reached for his wallet, he noticed the manager's hands were shaking. "I'll need a single, king-sized bed, non-smoking, preferably away from the pool. I trust you have a bar?"

"Yes, sir." The manager was definitely beyond terrified now. Sweat was breaking out on his forehead, forming a droplet at the end of his nose. As he bent over to scan the reservations screen, he caught Moss's eyes and jerked his head in the direction of the room behind him which had a curtain covering a small alcove.

For a big man, Moses moved fast. He weighed close to two hundred pounds but, when motivated, could pounce like a lynx on a rabbit. He cleared the counter, Glock drawn, as the manager hit the floor and, in two giant steps, he had dragged the rat-faced man by the jaw from behind the curtain.

"Now, before I detach your ugly head from the sorry ass rest of you, where is the lady? I hope you haven't hurt her, 'cause if you have, you gonna be even uglier when I get done with you, ya hear?"

Ratface could only squeak in terror with his jaw in a viselike grip, but he kept rolling his eyes toward the door. As Moses dragged his quarry past a couple waiting in line to register, the woman asked. "Aren't you going to read him his rights?"

Glancing at the couple without apology, he said. "So sue me. His kind gave up his rights when he got kids hooked on heroin."

Kenya had almost succeeded in getting one hand free when Moss came through the door dragging Ratface with the motel's manager following in their wake. The woman had fallen asleep watching TV and let out a bloodcurdling scream when Moss yelled. "Don't move!"

The manager freed Kenya and helped her to her feet. "What took you so long, Memphis? And I thought *Georgia* cops were slow," she said as she toddled off to the bathroom, "but you win that contest hands down."

Quade Walker answered the 911 call, beating the Highway Patrol and the ATF guys by a good fifteen minutes. He took custody of Ratface whose name turned out to be Raul Dalton, aka Ralph Jimenez, and about five other names. His deputy took them into custody.

Meanwhile, Kenya was holding an icepack to her head while the EMTs applied first aid to her wrists and ankles, which were bleeding from being bound so tightly. Moss couldn't help admiring the coolness with which she gave her statement to the hulking Julia Springs detective who, it turned out, was also the chief.

"Was there any other connection with Holly Simpson other that an attempt to extort money from you?" Quade looked in Kenya's smooth, heart-shaped face, seeing the frightened young girl he had known over fifteen years ago. "I know she was into drugs, among other things. You don't remember me, do you? You told me to ask the girl I was crazy about to marry me and I did, remember?"

A look of recognition, then a smile broke through the worry and pain on Kenya's face. "Detective Walker! Sure I do! How are you? That was your daughter I met yesterday. How is Isis?" At that point, she broke into tears. "I'm so worried about Sheldon. He's my little man, my son. They threatened to kidnap him, said I'd never see him again!"

"Wait a minute! Walker? You don't remember me, do you?" Moss stared at the big man with the soft voice and scarred face. "Sergeant Grover Moss, Rangers, Second Division, Feluga, 2012. I was behind you when your Humvee hit that landmine. 'Course you wouldn't remember, you were pretty tore up."

It was Quade's turn to stare at the big, balding man in casual clothes, packing a shoulder holster under a loose jacket. "You're right, I was, but I remember knowing we were still under fire, and somebody, I don't know if it was you, dragging me out of there."

"It was me. Damn snipers kept picking off the survivors left and right. So I kept my head down and got to the nearest one that just happened to be you. Anyway, how are you?"

Kenya got busy packing her suitcase. "Look, I hate to breakup what looks like a happy reunion, but I'm so worried about Sheldon. Is there any way you can send a guard out to my house until I can get back to Memphis? I'd even pay for a private security guard."

The two police officers exchanged looks that said we'll talk later over a drink and turned to the matter at hand—a nearly hysterical woman, a forced entry by two types with rap sheets a mile long and enough charges to put them away for three years easy. Quade decided to lean on the transgender cross-dresser or whatever he was. Quade told Moss his plan and the big detective agreed.

"I'll escort Miss West back to Memphis and see what I can shake loose up there."

Kenya corrected him on the spot. "You'll make sure Sheldon's safe first off or I'm driving to Atlanta and getting the first plane back to Memphis by morning, before he leaves for school."

Moss already had his phone to his ear. He waggled his thick brows at Quade. "She ought to be head of the department. What's your address, Miss West? And who's with your son?"

She slipped him a card saying Chantal West R&B Princess, Songstress, and Entertainer Extraordinaire in bold, flowery script. Under that was her website and a phone number. She had scrawled her address in pen on the back and another phone number. "That's for you only. My private phone number. I don't want it to get out or anything."

"Don't worry, I'm not going to put it on the Net." He stuck his finger in his ear and addressed the phone. "Hello, this is Moss down in Georgia...yeah, well, it's a long story. *Cherchez la femme* or something. Look, can you send somebody out to this address? Yeah, surveillance. Joey'll be perfect. Keep him out of trouble. Just make sure nobody messes around outside, there's a little kid who needs to get to school in the morning. Make sure that happens, okay?"

With all the fury of a mother lioness protecting her cubs, Kenya attacked. "You think this is a joke, don't you, Moss?"

The detective somewhat wearily said goodbye to whoever he was talking to and pocketed the phone. "That's Detective Moss. And no, there's nothing funny about a kidnap threat. I agree with you about that, Miss West. Okay, Chief Walker, we're out of here. Miss West, stay in touch." His eyes said more than that but Grover Moss was a quiet man and Quade taciturn to the point of monolithic. Quiet inside, but for both men, it was hard won, the hardest battle they had ever fought.

Kenya saw that it was useless taking out her fear and frustration on either of them, so she glided away to pack like a harmless snake, aware of her power to frighten people, but also aware that people hated snakes. "Whatever." She slammed the door to the bedroom, making the windows rattle.

"Bitch," Moss said softly, but she seemed to be listening out for his reaction.

"I heard that," she shouted through the flimsy door.

"I was talking to my cellphone!" he shouted back. "Can't get no signal in here!"

Quade was enjoying the show. He wiped the smile off his face, telling Moss he'd let him know what he found out from the two he had taken into custody. "Write down your cell phone number here," he said, handing Moss a sticky notepad and a pen. "That way, we'll keep it unofficial until we nail Holly's killer. I get the feeling there's some kind of connection between here and Memphis that brought these two rats all the way down from the big city. Now, we need to find the bait that will attract the big cheese."

"Looks like you learned something in 'Stan about setting traps."

"I wish I'd known how before I went over there. Turned out I was the bait. You see any action?"

"Yeah, mostly in the kitchen." What he didn't say was his forward kitchen unit had been hit by a missile, killing all but a few soldiers in the mess hall. Moss, a national guard private straight out of high school, grabbed an automatic weapon from one of the dead guards and rushed out just as the second missile hit, killing all but three.

What happened after he qualified for the Rangers was a blur in Moss's memory—a blip that earned him a bunch of medals and a whole raft of nightmares, shakes, flashbacks, as well as a promotion to lieutenant.

Chapter 5

Chris Bjorn turned out to be exactly who he said he was, a doctoral candidate in Biomedical Technology working as part of his assistantship in the Technology Department of the university. Satisfied with his credentials, Faun let him try to unscramble the seemingly hopelessly tangled files adulterated by the hacker's malware virus or viruses, it was hard to tell.

"My scanner isn't having any luck identifying what sort of program they used, except for one peculiar thing," he said.

"What's that?"

"Well, it keeps saying the origin of at least one of the viruses came from a computer used in this very lab. One of your techs have it in for you?"

"No." Faun was aghast at the suggestion. "That's impossible! I made strict rules that these computers are dedicated to our program. Under no circumstances are they to be used for outside work."

"Can I ask what kind of thing you're working on? Just ballpark it for me, general idea, that sort of thing."

"Sure. My partners invented an app that will tell you, after some input, whether you've got a genetic deposition toward several neuromuscular diseases like multiple scle-rosis or Lou Gehrig's disease."

Bjorn's eyes glistened in the growing light from the windows. "I knew it was a matter of time before someone did that, but I never thought I'd meet them, much less fix their computer. That's brilliant."

"Patent ap's still pending, but we've already got of-fers to sell."

"Are you going to? Sell or keep working? None of my business, I know, but I'm just wondering if I were in the same boat what I would do."

Faun looked up from her work and their eyes met, blue on blue. Then they both looked back at the screens they were working on, without knowing why.

She spoke without looking at him. There was some-thing disturbing about looking at him directly. "Funny you should say that because that's just what I—we've been trying to decide. Of course, the grant we got will want a share of anything commercial that comes out of it."

He was apologetic, but she wasn't buying it. Bio-technology was an incredibly competitive field. He could be scoping out the competition. Great setup, working as a tech assistant. That gave him access to every research project the university funded.

"Look, I didn't mean to pry. It's none of my business and I shouldn't have asked, it's just that I've been work-ing on something myself as part of my dissertation—sort of, and I wondered, that's all."

She found herself immediately drawn to this young man, in spite of the fact he was a perfect stranger until three hours ago. One thing was for certain, she could tell if he was the real deal, a science nerd just like her, not in it for the money, just the discovery of something new. He really knew his way around computer systems. Bjorn's fingers flew over the keys like a concert pianist playing Rachmaninoff, running a program and then discarding it halfway through, only to initiate another one.

Faun glanced at him sideways, as if he was standing in deep water and she was wading out to him slowly. "What's your dissertation on?"

"You really want to know or are you making idle chatter?" He was intent on the screen in front of him.

Typical male assumption. "I don't make idle chatter," she said smartly.

"My bad. I forget who I'm talking to. Damn! Thought I had it then. Sorry, um, it's a hell of a long title. Let me see if I can even remember…it goes 'The Impact of Electrolytes on Autonomic Nervous System Dysfunction.'"

"Biochemistry?"

He looked at her and blinked. "Why yes, I thought I told you. That's why they sent me. Didn't think it would matter, seeing as how some of those geeks they've got in IT wouldn't know a genome from a gnome. We all specialize, see?"

She was about to ask him if he would consider joining their lab when he looked at the screen if front of him, and said. "Bravo! Looks like we're making headway. Come take a look."

Leaping from her chair, Faun crouched behind Bjorn, unaware of anything but the file reshaping in front of her eyes. "That's my file! That's it!" She hugged Bjorn's shoulders and kissed his cheek. "You got it back! Awesome!"

In the back of her mind, Faun was aware he smelled of soap and water and some kind of after shave. *Spice*, she thought. *Poor but wholesome, just like him*. She wondered if he had a girlfriend, checked his left hand. No ring, but that didn't mean anything these days.

"That makes being called a terrorist well worth it!" His beard was blond stubble like mowed hay. "Of course, you know they copied your research file, right?"

"That's okay, the patent application 's been filed so it won't do them any good. You're a genius," she said. "Wait until I get hold of Steve."

"Who's Steve? Whoever he is, he's working for the competition, I'll bet you."

Faun was on the phone. "My lab manager. Was my lab manager. He's being fired as of now."

Bjorn's expression was disapproving, but Faun noticed he kept his eyes on the screen where file after file was reforming. "A bit hasty, isn't that?"

"Why? He was the only one here. I figure he did one of two things. A: He left the lab to get something to eat when there was no one covering it. Or B: He was surfing the Net like I gave strict orders not to do it on these computers. He's got a laptop. He should've used that if he wanted to look at porn."

"How do you know he was looking at porn?"

"Because he always does when he takes the night shift. He's probably gone to class." The answering machine played the first bars of a reggae tune. Faun left a terse message and hung up.

Meanwhile, Bjorn had risen from his computer and stretched. "Let this program run until it goes through all the files. Don't touch it or turn it off. Some of these viruses are programmed to erase the system, hoping you'll copy the files to a folder. Thing to do is take them off on a jump drive, but even that's tricky because you can copy the virus that way. I'll be back about five. Got to teach grunts in the lab this afternoon, bless their little pointed heads. And don't fire Steve for getting the odd sub sandwich and a beer. It probably wasn't his fault. Whoever did this was up to no good, determined to shoot you down. No doubt. Whoa, what's that? Holy crap, you weren't kidding! He's into porn."

Faun looked over his shoulder. The file had stopped running and there on the screen was Holly Simpson. At least, Faun recognized her face from photographs she had seen at the funeral. The rest of her could have been anybody, posed in a lascivious position.

Chapter 6

Grover Moss knew better than to argue with a woman who thinks her child is in danger, especially someone as high-powered as Chantal West. He didn't know what it was about her, but she could shrivel a man's *cojones* with one look of those chocolate-brown eyes.

Like a bloodhound on scent, he followed her Escalade up to Atlanta, then like a comet's tail, up the turnoff to Memphis. His eyes ached, his body ached—no, cried out for sleep. But he had to keep following this crazy woman as she drove at nearly 100 mph through the night. To keep awake, he got to rehearsing what he would say to the highway patrol officer who would pull them both over for speeding. *Good evening, Officer, I'm escorting Miss West here to my precinct back in Memphis, (flash your badge) to swear out a warrant stemming from her assault and attempted abduction by two suspects.* "Bogus, that would never fly," he said out loud.

The trooper probably would let them go with a warning and in the morning, call his supervisor who would ask why the hell he was chasing a broad up a Georgia highway in the middle of the night when he was supposed to be on R&R. If that was his idea of R&R, then he could come damn well come back to work.

About three in the morning, West pulled into a rest stop for gas. Moss pulled in behind her.

Moss looked at the sky, expecting the worst. "Big storm coming this way. Could be funnel clouds."

She looked at him as if he was speaking Mandarin. "Say what?"

"Tornado coming. Didn't you hear the warning?" He could see the headlines *Law Officer Caught Trying to Lure Driver into Motel*.

She looked so fragile, holding on to the gas pump, he thought she was going to pass out. Except black girls don't pass out, they have sinking spells.

"Oh, my god, really? I was listening to my CDs. Can we get a motel here, do you think? I need some sleep. Just a couple of hours, that's all."

"I guess it will be all right." He had prayed for a miracle and here it came. "Only for a few hours. You have to get back in time to see Sheldon off to school, you said." Moss tried to appear casual like the idea was a novelty to him, but he could hardly keep from shouting *Sweet Jesus!* "There's a pretty high-dollar one right across the street. I'm fine in my car."

He counted on her to say. "No, come in with me. I'll get a suite and you can sleep in the living room. I'd feel safer that way."

The River Princess didn't fall for it. Instead, he spent the rest of the night in his car.

She slept until nine the next morning. Moss was already up, getting two large coffees when, he got a call from Quade Walker.

Quade told him about the attempt to destroy his daughter's files and Moss listened intently, trying to understand what all this had to do with him.

Then Quade dropped the bomb on him. "I know you're wondering 'What's all this got to do with me?' right?"

Moss was keeping one eye on the parking lot, expecting to see a ruby-red Escalade go tearing out any second. "Yeah, kinda."

Quade told him what it had to do with him. "Seems whoever did this crap to my daughter's research was also into pornography and knew enough about Faun's research to use some pretty sophisticated programs to get into her files, and had a signature screen with a picture of Holly on it. You can only guess how she was posed. I wouldn't tell Kenya if I were you. She's kind of protective of Holly. Whoever's behind this is a pretty smart operator. I'd just like to get ahold—no, I'd like to wring his neck for doing that to my kid, let alone Holly."

"I heard that, loud and clear, Chief. He's got to be in my neck of the woods, unless you got another idea. Memphis is a good place to start, anyway. Plenty of opportunity to get into a mess of trouble in that city. Anyway, stands to reason, if the two you've got in custody are working for the Porno King, he's got to have more boots on the ground than those idiots."

"I intend to find out. This morning. By the way, I'm not recommending bail to the judge so they'll stay right here until you get back."

"Back? I wasn't planning on coming—" The ruby Escalade tore out of the motel parking lot as if it was late to a fire. "Hey, later, man! There she goes, and I've got to be right behind her in case the highway patrol needs an explanation of why she's breaking the sound barrier."

Quade's slow drawl came over the miles with a laugh inside. "I ever tell you Kenya once wanted to drive stock cars? Go on. We'll talk."

Chapter 7

Sheldon Grey was a big boy for his age. Taller than the rest of his classmates in the first grade at St. Mark's, he looked like a reedy sapling shooting skyward. That's why, when Mrs. Davis wanted to hold his hand crossing the street, he jerked it away.

"I'm not a baby," he said to the large girth of Mrs. Davis looming above him. He put his hands on the straps of his backpack just to make sure she wouldn't grab one, hoisting him across the street like a poodle on a leash. "I can walk to school by myself." His defiant voice floated back to her as he hurried ahead."I got Show and Tell this morning!"

"Sheldon William Greyson, get back here this minute or I'll give your mother a bad report on you," Davis shouted.

"I'll be late," he shouted back at the lumbering, red-faced woman. "You're too old and slow…and fat. You'll take all day."

The crossing guard blew his whistle to let Sheldon cross the walk, and then held up his hand to stop her. "Hey, Manny, I'm with him. That little guy who just ran across."

But Manny didn't hear her above the traffic noise and waved the cars on by. It was several minutes before Mrs. Davis climbed the steps to the school where the smiling principal stood greeting the river of children.

"Have a good day! I don't want to see you on the bench this morning!" she said to each one through the her frozen smile. St. Mark's was a private school and the parents expected the personal touch to everything from the lunch menu to the hand towels in the bathroom.

"Have you seen Sheldon Grayson go by?" The nanny had to pause to take a breath. "He's a first grader."

The principal's fixed smile said she was very familiar with Sheldon Grey. She took in the exhausted woman's wheezing and disheveled appearance with sympathy. "Sheldon? Yes, he's here. So punctual. Hates to be late. Have a nice day," adding silently, *if you can.*

Mrs. Davis turned and went down the steps. "Wait 'til I get hold of that little shit," she muttered, charging past Manny, the crossing guard. "And don't tell me what kind of day to have!"

Sheldon never got to his classroom to do Show and Tell. He was headed down the long hall to the lower grades classrooms when a neatly dressed man in a business suit and tie stopped him. "Son, could you direct me back to the side parking lot? This place has got me so turned around I forgot where I came in."

"Sure," said Sheldon, pointing back in the direction of the front door. "See those double doors? You turn left and go straight down that hall, then make a right."

The man shook his head, as if fighting confusion. "Would you show me the way, kid? I'm kind of in a hurry and I don't want to keep going in circles. I'd sure appreciate it."

When they got to the second set of double doors leading to the parking lot, the stranger showed his appreciation by snatching up Sheldon and tearing out to a waiting car.

As they approached, a large, thick-bellied man got out of the front seat and moved to the back.

"I'm sure glad to see they're raising kids right these days," he said to the man in the back seat. "Hold him tight, Lolo. We wouldn't want anything to happen to him." Shoving the frightened child into the back seat beside the stranger, his captor got behind the steering wheel. "A real little gentleman, this is here."

The little gentleman writhed and kicked. "Let me go! I gotta get back to Mrs. Peabody's room to do Show and Tell. Where're you taking me? My mama said she'd be home this morning and she'd check on me. She's going to be mad if you don't take me back."

"Oh, that's okay, kid," said the paunchy man beside him. "Your mama wanted us to take you to the zoo."

"I hate zoos. She knows I hate the way they smell. Zoos are nasty. I don't want to go. Take me back to school." Sheldon opened his backpack and fished around.

"What are you looking for? Your gun? Hear that, Earl? He might be packing heat!" The man with his belly hanging over his belt rocked with laughter. "A real gentleman, this is."

"Shut up, Loquacious," the driver snapped. "We don't use no names, remember?"

"Relax, Earl, he's just a little kid. What you looking for in there, kid? Your game-a-thingy?"

Sheldon looked at the man beside with scorn. "You really are stupid, mister. I'm looking for a tissue. I've got to blow my nose." Instead, his fingers were forming a rudimentary text on his cell phone. *I don want to go to zoo. When you coming to get me? Who r these dombass guys?*

"Well, why didn't you say so? Here, use mine, kid."

The man beside him produced an ironed purple linen hanky, which he held out to Sheldon.

Sheldon regarded the hanky with distaste. "That's not a tissue. That's unsanitary! It looks like a piece of a tablecloth."

"No, it's not, you little shit, but use it anyway, ya hear? You got no manners, you know? Your mama ought to teach you better." The fat man waved a finger under Sheldon's nose.

What followed was a scream from the man in back seat as Sheldon's teeth clamped down on his finger with the force of a sabretooth tiger. Sheldon's incisors, being somewhat oversized and destined for the orthodontist, were able to produce a very loud scream from the very large man beside him. When the finger began to spurt blood, the man slapped Sheldon in the head so hard he spat out the finger and attacked the nether parts as his mother had taught him to do on just such occasions.

This produced screams in the high-C range from the fat man called Loquacious.

The driver meanwhile was swerving all over the road as he glued his eyes on the rear view mirror. "What the hell is going on back there, Loquacious? Can't you even handle a skinny little kid, for God's sake? What's he doing?"

Loquacious made a series of squeaks before forming actual words. "He's—he's got my balls, goddammit! Let go, you little motherfucker! Let go! Make him get off me! He's killing me, dammit! Do something, Earl!"

"I heard what you said about my mother!" exclaimed Sabertoothed Sheldon, coming up for air. "Nobody says that about my mother! And don't call me a little kid!" He latched on to an ear lobe just as they hit another car.

The safety locks flew up and Sheldon was out the door, darting between the line of stopped cars who had seen the wreck coming for two blocks. He ran in to Zip Cuts Barber Shop, because it was full of people who looked like him.

"Help!" he screamed to no one in particular.

"It's the man!" A kind brown face bent down to greet him. "Hop up in this chair, man. I'll do you a fade that will set the young ladies a-twittering like birds in the trees."

"I want to call my mama, to tell her where I am." It was apparent that Sheldon was about to lose it any minute. His lip was trembling and his fists were clinched, ready to punch out anybody's lights that gave him a hard time, regardless of size.

"She's probably wondering why you aren't in school, maybe. Why aren't you in school, by the way?" The barber got out his phone and made ready to dial. "Just in case she asks. You know how mamas are. Always checking up on you." He winked at the other curious brown faces with their beards of shaving foam like a bunch of ethnic Santa Clauses.

"Because the kidnappers asked me to show them the parking lot and then—" That was when Sheldon let out a long wail any first grader would have been proud of. "—they shoved me into their car and drove away from St. Mark's and I was supposed to do Show and Tell this morning in Mrs. Peabody's room."

"That's the kid they've got the alert out for this morning," said one of the shaving cream Santas. "I bet a fiver that's him."

ɔᔆɔᔆ

He was waiting at police station when Detective Moss got there with Kenya. She'd had to leave her car at a truck stop on the way to Memphis when St. Mark's called her to say that Sheldon was missing. She subsequently had a certifiable meltdown, at which time Moss had to fit her with all her luggage in his compact car to take the distraught Miss West back to the city. He wondered privately, and couldn't imagine, what the hell she thought she was going to do with all those clothes down in the Boonies. *Maybe have a yard sale after the funeral?* Moss amused himself with options while Kenya "Chantal" West convulsed beside him.

Shortly before ten, as they were reaching the outskirts of the city, he got a call from the station.

"We got the kid here. Come get him quick before he destroys the place."

Moss could have sworn there was a note of panic in the officer's voice.

"Is he okay?"

"Fine. Just fine. It's the rest of us I'm worried about."

He glanced at Kenya who managed to look up from her hanky to give him one of her 100-kilowatt smiles.

"Sheldon?" came the quavering voice of the devoted mother. Kenya snatched the phone and shrieked. "Sheldon, you little shit, you better behave 'til I get there or so help me God I'll wail your behind!"

"Mommy? I'm okay. Eating ice cream and driving the policemen nuts."

Chapter 8

Come on, Dad. It won't hurt," Faun pleaded, holding out a tongue depressor. "Just scrape the inside of your cheek."

"What do you hope to prove by this? I mean, I don't know anything about my family—what killed them and all that. Probably wound up at the wrong end of a shotgun, most like." Quade dutifully did as he was told, scraping the inside of his cheek and putting the cells on the slide his daughter handed him.

"Mom, now you. You've got to be part of this experiment. It's totally anonymous."

"I'm not a laboratory animal." Isis had her hands in the bread she was making for morning delivery. Lesbos, the female-only compound/company her mother Lois had started in the Thicket, was delivering a number of organic products and baked goods to cities as far as Atlanta, Chattanooga, and Birmingham.

In spite of local gossip, the chief of police allowed his wife to participate in the lesbian enterprise. Some said he was afraid of his mother-in-law, although not within earshot of the chief himself. Others, who knew Walker better, said he was just trying to keep the peace which was what Julia Springs paid him to do. Nobody pointed out that the peace was among a bunch of headstrong women.

Nobody needed to.

Now, it was shaping up to be a battle between two hardheaded women, his wife and daughter, and, if he had to pick a winner, Quade bet Faun would get her way. After all, she had time on her side.

"What's the big deal, Mom? You act like your DNA is sacred or something. It's just for research, to help people with chronic diseases."

"I'm busy now, Faun, can't you see that?" Isis was beginning to feel cornered, Quade could tell from the note in her voice. "Go pick on someone else, your grandmother, for instance."

Quade tried the humorous approach. "Does that list of diseases include chronically poor? If it does, my DNA ought to count double."

"Funny, Dad." Faun stalked away. Her father marveled at her strategy. Playing hurt so Isis would give in and contribute her DNA to scientific research.

'"She'll be back, you watch." Isis could always tell what he was thinking.

"Sure, she will. Better do like she says. Maybe you can take it off your taxes as a charity donation." Quade took a last sip of coffee and a fleeting glance at the local newspaper.

His wife covered the loaves with clean dish towels to rise and rinsed her hands at the sink. "Don't joke about it, Quade. It's not going to be funny when she finds out."

"Finds out what? That you've got insanity in the family? Everybody's family has got somebody that's two bubbles off plumb. You're not scared of that, are you?"

"That's not what I mean." Before he could ask what she did mean, Isis had left the kitchen.

eɔeɔ

The following night, after the last show, Kenya left Memphis in a hurry.

She packed enough clothes to get Sheldon through the summer, shut the condominium, and told the cleaning lady she was going on a cruise. The last thing she did was text Grey Grayson, leader of the Shades of Gray, she was quitting the show. Personal reasons. He didn't seem to be broken up, said to let him know when she was ready to perform again and he'd try to schedule her back in, that he would deposit her check in the bank and even add a couple of hundred even though she had broken her contract. "Oh, and by the way, where can I get in touch with you?"

"Same place you always do, my phone," Kenya replied.

Grey was married with three kids and a jealous wife who resembled a professional wrestler. She knew about Kenya's affair with her husband and just wrote it off as she would a business expense. Grayson could sew his seed outside the family plot as long no fruit came of them. His wife had once been his lead singer and knew how that drill went. She had taken Grey from his first wife and she wasn't about to support a bunch of little Grayson bastards.

Kenya told herself she didn't mind any of this. In fact, in daylight and sober, Grey was hardly the man of her dreams. The fact was, there wasn't any man of her dreams because she didn't dream about men.

Kenya dreamed about a place where she and Sheldon could be safe, surrounded by her sisters, cousins, children, and parties—birthday parties, Christmas parties, parties where everyone received the gift they had always wanted. And she, Kenya Jones, would play Lady Bountiful, bringing pleasure. Never disappointment. That alone was what Kenya dreamed of because she had never had been part of that dream. Her life had been a desert, devoid of mirages or miracles.

No, men had only brought her pain to which she was now immune. The only man in her life now was her son, who was a gift from Holly Simpson. Grey Grayson had given Sheldon his name because he thought the boy was his which was all right with Kenya. Grayson hadn't even bother to do a paternity test, so much did he play around. Served the bastard right, Kenya was fond of saying to herself.

Grover Moss shared that sentiment although of the opposite gender. His ex-spouse had been caught in bed with his partner on the force. No telling where else she was playing because she came down with an STD as a result. Grover gave her everything—their daughter, the dog, the furniture, and the flat screen TV, and moved back in with his mother who'd told him not to marry that whore in the first place.

"But oh, no, you don't listen, do you, Grover? You are just like your father, God bless him."

After enough of being reminded of how much like his father he was, Grover moved out to a tiny apartment where he spent so little time the neighbors called the police one night when he came home late, not recognizing him for a tenant. Memphis was full of strangers now. The city was not the same place where he grew up, running in the street, doing the shuffle for spare change. Now, it was all pimps, drug dealers, and petty gang bangers. Moss was tired, tired of life, and he had a lot of it left to live.

Until he met the craziest, most beautiful, most mixed-up bitch he had ever had the misfortune to fall in love with. What else could he call it?

She was mercurial, imperious as his mother, had a

brat for a son, and, her saving grace, a weak spot as soft as a caramel crème. Oh, yes, and she was beautiful. He couldn't imagine her wanting a lump like him. He was a good detective, a good friend to those who knew him well but, nevertheless, a lump.

So he called her on the flimsy pretext of wanting to interview Sheldon, knowing she would guard her only man-child like a mama lion. He got the reply he expected.

"Absolutely not! And I haven't got time to talk, I'm leaving town directly."

"Can I ask where you're going? You don't seem to realize you're in danger, Miss West, and you need to stay here where I can keep an eye on you until—"

Bad move, very bad.

"Oh, uh huh! You keeping an eye on Sheldon only got him kidnapped, and it was only by his quick-thinking that he saved himself. Hell, he's only six years old!"

"Seven," Sheldon's voice said in the background.

She hardly drew a breath. "I'm in danger, all right! Your police force is more dangerous than the crooks! That's why I'm getting the hell out of Memphis before they decide what they are going to pull next," the unobtainable Chantal West said.

"And have you decided who 'they' are? Have you any clue? Because you lured me down to Georgia to that little po-dunk town—I've even forgot what it was called—on the pretext of giving some names of drug kingpins who were responsible for your friend's death. Or have you forgotten?"

Miss West sounded a little less sure of herself. In fact, she sounded like your average scared-as-hell-but-defiant independent woman. "Oh, yeah, I did, didn't I? Well, someone must have overheard our conversation, too, to follow me home like that. But Quade Walker has them in custody down there, right?"

"So you're telling me you were lying to get me to follow you just in case there was trouble, is that right?"

"Well, not exactly lying. Holly did mention some names over the years..." She trailed off. "Look, Detective, the longer we keep talking, the longer Sheldon and I are in danger. I got to get on the road. Can we talk later?"

"Yes, ma'am, but keep in touch." She had passed through his life like a comet, breathtaking beautiful but solid ice over rocks.

"Definitely. And I promise I'll give you those names. Just in a safer way of communication."

He could tell this woman thought the whole world was out to get her. Like the thugs didn't have nothing else to do but hunt her down. "Carrier pigeon, maybe? Far as I know, they haven't hacked into the birds yet."

She made that little "tsk" noise his mother used to make when he said something stupid. "No, by US mail. Goodbye, Detective Moss."

Chapter 9

Six trials later, Faun got her answer, thereby making her own invention the key to her eventual destruction.

She had finally gotten her mother to give her a DNA sample, albeit reluctantly, as if Isis knew what her daughter would find. It was positive for—among other things—Amyotrophic Lateral Sclerosis, the debilitating brain disease, known to the general public as Lou Gehrig's Disease. The most common hereditary type was found in people of Scandinavian descent. Her grandmother's name had been Lindstrom. Lois Lindstrom, before she took the name Slade.

It was a balancing act and her own life was on the scales. Her father turned out positive for nothing, except diabetes on his mother's side, the white side. She took her father's blood type one step further. Typing it for genealogical origin, she found he had the standard Amerindian blood type: mixed European with Native American haplogenotypes.

A man's voice cut through the wall of her consciousness. "You living here?"

She was startled to the point of letting out a scream,

which she quickly squelched. Scientists didn't scream, they didn't even notice they'd been interrupted. Still, when Faun turned to face whoever it was, she had disaster written all over her. "What time is it?"

Bjorn stepped into the light from the computer. "Close to midnight. Thought I'd check. Just got off myself. My god, what's wrong? The program go down again?" He sat beside her, big and tangible, and with an expression on his face as if he understood everything.

Faun did what she never thought she would do, she blubbered. His arms went around her, and Bjorn, Scandinavian to the last blood cell, pulled her to him. "There, cry it out. It can't be all that bad, whatever it is. Come on, tell Papa what's wrong."

"I'm never going to have children! And I'm going to get ALS and be a screaming mess!"

Through great hacking sobs, he got the message. She had opened the Pandora's Box of DNA and let the evil genes out.

"Faun, listen. *Listen.*"

Gradually, the sobs subsided and then stopped altogether. A little voice said, "What? There's nothing you can say that wouldn't be a lie."

"Yes, there is. Just listen. Don't try to suck it up. Don't try to minimize it. Just listen, okay?"

"Okay, what?"

"Well, for starters, you're talking about a disease that affects one percent of the population or less. Neither of your parents or grandparents had it, right?"

"No, but I found the gene on both sides, my mother's and my maternal grandfather's. Everyone knows—" She stopped and sat up, wiping her face with her blouse.

"Everyone knows what?" Bjorn studied her face, exquisite in its unawareness, without artifice or coy expressions. "Faun?"

She turned in his direction and he thought he was looking at love for the first time. In the past, there'd been plenty of girls, plenty of sex, but no love. Not like this. Bjorn couldn't resist kissing that face.

It was like he had set off a security alarm.

"Don't!" Faun drew back as if had he punched her. "No!" She stood up so abruptly, her computer stool flew backward, colliding with another chair.

Bjorn was suddenly embarrassed by his impulse. "Sorry. I just...I don't know..." He hid his confusion by retrieving her chair.

"Felt sorry for me, is that it? " She aimed an expert kick at the stool, sending it in just the right place before the computer god. "Well, don't bother. Because I'm going to find a cure for ALS if I die trying!" As if taking a vow of devotion, Faun plopped down on the stool. "Now, let's get to work. I've got stuff to do, and I know you do."

She left him wondering what everyone else knew and he didn't. Then Bjorn replayed that entire extraordinary conversation until he came to the part about inheriting the ALS gene from both her mother's and maternal grandfather's sides. *But, of course, they would be one and the same, right? Unless—*

"Oh, god," he said in a voice so soft at first he thought she didn't hear him.

"What?"

"Nothing, this virus is just duplicating again. I'm on it, though." *Nice save.*

"Let me know if anything turns up," she said idly. It was clear she was distracted by something else.

"I'm afraid it has."

On the screen in front of him were there words *So now you know* in some esoteric font. It was accompanied with a cartoon character, a fat man in some kind of rocket chair going "Ha! Ha! Ha!" and then turning into a shark eating up more photos of Holly—Holly shooting up, Holly pleading for her life, Holly with a rope around her neck doing S&M.

"Don't look," he said, but it was too late.

She saw the shark eating the last photo of Holly from where she stood across the room.

Just then, the shark regurgitated all the photos across the screen.

෧෬෧

Quade was just getting comfortable in bed, adjusting his six-foot-three frame around his wife, when the phone rang. It was Faun, trying to sound like a scientist, with a telltale tremor that told him she was still a kid.

"It's happened again. He hacked through our security system, the firewall—everything. It's like you can't stop him. Then it just disappears."

"You're sure it's the same hacker? You know, once they get in—"

"Dad, he has pictures of Holly, of her doing things you wouldn't believe."

Quade sighed. By now, he would believe anything. "Call your campus tech and then the campus police."

"The tech was here when it happened, and we already filed a hacking report with the police. They said this program has a virus embedded in it that makes the computer crash once it works its way through the files. All that data is compromised, and on top of that, whoever accesses it, gets the virus on their computer, too."

"But you backed up your data files before this happened, right?"

"Right. Since it happened, I've been doing double entry on the lab program and on my laptop." Her voice began to waver. "I'm so tired, Dad. I didn't even know Holly. Why am I the target?"

"Because whoever is doing this knows you're from Julia Springs, like Holly was. That's the only connection, I see."

There was a sigh on the other end. "Maybe," she said, "but could you call that detective from Memphis again. I think he ought to know."

His wife was awake by then, sitting up like an older version of her daughter. "What's wrong? Is it Faun?"

"She's okay," he said, covering the phone. "Some-one sent her more pictures of Holly Simpson. Go to sleep. That goes for both of you."

"And, Dad, I was talking on my phone when it happened. I got pictures of most of it."

Bjorn, who was listening, interrupted."Hello, I'm the tech and I think we've been hacked by an international organization, not just some sick criminals."

"Okay, I'm coming up there tomorrow. Get some sleep." Quade put the phone down on the nightstand, but this time he didn't curl around his wife's body. He lay staring at nothing but the shadows dancing on the wall from the spring wind outside.

When he was little, his step-father told him those were the shadows of ghosts scratching at the window to get in. He remembered asking, 'But they won't get in, will they?' 'Only if you're bad, then they'll come and get'cha' was the asshole's reply. Now, Quade lay awake wondering what evil ghost from the past was trying to get in and hurt his family.

ひとひ

Kenya was on her way to Birmingham, speeding down the interstate, when she noticed another car had fol-lowed her through the turnoff south, a black SUV with smoked windows.

Moss finished his drink at Muley's waiting for his

tipster Bobo to show up. He finally went home, watched Leno and then fell asleep in his chair in his pajamas and slippers. In his dream, Chantal West was snuggling close to him, whispering words you couldn't say out loud. He was wakened at three in the morning by none other than the crazy beautiful woman of his dreams shouting something about a black SUV.

Moss responded automatically, trying to equate this shrieking bitch with the siren in his dream. "Call 911. Or the highway patrol. Whatever you do, keep moving."

"Thanks a helluva lot!"

The phone went dead.

"Damn," he said softly, "that's some kind of a hot-headed woman."

She pulled over abruptly on the first emergency shoulder she came to, letting the SUV swoosh by. Three semis passed in succession before she got back on the road.

She spent a sleepless night, watching over her son, and found Quade in his office at the police station the next morning. Sheldon was still in his footie pajamas, carrying his blankie and teddy bear when she carried him into the station.

Quade had his usual Styrofoam cup of coffee by his computer and was pondering his mail when he looked up. "How are you, Shekenya? Good to see you."

"Call me Kenya now, if you don't mind, and this isn't a social visit, Quade. I'm scared to death." He nodded attentively, knowing her flair for drama. "Know a place that's for sale around here? Some place I can make secure? Big enough for my little sisters to come live with me, too. Only not so little anymore. Baby Pearl is starting college. First one in the family to get past high school, can you believe?"

"As I recall, she was a toddler when I saw her last

time. And you were singing gospel." He didn't mention the Reverend Jeremiah. By the looks of her, Kenya had left the past way behind.

She filled in the gap with. "They say time waits for no man...or woman."

Walker nodded, then said, "Only place in old town is Ham Phillip's old place, Magnolia Alley. Ross Tanner has a bid in for it. If he gets his way, he'll tear the old place down and make it a gated community for, get this, horse owners with riding trails and barns and a nine hole golf course. A kind of rich dudes' playground."

"Has anybody else put a bid in, do you know?"

"Nobody's got the money to develop it but him. It's kind of a mess. Orchard gone wild, vandals have done a right job on the house. But talk to Cameron Bulloch, he's the realtor. I warn you though. Probably got some of old Ham's robots running around the place still. You'd like that, wouldn't you, son?"

He glanced over to where Sheldon had been sitting when his mother had come in. It was empty.

Kenya jumped up, despite her exhaustion. "Sheldon, come here right now, ya hear? If I have to come get you, you're going to feel it!"

"He's all right, Kenya. Let him go. He can't hurt much of anything."

A splintery crash made that a lie. Sheldon came running back from the inner office, his eyes wide. "I didn't do it Mommy! The computer just fell over by itself. Honest!"

Kenya closed her eyes. "I'll buy you another one, Quade. Hope there wasn't anything important on it."

ℰᴔℰᴔ

Cameron Bulloch was smooth, white, and rich like his parents. Melissa Bulloch Etheridge Mallory Tanner was now eighty-seven with a hearing problem and a boy-friend seventeen years her junior. "Just waiting for that old thing to die so he can get his hands on all that money," was Saranjii's opinion of the situation. "Hell, she's got more plastic in her than a recycle bin."

Cam's father had been one of Melissa's four husbands—all wealthy and powerful, all except Jordan Tanner. "That one was for love," Melissa was fond of saying. "Love keeps you young—younger than the best plastic surgery and it's free."

Kenya introduced herself as Chantal West and Bulloch's smooth face instantly lit up with a patronizing smile. He was on his feet like a head waiter in a five-star restaurant. "Yes, I've heard of you, Miss West. In fact, I've seen you perform at the Memphis Jazz Club, right? To what do I owe this honor?"

With one eye on Sheldon, Kenya was wasting no time. "I'm interested in buying Magnolia Alley. I'll match your best offer and raise them ten thousand if they try to overbid me."

Cameron Bulloch, she told Saranjii later, looked like he'd been punched in his substantial gut. By this time, she'd checked into a motel, gotten Sheldon a new game on his tablet to keep him out of trouble, and called Detective Moss back to apologize, also to ask him to run a trace on a black Ford SUV with the license ALS134.

"Could I ask why?"

"Because that's the one that followed me from Tennessee until I lost them in Alabama."

"What were they doing?" He tried not to lean on the word "they" again. "And what state? Tennessee, Georgia?"

"I couldn't see. They were going the same direction as I was at three in the morning and staying right behind me."

"And were you breaking the sound barrier like you always do?" As usual, his attempts at humor ended the conversation. Abruptly.

Now, with Sheldon in tow, she was at the realtor's office doing a good job of looking as if she could afford a house as big as she remembered Magnolia Alley to be.

"Call me Cam, please." Bulloch appeared as though he was about to wet himself.

"Only if you call me Chantal." Kenya smiled sweetly. 'You probably don't remember me, but your stepfather, Jordan Tanner, did me a favor once. I just want to do something for him in return. I know he and Mr. Phillips were friends. He wouldn't want to see that old place torn down. And he wouldn't have cared if my family bought it. Mr. Jordan was also friends with my Aya—grandmother. They used to call her Root Woman because she was what they called a healer."

A look came over Bulloch's face, as if he remembered some scandal attached to her. "Now I remember! She founded the church—Glory Road, wasn't it? Weren't you—"

"Yes, that was me. Can we get down to business fast, Cam? My son is getting restless and I don't want to pay for any more damage than Chief Walker's computer if I have to fix up Magnolia Alley."

Bulloch reacted as if he'd been stuck with something sharp. The figure she said didn't matter, the house did. It had to be well off the road, up a long drive, at least two stories, lots of land—in short, Magnolia Alley.

Cam Bulloch's smooth, pink face got smoother with shock. A black person wanting to live in an ante-bellum mansion undoubtedly partly built with slave labor. "I believe there's already a bid on that place, Chantal. Oh yes," Bulloch said with relief, "seventy-five thousand. That place is badly in need of some repairs. Full of scraps and junk Hamilton Phillips left when he passed. Lord, that man was eccentric, but a genius nonetheless, I'll say that for him."

She spoiled his attempts to change the subject. "I'll bid one hundred. Thirty down. As is. And tell Mr. Tanner, I'll overbid him whatever he bids. Within reason, of course."

Bulloch conveyed that message to Ross Tanner who said Chantal could have it for seventy-five and good luck. The richest man in two counties could afford to be generous. He owned more land than he had any use for anyway. "History comes full circle. The master becomes the slave, right, Bulloch? Is she pretty, the little songbird?"

Although he talked a good game, it was just talk. Everybody knew Ross Tanner was queer as a two-dollar bill."Beautiful. But she's a hard-nosed business woman, I tell you what, Ross. Pretty soon, she'll own the whole damn town."

That's just what Kenya was thinking as she set out for Magnolia Alley. "We're going to put this place on the map, baby." Sheldon remained ominously quiet in the back seat. He was engrossed in dismantling his tablet to see what made it work.

Behind her shades, Kenya rolled her eyes. *Oh well, at least he's busy.*

She had sent Toya and Baby Pearl money to come down from Atlanta, to stay if they wanted to or not, the choice was up to them. Like her, they had grown up in the foster care system. After Lewis Spencer was found dead in the quarry, Pearlene just couldn't cope without a man. Whatever and whoever would feed her habit, she was dependent in more ways than one.

Toya was twenty-three now and had a job, and Baby Pearl lived with her. Baby Pearl, now known as Ashley and was just a baby when she left them, turned twenty this month. They would have a big birthday celebration for her with presents and balloons at Saranjii's so everybody could see Kenya Jones was no longer a thing to be spat upon—cursed by her own mother and, by extension, the whole town—nor regarded as trash.

Root Woman would have been proud of her.

Aya, keep watch over me.

Chapter 10

While Quade was driving up to Athens, he called Moss in Memphis. "Looks like our boy has struck again," he said to the speaker phone. "Sent a virus to my daughter's computer that shut down her program. I'm on my way to look at it now. Had some porn shots of Holly Simpson with it. Not anything I want my kid to see, but smart girl that she is, she got a picture of the last screen with her phone. I told her not to send it to me by e-mail, I'd come get it. Says the tech guy got even more."

Moss grunted approval. "Hey, Walker, I've got some leads on this creep, myself. Word on the street says the kingpin is in some legit part of the pharmaceutical business. A white dude. Gotta be."

"You got a name?"

"Not yet. Tipster didn't show up last night, but Miss West called. She thinks some SUV was following her down there. Got the license plate number."

"I saw her this morning with that kid."

"You met Sheldon and lived to tell about it?" Moss let out a belly laugh that made his co-workers envious.

Walker smiled, thinking what effect a detective

laughing must have on those around him. "Yeah, but my computer didn't."

"Kid's a monster, but don't you dare tell her I said so. Anyway, she got the license number of the SUV. Turns out it's leased to a corporation. A Biopharma Co. I called information and it's listed as having offices in thirty states. So I called the one in Chattanooga, right? Asked where the corporate headquarters was located. They're a subsidiary of another company located somewhere in Europe, but corporate headquarters for the States is right outside Greenville."

"A conglomerate that has shell companies sprouting up like mushrooms all over. That figures." It was a statement insinuating they were helpless, a fact of life that people had accepted—except people who didn't know any better, like him.

"Exactly." Moss sat back in his swivel chair. "The kind with an army of lawyers to do their dirty laundry, mostly in large bills."

For a long minute, neither man said anything, then Quade said. "You know, Faun asked me why she was the target. Maybe that's why. Because she's trying to develop this app that will tell you whether you have a chronic disease or not."

"Sounds cheerful. She's into that sort of stuff, correct? Biomed stuff?"

"Yeah, way over my head. Look, I don't give a rat's ass what this company does or how big they are, but if they're trying to hurt my daughter, I going to take 'em on." Quade sounded more like an army ranger, less like a police chief.

"I hear you." Moss was thinking about Kenya West. Her frantic calls for help in the middle of the night. Her friend Holly Simpson and all the Jane Does he had seen—more than ten with the same tattoo, a shark riding some kind of a jet-propelled chair with *I kill the things I love* scrolled underneath. All had been bound and tied like Holly, all women, all victims of sadistic torture, and all dead, except for West and Walker. The end of the alphabet. He tried to sound casual "Give me the week to wrap things up here and I'll be down by the weekend, okay? We're in this together, man. Meanwhile, keep in touch with anything you find out. And Walker?"

"Yeah?"

"Don't go gunning for them just yet, okay?" Something in Quade's tone was making Moss hold his breath.

"I won't. Not yet."

Moss exhaled noisily, saying, "Good man," then hung up.

He leaned back in his swivel chair, staring into space until someone shouting his name brought him back to earth. One of the sergeants named Jackson waved him over.

"Isn't this your man on the street? The one who used to hang out at Muley's, Bobo or whatever?" Jackson shoved a glossy photo of a battered corpse under his nose. "Found him in a dumpster over on Third and River. Needle tracks says he was on horse. Look at the tattoo on his chest. Fresh."

Same tattoo minus the heart. Apparently the perp had a thing for tattooed women, but not down-and-out musicians.

Grover Moss looked at what was left of his snitch. "He's got a name, Sergeant Jackson. It's George. George...something. I got it! George Waddell. Used to be a musician. Played trumpet with some pretty big names until..." Moss froze, without finishing the sentence.

Waddell, West, and Walker. That did it. Grover Moss got to his feet and lingered a few minutes, trying to appear casual. Except those who knew him well, knew he was going after somebody. "Tell the super I'll be out of town following a lead. I'll call him."

Sergeant Jackson looked at the glossy photo in his hand. "Played the trumpet, huh? I play a little trombone, just jamming, parties, stuff like that. Think I'll surf the Net, see what they're saying about ol' Bobo...excuse, George." When he didn't get an answer, Jackson looked up and found he was talking to himself.

Moss was gone.

ᔕᔕᔕ

Bulloch was at least honest about the house needing repairs. It looked so much like a haunted house at Halloween, Sheldon wouldn't even get out of the car.

"Do zombies live here, Mama? 'Cause if they do, I don't want them to eat my brains. I like my brains to stay in my head."

But Kenya was only half-listening. Leaving the keys in the ignition and the door wide open, she stared at the house. She didn't see the peeling paint, the shutter flapping in the breeze, the piles of old car parts, metal bed frames, and just plain junk. She saw herself on the columned porch, waving to admirers, dressed in gossamer clothes. She saw a Creole princess holding court, fluttering her fan and smiling because life was all roses and Daddy loved his little girl.

Then, walking slowly up the long shady drive as if that dream were leading her inside the etched glass doors, Kenya entered Magnolia Alley.

She only heard the engine start on her Cadillac too late, too late to stop Sheldon, who had slipped behind the wheel, from putting the car in gear and rolling down the driveway.

She raced out to the porch just as he rolled past her,

an expression of horrified glee on his face, which disappeared when the car rolled into a peach tree. When she reached into the car and turned off the ignition, her son was rubbing a bump on his forehead. Green peaches were still dropping like green hailstones on the ruined vehicle as if the peach tree were trying to defend itself.

"There's more than your head that's gonna hurt, boy! Look what you've done now, Sheldon! Just look at my new car." He squinted through his tears. The hood was crumpled and there was steam coming from the radiator. "What did you think you were doing, anyway?"

"Saving you from the zombies, Mama. I thought they had got you." He burst into sobs. "I didn't want them to hurt you. Eat your brains."

She grabbed him in a hug so tight, he couldn't breathe. "Them old zombies would sure be disappointed if they got into my head and found nothing to eat. 'Cause anybody with any brains wouldn't have left the keys in the car. But that's mighty brave of you, honey. You're Mama's protector, that's what. Her brave little boy." Kenya kissed the bump on Sheldon's head and called for a tow truck. After pocketing the phone, she took Sheldon by the hand. "Come on, let's explore. All this belongs to us now."

"And Auntie Toya and Baby Pearl and Uncle Freddy."

"Yes, and them, too. Now, let's go explore our new old house."

᪉᪉᪉

By the time Quade Walker got to the university, things were back to normal in Faun's lab. He realized that sending a virus that destroyed all the data in your hard drives and had dirty pictures popping up on the screen was the norm to kids these days. That it had information that might lead to solving a murder was secondary to what it could do to their grades, if they didn't turn in a project.

That was basically what the lab techs going about their business as usual thought.

He felt like an over-reacting small-town policeman who needed an excuse for a road trip, until he met Chris Bjorn. He was hanging around the lab, watching the techs scurry in and out, putting on or discarding lab coats and gloves in a bin by the door. A few of them stopped to say hello and shake his hand, although he wasn't sure what they'd been touching.

One of them was the odd girl named Angela. She was the only one that mentioned the virus "Hi, Officer Walker. You here about the virus?" Head down, she threw the words at him as she went out the door.

"Yeah, and just to check on Faun. How's it going, Angela?"

She stopped and looked up, her eyes wide. "You remembered my name?"

"Sure, I always remember pretty girls." He didn't expect that old line to draw the reaction it did.

Angela acted like she didn't know where to look, readjusted her thick glasses, and scurried out the door with. "Goodbye, Mr. Walker. Have a good one."

"She's a strange one." A tall, blond young man was standing nearby. His campus ID badge said he was Chris Something, IT Department. "It's Bjorn if you're wondering. Chris Bjorn, and you're Faun's father, I'll bet. I usually get referred to as the tech."

They shook hands. "You're the one who got the video, I take it. Nice work, Mr. Bjorn. That took fast thinking on your part."

He didn't have to have Isis with him to tell this

young man was a match for Faun. Tall, blond, with intelligence oozing out of him, Bjorn had a steadiness about him that Quade recognized in himself. An ability to take flack and keep a steady hand on the trigger.

"Actually, it's part of my job, really. Keeping the camera on to record what actions these viruses are taking so we can reverse them."

"And can you? Reverse them, I mean."

"In some cases. At least we can sort of tell what program they're using, just in case they're going to self-destruct."

Quade pondered the "sort of" generation. In his day you either did or you didn't. No sort of about it. "Sounds complicated."

"It is, unless you consider it a game." Bjorn grinned. "I know, hard to play games with somebody's life's work, right? But if you get up tight, you lose even bigger. Object is to stay loose."

"Spoken like a true gamer."

"Hey, I'm a graduate of the arcades of yore, Chief. Ah, here's the boss now."

Faun came in, looking exhausted. Quade recognized that look. She used to get it when she did homework until one o'clock in the morning. Driven, Isis called it. When she saw Quade, his daughter hugged him wordlessly. He looked at Bjorn over her head. In those Nordic blue eyes, he saw concern, however guarded. *Much as a man in love can guard anything,* Quade thought. "Come on, I'll buy you both lunch."

At the burger joint off campus, Faun picked at her French fries, while Bjorn devoured his double cheeseburger. At the same time, he asked Quade about forensic science's role in detective work. They had a discussion about blood typing and DNA playing a significant role in solving crimes.

All the while, Quade watched his daughter with concern. It is as though the young man was trying to protect her from something, some unseen menace. As a parent, Quade resented that because it implied possessiveness. At the same time, he understood because he had always felt that way about Isis.

Just then, Faun came alive. "Pop, your DNA is consistent for Amerindian ancestors and Caucasians from Northern Europe, Scandinavians, in fact. Where'd the Scandinavian come from?"

"Whoa!" Quade sat back in the booth, blinking. "Say that in English, baby."

"Sorry, I didn't mean to spring that on you, Pop. It's just that it's kind of become important to me lately." Faun regarded the fried potatoes with disgust. "These things are crawling with polyunsaturates," she said, shoving her plate away.

Quade pretended to study his daughter's discarded plate. "Where? I don't see any."

"You wouldn't, Dad. Trans fats are invisible to the naked eye, but they clog arteries and they're in just about everything we eat." Faun caught the amused expression on her father's face. "Oh, I see. Joke." She and Bjorn gave a knowing look to one another that said old people's joke, then sputtered with laughter.

"That's better. Order something else, okay?" Quade knew what Isis would say, "You indulge that girl too much."

But then his wife wasn't here, hadn't seen what Faun had seen or done the things Faun had done. Isis had always hidden away in Julia Springs, expanding her mother's growing business worldwide, but naively far away from anything that she thought could hurt her.

"Let's see here, those deli sandwiches look good," he said, taking up the menu.

"Dad, you're making such a big effort to change the subject."

Bjorn unfolded from the booth, towering over them. "I'll go get the sandwich. Pastrami or turkey on—"

"Turkey, Pita bread, lettuce, tomato, no mayo. Thanks, Chris." She might as well been talking to the girl who took orders.

"Only if you'll let me have your fries. My arteries could stand a little plaque. What the hell? You only live once."

"Sure, your funeral." Shoving over the fries as if they were nuclear, Faun leaned forward on her elbows. "Now, Dad, tell me what I'm missing here."

"You know, I like that boy—young man, and I can tell he likes you, baby."

"Chris? He's okay. Very sharp." For Faun, that was high praise at least. "Knows his way around computers. Now, Dad, the story."

Quade slouched back against the padded booth. "Okay, you know the story about my dad, Lou Owl. He never married my mother because white girls didn't marry non-whites in those days. Besides, he was already married, had a whole slew of kids."

Faun's smile sensed scandal. Her generation wasn't shocked by anything. "Sounds like quite a swinger. Go on."

"After he was killed in the big storm, I found out later he had won the Purple Heart and a whole bunch of other medals fighting in World War Two." He tried to make it relevant to her, knowing his daughter wasn't interested in the past, even his past. Quade felt sorry about that, as if he had failed her somehow. "You know your cousins Dan and Mitchell are doing real well at school. Mitchell is in pre-med at Georgia—"

"I know. I run into him occasionally, on-line, I mean.

We text. Go on." She poked a French fry as if it had germs.

"And Dan is at Tech."

"We text."

"Yeah, well, you probably know them better than I do, then."

"So tell me about Grandma Owens then. What was her maiden name? It doesn't matter about her husbands, just her."

Bjorn was back. "They'll call your number out when it's ready."

He slid into the booth beside Faun. Quade couldn't help thinking how much they suited each other, with their blue-eyed intelligence and insouciant expressions.

"Swenson. She was born Eileen Swenson," he said.

"We say Svenson up in Minnesota. Spell it that way, too." Bjorn sampled the cold fries, making a face. "You're right, too greasy." Faun was looking at him as though he had brought a live grenade back to the table.

"Say that again." For the first time, Faun acknowledged him.

"Too greasy? Sorry, I didn't mean to interrupt." Bjorn looked from one of them to the other, still holding the limp fry.

"No, the part about Minnesota." It was hard to ignore the urgency in her voice.

Quade filled in for him, hoping he'd take the hint that they were talking about genetics. "That's where she was born. Way up in Minnesota. Family came down here with the Mennonites to farm. Are you Swedish, Chris?"

"Norwegian. I get it now." Bjorn leaned back, his eyes straying to the girl beside him as he chewed. "Faun thinks we Scandinavians carry a hereditary gene for ALS. Lou Gehrig's disease, we call it after the ball player who died from it. They haven't found a cure for it yet. I tried to tell her—"

Faun cut him short with a wave of her hand. "And I found the gene in mother's DNA. What aren't you telling me, Dad?"

Quade cleared his throat and eased back against the seat. Faun was being downright rude and imperious. He didn't like that superior attitude and let her know that by taking his time answering her.

"I'd better leave this discussion up to your mother, baby, 'cause that's all I know. You're asking the wrong person about family. I got my own family. They're happy and healthy and that's all I care about." He sought safety in changing the subject. "So, Chris, what have you got for me? You said you videoed this sequence on your cell phone."

Bjorn reached into his pants pocket and pulled out a key ring of flash drives. Detaching one, he shoved it across the table. "Here. I downloaded it for you. That way, the boys at the station won't think you're going to naughty places on the Web."

"Good man. Nothing the deputies I've got haven't done already, I'm sure. Any idea who's behind this?"

Abruptly shoving her plate out of the way, Faun slipped out of the booth, her face flushed with anger, her eyes filled with hot tears. "I'd better get back to the lab. Thanks, Dad." She rushed off before either man could say anything.

Left alone, they exchanged male looks and Bjorn said, "She's upset. It doesn't take much these days to set her off. She really ought to rest up this summer. Take a long break. Grad school is a big strain, much less under pressure of a grant."

"I don't know. She's always had things her way, Faun has. Lately, she's developed this attitude like some

big-time CEO or something. There's no excuse for rudeness, I don't care how smart you are. And she was rude to
you *and* to me."

Bjorn shrugged. "She'll learn. She's so young and so
smart. Sometimes, it's hard to put up with other people
getting in your way."

Quade threw some bills on the table, annoyed because he was annoyed with his own daughter. "I don't
care how smart you are, that's no excuse for rudeness.
You'd better believe I'm going to get in her face big time
about it. But I thank you for excusing her. Now, you were
saying you can possibly trace the origin of this hacker
guy?"

On the drive home, Quade tried to concentrate on
what Bjorn told him he had found out about the hacker or
hackers, since he couldn't rule out the possibility that this
was a gang as Moss suggested They were expert pro-
grammers, animators, interfacers, and, on top of that,
were using some weird computer language that was possibly of foreign origin. All that meant nothing to Quade,
except one thing—whoever was doing this, was driving
his daughter to the edge of a nervous breakdown by his
attempts to compromise her work.

Quade didn't know why he was thinking that whoever was doing this were men. If it was a woman who hated
women and also was involved in genomic research,
which would really mess up some statistics.

When he had said as much to Bjorn, the young man
talked around a mouthful of fries, "I think somebody is
trying to send a sick message. Look at what I gave you
and you'll see. In both videos, this signature image of a
round fat man in a rocket-propelled chair keeps popping
up. Then he turns into a shark that eats up the program.
That could be a caricature of himself destroying someone
else's work. Somebody who's also into ALS research,

porn, and drugs. Also a sicko sort of sadism." Bjorn toyed with the fries, obviously uncomfortable talking about something as intimate as pornography with a policeman. "A person who gets off on other people's pain. Like he can't feel anything himself."

'They know or imagine they know the victim.' His own words formed an earwig in Quade's head on the long drive home—that is until he called his wife.

"Finally!" Isis answered. She always said that when he went somewhere out of town, as if it had been days since she'd heard from him instead of just hours. "How's our girl?"

"Tired. She didn't eat anything."

"Never does. She must live on air like bromeliads."

He didn't have time for small talk. "Did you ever tell her about Michael?"

He imagined her freezing, wondering why the subject should come up now. After a long pause—too long—she asked. "No, why?"

"Because I think she's finding out, darling. The hard way. You'd better tell her before that happens. Where is he, anyhow?"

Another long pause. "I don't know, Quade. I honestly don't know. I've even called the Children's Home. It's closed. Why are you asking all these questions? He hasn't...done anything, has he?"

"Not that I know of. Look, baby, we'll talk when I get back. Everything's all right, then?"

"Fine, except Rudy needs money for prom and Kenya needs help renovating Magnolia Alley. That shyster Cam Bulloch sold her a white elephant, if you ask me. Place is falling down."

"Tell Rudy to get a job and Kenya to ask Cam Bulloch for a list of contractors who won't take advantage of a woman. Come to think of it, that's like asking the fox to watch the hen house." Quade allowed himself to have a chuckle at the expense of women on their own. In a millisecond, he was reminded of how his wife had been raised.

"Never mind, I'll get the team from Lesbos to do it. Forget the fox. I'll get the henhouse on it."

He called Grover Moss next.

"Moss, here." The detective sounded grumpier than usual.

"I catch you at a bad time?" There was the unmistakable sound of a police radio in the background.

"Damned Alabama troopers doing the thing they do best, calling the department to see if my badge is fake. And asking them if I'm here on official business."

In the background, Quade heard a voice say. "Here's your license back, Detective. Sorry about that. We had an alert a while ago to be on the lookout for a stolen vehicle. Driver was posing as a detective from Memphis."

"Funny, I got the police radio right here and I didn't get any alert."

Another voice joined the first. The trooper's backup, Quade guessed "Hey, Grover Moss. Didn't you used to play for Tuskegee?"

"Crimson Tide," said Moss with a snap. "Alabama."

"Roll Tide. Have a nice day."

Quade imagined the officer tipping his Smokey hat brim to Moss. He smiled into the phone. "You quarterbacked. Ran for a twenty-one-yard touchdown."

"That was then. This is now," Moss muttered into the phone. "Bastard! I'll tell him what kind of a day to have. Okay, Walker, what's new?"

"I got the video and some leads, I think. Where did you say that holding company Biopharma was based?"

"That's the thing, it was all over the world. Local companies had sold out to it, but retained their own names. Sort of holding companies, probably for money-laundering, among other things. The main office has got to be in Switzerland, and the US office in South Carolina, somewhere around Greenville."

Quade couldn't stifle a laugh. "I don't want to spoil your day. Tell you when you get here. Drive safe. And watch those Alabama boys."

"Roll Tide, my ass!"

Chapter 11

Not a thing in this whole damn place works! Not even the toilets. And I've invited my sisters to come and stay here! They'll turn around and leave when they don't have cable, much less be able to flush toilets."

Isis had answered Kenya's distress call personally. Now she stood in the great shell that used to be Magnolia Alley. Even its ornate molding was blacked with soot from squatters' fires. "That's probably because the water hasn't been turned on in ten years. That's about how long ago Ham Phillips died. You're sure the well is working?"

"Well? I haven't heard that word since I lived on Mcfarland's farm." Kenya stood there in the waning afternoon light coming from French doors. "I need a stiff drink."

"I'm sure this place isn't on city water. Kenya, you still haven't signed anything. You can still back out of the sale."

"And let Cameron Bulloch and Ross Tanner and all those other snobs sneer behind my back and say, 'She's just the same ignorant country girl she ever was. Didn't any of those city smarts rub off on her? No, siree, she's just a jumped up field hand, with a fancy name she made up.'"

Isis shrugged. "What do you care what they say? You've made it, they're just stuck in the same old place. Now, get moving, Queen of the Blues or whatever they call you. Quade will be home soon and he'll get somebody to help you. Or I'll call in the crew from Lesbos."

Just then Sheldon burst into the room. "Mama, I love this place. It's more fun than the kid's science museum back home in Memphis. Just meet my new robot. I'm going to name him Piglet."

He was followed by a whirring, lurching vacuum cleaner motor on which perched a pot with two mismatched eyes rolling in opposite directions. "Meet Piglet, Mama and Auntie Isis."

"Hello, ladies. We've met," said the lurching junk pile, "when I was much younger. I could use some lubricants and new parts. Where is Dr. Phillips? It's been awhile since I've been serviced."

Kenya giggled. "That makes two of us, honey."

Isis recovered first and replied with unruffled dignity. "You remember me, don't you?"

The machine turned its mismatched eyes with a grinding noise like fingernails on a chalkboard. "You've gotten heavier and also happier since we last met the night of the big storm. You are Isis. Lesbos is your home. Your mother is Queen Sappho otherwise known as Lois."

"I'm glad Dr. Phillips taught you to be truthful." Isis smiled. Quade would have just said there was more of her to love in the right places. "Dr. Phillips has been...recycled. Sheldon and Isis are your new owners now. You must serve them as Dr. Phillips would have wanted."

"I didn't know you knew robot speak. I'm impressed." Kenya gave Isis the elbow. "Hidden talents."

"Auntie Isis, you can make this thing talk?" Sheldon was dancing around Piglet, pushing the buttons on the little machine's aluminum torso. "Show me how."

The junk pile reacted sharply. "Mind your manners, boy! Stop poking at me! I'm not a dartboard. I'm a machine and proud to be one. And quit hopping! It makes me nervous."

"And me." Kenya stepped forward into Piglet's off-kilter laser scanner. "Do you know me?" Surely this machine couldn't see through years of plastic surgery.

There was a noise like a truck shifting gears. "I know the voice, not the face. You are the granddaughter of Root Woman. Your name is not in my vocabulary at this time. You may add it. You used to sing all the time. You have become...stronger. Yes, that's the word. Strong. Inside strong."

Sheldon immediately stood still. "I think I'm going to like this place. A whole lot! Do you fight zombies?"

Piglet swiveled with a creaking noise. "Of course, if that is your command. What are zombies, please?"

"Oh, brother, you've got a lot to learn. Come on, I'll show you a video game with zombies fighting humans, so you'll know if one is hanging around the house."

"Strong, my ass. Can I have that drink now?" Kenya sank down on a window seat and just avoided falling all the way through the rotten wood.

"I just happen to have a bottle of Mama's peach brandy in the truck and two paper cups. Come on. Sheldon will be all right."

"But I'm not sure that Piglet will."

They went outside into the late afternoon sun which patterned the broad veranda with leafy shadows.

"At least he didn't say you were fat," Isis giggled. "I'll have to lose twenty pounds before I get up the nerve to come back here."

"Honey, don't you wait that long or you might find me replaced by a zombie."

Two glasses of peach brandy later, Kenya decided she had a home for the first time in her life. They ordered chicken baskets delivered from the chicken place on the highway and went through the house room by room with sagging paper cups full of Mama Lois's peach brandy, doing imaginary decorating as only two women can do half-smashed. Sheldon gnawed on a drumstick, activating every robot he found in working condition until they were crashing into walls, rocketing down the stairs, and bumping into each other. Kenya found a closet full of old clothes and clapped a hat on one robot as he passed by while Isis added a scarf.

"I never thought I would live to see robots in drag." Putting on another of Mrs. Phillips seemingly endless supply of wide-brimmed hats, Kenya swished around the room singing "Ain't Misbehavin'."

When they had dressed as many robots as Sheldon got working, all running around with hats and scarves trailing behind them, both women sat down on the stairs, laughing.

Isis sobered first. "I admire you, Kenya. You've grown into a strong women, you know that?"

"Now you sound like Piglet. Besides, I had a good role model." Kenya searched for the words that could encompass Root Woman. "She made me believe in myself. Holly's grandmother did just the opposite to Holly. She had her believing only what the preacher said she was—a sinner come from a sinner."

Isis nodded. "Lois said one was infinite. The other finite."

"I guess." Kenya nodded and hummed a few bars. "Like your mama. Lois is a mighty strong woman. I believe she could whip bears with a switch."

Isis sat up, frowning, and took a sip from her damp paper cup. "Yes and no. Yes, because she's got through the early years and has never looked back. And no, because she knew what my father was like and still kept us there in that awful place."

"You know what my Aya used to say. She used to say there are some people who cast spells over other people. A spell where those people can't make a decision, can't even think for themselves until something stronger comes along to break that hold. In your case, it was love. For her, it was all her kids that gave Lois the strength to finally fight free of your dad. She hasn't looked back since that day she packed up and left him. You should give her credit for that."

"I do. It's because of her that I could love Quade, a policeman for God's sake, after the sheriff hauled us screaming away from her and put us in foster care."

Kenya nodded, reliving forgotten scenes. When Quade had picked Holly up for questioning about a burglary, Kenya had been with her. "I remember telling him that you loved him. You should have seen that man's face. You'd have thought he won the lottery or something."

" But you were only a teenager then. How could you have known?"

"Honey, I got news for you. Fourteen is the new thirty." Kenya's smile swept away all the shadows. "I'd had my first miscarriage by then."

"I only wished I had." Isis raised her eyes to look at Kenya. 'That's why they took us away."

At that point, they heard a voice downstairs yelling. "Is anybody home? Hey, Kenya? We're here. It's Toya and Ashley."

Kenya stopped, eyes wide. "Oh, almighty shit! They're here already."

"Who is?" Isis was feeling no pain by this time. She tried to get up and sat back down hard on the stairs. "Tell them to go away unless it's the chicken basket."

"Can't. It's Toya, and Pearl, s'cuse me, Ashley. That a white people's name, for godsake." Using the railing for support, Kenya tried to negotiate the steep stairs, but like Isis, ended by sitting half way down. "Hey, you two! Up here!"

Her sisters were looking around the front room, taking in the cobwebs, peeling paint, and crumbling plaster. Toya, tall and slender balanced on four-inch heels. "Is this place a dump or what? Kenya, you have lost your mind, bringing us down here. I thought this was some kind of grand place like the movies, not a freaking haunted house." She put her hands on her narrow hips in a pose that reminded Kenya of her mother. "I'm sure not bringing my baby down here. I'm glad I left him up in Atlanta, right, Ashley?"

"Does it have ghosts?" Baby Pearl looked around wide-eyed as though she expected something to snatch her into the dark beyond at any moment. Just then, Sheldon sent Piglet to the top of the landing dressed in Mrs. Phillip's wide-brimmed gardening hat, flowing scarf, and a child's dress. Baby Pearl dropped her purse and ran screaming into the next room while Toya just stood there openmouthed.

"Jesus! What's that?"

"Only a robot." Kenya spread her arms wide. "Come give me a hug, little sister."

But Toya stood teetering on her heels, her painted toes like reflectors on her feet, her doll face pouting with resentment. "I'm not going near that thing. I rode all this way on a frigging bus just to come to a damned crazy house. I should have known better, seeing as how it's my frigging, crazy-ass sister."

"In that case, I'll get Freddy to take you all back to a motel for a couple of nights, since it'll take about a week to whip this place into shape."

Isis couldn't believe the conciliatory tone Kenya was using, almost wheedling in the face of her sister's rudeness.

"I'd drive you to a motel but Sheldon drove my car into a tree. You remember Freddy? He's working at Saranji's now. He'll come get you."

"A week? More like a year to get this dump fit for humans to live in. Come on, Pearl. Let's get out of here!" Toya turned on her heel, clip-clapping across the floor, sunlight flowing through her short dress as she went out the door.

Edging back around the doorway, Baby Pearl looked at Kenya, as if she wanted to say something else other than "Bye, Kenya, bye, Sheldon." Instead, she followed her sister like an obedient puppy out the door.

"Why did you let her talk to you like that?" Not trusting her legs, Isis scooted downstairs, landing beside Kenya. "That girl's got no right."

"I guess she has a right 'cause I went off and left them." Kenya put her head on Isis's shoulder. "'Cause I promised to come back and I never did. But I did everything I could for them. Sent them money, presents, got them out of foster care and paid an aunt every month to keep them. But I'm too late, Isis. Just too little, too late."

The two women rocked on the stairs, thinking about what might have been.

❧❧❧

When Quade drove into the yard about nine o'clock, he found Isis passed out in the front seat of the truck. He smiled, seeing her asleep, her head pillowed on his old high school letter jacket like a love-struck cheerleader. He carried her back to the neat frame house they had shared for twenty-one years, ever since she decided to join mainstream society outside of hiding in Lesbos.

"Am I fat?" Isis sighed as he put her down in their king-sized bed. "Piglet said I was fat."

"Who's this Piglet that needs glasses?" Quade took off her sandals and rubbed her feet. He loved her feet, pressing them against his dark cheek. They always reminded him of white doves with pink beaks, something he didn't dare tell her except when they were deep into each other, thinking she would laugh.

"A robot. He's a robot." Isis curled up like a little girl when he tickled his fingers across her painted toes. "Don't! That tickles."

"That's the point. Remember ol' Ham Phillips was a bachelor. He didn't program those robots with a very good vocabulary where ladies are concerned. I'd say more like round, and only where it counts." He caressed her ample behind.

"That's what I thought you'd say." His wife snuggled against a pillow as if it were his body. He longed to feel her skin next to his, longed for the very scent of her. "Kenya's back," she said.

Quade stroked her long bright hair and then kissed her cheek, smelling peach brandy. "I figured."

৩৩৩

"Where's she staying?"

Quade was awakened at six in the morning by the gruff voice of the Memphis detective on the phone.

"Sorry to call so early, but I've got to make sure she's okay." Moss sounded like death warmed up.

"Magnolia Alley."

"Sounds like a hell-of-a name for a motel. Bet they don't get many visitors."

"It's the house she bought. Magnolia Alley." Quade got out of bed and padded across the floor barefoot to the bathroom. "She spent the night there. My wife said she can't get Sheldon to part with his robots. Gave her some camping gear she had in the truck. Sheldon drove that Caddy into a tree so she's got no wheels."

"Figured he would start driving young. I'll meet you for breakfast in an hour. That Saranji's Place still there? That's the only decent grits place outside of Memphis. That girl makes good coffee, too."

Quade smiled at Saranji being called a girl. The café's owner was pushing sixty by now and was on her way to becoming Julia Springs' first black female tycoon. What with her hair salon specializing in authentic African hairstyles, the deli next to that, and the boutique next to that, Saranjii could almost qualify as a developer. As she had bankrolled all these enterprises by herself, she was now considering opening a bank specializing in micro loans to black enterprises.

"Under new management, but it's where the elite still meet, brother. See you in a bit." Quade hung up, thinking how Julia Springs was changing for the better although there those who wouldn't agree.

"Who was that?" His wife turned over in bed and struggled up to one elbow. "Ow, my head. What on earth did I run into last night?"

Pulling on his jeans over his shorts, he dropped a kiss on her head. "Your mother's peach brandy. Don't get up. I'll bring you up your coffee."

Isis flopped down on the pillows with a moan. "And two aspirin with it."

☙☙☙

Meeting the detective from Memphis at Saranjii's, Quade showed Moss the video which he had put on his laptop for safe keeping.

"I see what you mean about that cartoon character. They usually leave some kind of signature, those stalkers, even cyber-stalkers like this guy." Moss took out his phone and flipped through the pictures. "See this tattoo on Miss Simpson's abdomen? It matches the one this guy sent your daughter. These guys always leave their signature somewhere. Same one I've seen on bodies of prostitutes, Jane Does, even a tipster of mine. Shark in some kind of a flying chair."

Quade felt his stomach roll and pushed his heaping plate aside to concentrate on the coffee. Seeing someone he had known all carved up that way made him feel like killing something. He hated the thought, pushing it away like his bacon and grits.

Moss sensed his repulsion because it echoed his own. "Like you said, he's using these pictures of Holly to threaten your daughter, mess up her program, and to scare Chantal/Kenya West into silence about Holly's drug connections." Moss sat back and sipped his coffee. "That's decent, very decent coffee."

Shutting the laptop, Quade put it aside. "Looks like Holly was into more than drugs."

Moss shrugged. "People with a habit start going down the slippery slope fast. She was into porn for the money, and that usually leads to prostitution. I had her pimp put in the slammer. Told him the only way I'd get the DA to let him out was if he gave me his list of Johns and her supplier. We started asking around on the street, following up on the leads. He got real messed up by some thugs a week later and had to spend some time in the hospital. I lost my snitch yesterday. Whoever this is doesn't want to be found, and it's not the Mexican cartels either. Whoever these guys are, they're daring us to go after them like 'bring it on, man.'"

"You said Chantal called from the Interstate?"

"Which time? She calls me a lot from the Interstate." Moss feigned a note of weariness in his voice. "Oh, about the thing with the black SUV with the ALS1 License plates?"

"That's the one."

Their plates were getting cold—bacon, hash browns, grits, and eggs over-easy for Moss, pancakes for Quade. There were fresh biscuits and local honey. There was a long silence while both men tucked in, as if it were their last meal before a hunger strike.

"More coffee?" The young waiter looked familiar, but Quade barely glanced up from his plate.

He shook his head. "No, thanks, son."

"You don't recognize me, Chief Walker?" The young golden-skinned man smiled. "I guess that's good in a way. Means I've stayed on the good side of the law."

"Frederick?" Quade took another look, nearly choked, then took a sip of coffee. "Frederick? I thought you were still away at graduate school, but I guess I've lost track. Freddy, this is Detective Moss of the Memphis Police Department."

They shook hands. "Pleased to meet you. To catch you up on the last ten years, I graduated with a double Master's in History and Biology, couldn't find a job, went to culinary school, and now I'm a chef."

"Here? At Saranji's?" *And you went to school for that?* was the question in both men's minds. They stopped chewing and stared at him.

Freddy grinned, as if he'd been asked that question a thousand times. "I know. My day job. At night, I work for The Cordon Bleu in Macon. As the sous-chef."

"You know, Kenya is back, right?" Quade changed

the subject. He was not good at making small talk, Moss noticed.

"I found out last night when I had to give her two sisters a ride to a motel. Seems like Sheldon drove her car into a tree. I thought she was mad at me because I missed Holly's funeral. Then all of a sudden she says she's here. In Ham Phillips' old place. One thing about Kenya, when she moves, she really moves."

"She does that," Moss affirmed. "Tell you what, you do deliveries, right? Like for the homebound?" Walker smiled when Moss held up a folded twenty. You can take the man out of the city, he thought, but not the city out of Moss.

Freddy looked over his shoulder at the kitchen. "I guess we do. Where to?"

"Tell him, Chief, I don't know where the hell I am, let alone this Magnolia Alley. What does the kid like to eat?" Moss's shoulders shook with silent laughter. "I've heard some stories that would curl your hair."

Quade gave Freddy the order and directions to Magnolia Alley on a napkin and Moss handed him the twenty. "Gas ain't cheap here."

"No, thanks. It's on the house." The young man had his grandmother's dignity and let everyone know it. "And if you mean Professor Phillips's old place, sure I know. I've lived here just about all my life. Nice meeting you, Detective."

Putting Moss neatly in his place as an outsider, Freddy topped their coffee up and gave them extra biscuits, then took off his apron, disappearing into the kitchen.

Moss frowned, tucking the twenty back in his shirt pocket. "Is it something I said?"

Quade didn't apologize for Freddy's abruptness. "He's doing it because Kenya is his cousin, not because you offered him twenty."

"My bad. My relatives would have taken the twenty and run right down to the track."

"Mine, too. Now, where were we?" With the diligence of a bird dog on the scent, Quade picked up the thread. "You were telling me about the ALS license plates."

Moss seemed distracted for a moment, as if he was processing some indigestible thought. "It seems so funny to hear her called Kenya, you know? Around town, she's billed as the glamorous Chantal West." He shook his head as if to clear it while Quade smiled inwardly. If he had ever seen a man falling for a woman, it was happening right in front of his eyes. "Oh yeah, so I traced the ALS plates. It was registered to the subsidiary for this Biopharma outfit in Switzerland. At least they have an office in Switzerland and everywhere else in Europe."

"That figures."

"It does? It's like fighting with Jell-O. There's nothing there when you try to get hold of it."

"Maybe, maybe not." Quade told him what Bjorn had said—that the virus seemed to come from a foreign source, something about the programming language.

"This tech guy thinks he can trace it back to the source?"

"He's going to try. Chris is a smart cookie. If anyone can do it he can. Meanwhile, I've got the campus police working on it and the Athens police."

Moss took another biscuit, his third, then decided against it. "Got to watch the carbs. Since I got out of the Army, I'm carrying an extra fifty and not in a backpack." He took a piece of crisp bacon and wrapped them both in a napkin. "For a snack later."

Quade nodded in agreement and then stuck to the subject. "We can't deal with something international. That's for the G-men. What we can do is deal with the bodies on the ground, the similarities in the killers' MO, and their connection to Holly and the games she was playing that got her killed. The fact that she might have confided in Kenya puts her in the hot seat."

"I see another connection. Your daughter is working on this project that involves ALS, whatever that stands for."

"Acute Lateral Sclerosis. I know because she identified my wife as carrying the gene. It's tops on her list of chronic diseases this app screens for. If she finishes it, the app I mean, it'll be a big breakthrough in early detection."

"I don't know, Walker." Moss sat back from the table with a satisfied sigh. "I'm of the school 'what you don't know, don't hurt you.' Frankly, if I could survive Afghanistan, I think nothing short of a steamroller could stop me now."

Quade grunted in agreement. "But you know how this young generation has all this information at their fingertips. They don't want to leave anything to fate, seems to me. They think control is everything." He gestured at Moss. "What is that?"

Moss was drawing something on his napkin that looked like a target with a bullseye in the center. "I do this when I've got a case keeping me up nights."

Quade was quiet, letting the other man work his way through his thoughts. Then Moss turned the napkin around. Under the target, was written Julia Springs. Sticking out like arrows were names Holly, Chantal, Faun. It was connected to another target that said Memphis. That one had the names Holly, and Chantal.

"What's the connection?" Moss asked.

Quade cleared his throat and took a sip of coffee. "Let me tell you something, Moss. Outside, if you don't mind."

They paid the bill and left the air-conditioned restaurant to step into the May morning, which hung heavy with the threat of rain. Moss took out his handkerchief and mopped his forehead. "Does a day ever pass without raining here?"

"That's what peaches need most—and mosquitoes."

"Good for them," Moss said. "So what were you going to tell me in there?"

Quade studied the sky for a long moment. In the morning light, his shrapnel scars were clearly visible. Moss still relived the day he'd dragged bodies from the burning Humvee. He had thought Walker was dead like the rest of his crew until he heard a moan. It was hard to tell with all the blood. Moss shook his head, trying to get the picture out of his memory.

"I don't talk in places like that about personal stuff. People have nothing better to do than gossip. It's better than TV for some folks around here."

Moss took a few steps out on the cracked sidewalk. Quade joined him and they fell into lockstep. "I hear you. "Go on. I've heard about everything there is, that's for sure."

As they walked, treading on pools of white petals fallen from the flowering pear trees, Quade told him about Isis.

"See, my wife had a child by her own father when she was just fourteen. The child was a boy, but he wasn't quite right. As she describes him, he was destructive, crazy about killing animals, cats, dogs. Cruel. Social services took her and the rest of the kids into foster care and put him—his name was Michael—in an institution. Lois, her mother, finally got custody of the kids and established a home. Michael stayed in the institution."

Quade didn't go into detail about the compound called Lesbos run by women, which had gravitated into a business enterprise. "When Michael was eighteen, he signed himself out of the place and the family lost track of him. The reason I'm telling you this is because before he left, Michael was showing signs of ALS already."

Moss stared at the trees across the street. Bradford pears, bursting with white blossoms like fuzzy ice cream cones. *So much beauty, so much ugliness. God must have mood swings.* "So your children have this crazy half-brother is what you're saying, who could be anywhere—maybe even Switzerland," he said.

"I used to visit him when we first got married, but he would throw a fit when he saw me and yell, 'Get away from my mother, you freak.' He said I looked like a nightmare, stuff like that." Quade smiled his lopsided grin, his white teeth the only light in his dark face. "I know I ain't pretty, but I didn't want to upset him, so I finally stopped going after Isis could drive herself."

They had walked the two blocks of Main Street and to where the sidewalk narrowed, leading to the park. "Go on."

"Isis said he was brilliant. They tested his IQ and it was off the charts. She bought him stuff—a voice-operated computer, sports stuff, Wi-Fi connection. But when she tried to get him back, the State said we didn't live in an area where he could get the treatment he need-ed. See, they were trying out a new medication that was supposed to stop the progress of the disease."

"Did it work?"

"I don't know. Like I said, he signed himself out of there when he turned eighteen and we haven't heard from him since. Don't know if he's dead or alive."

Moss looked at the puffy thunderheads overhead. "Crazy, brilliant, and cruel. Sounds like our guy. Tell me something, Walker, did you know all this about your wife when you married her?"

Quade stared him full in the face. "Look at me, Moss. I scare people. She was, and is, the most beautiful woman I ever saw."

"Say no more." The man from Memphis rolled his eyes. "I know how that goes."

The two men walked back to Quade's police SUV. Quade patted it like a cowboy pats his horse. "Just so you know, Kenya had the same thing happen to her. Her stepfather got her pregnant. Like Isis, she was only fourteen. It explains a lot about the lady you know as Chantal."

Moss didn't look surprised, only sad. He had seen everything at least twice over. Once too many for his own health. "Hey, thanks for telling me. Yeah, that does kind of explain her attitude, for one. Like she can go it alone, 'don't need your help' thing. Just downright hostile, sometimes, other times, like a little girl lost in the woods."

Quade nodded. "Could be a description of my wife. No wonder they get along. Still want to go see her?"

"No offense, but I didn't drive 800 miles to look at the scenery or hear about your shitty life."

Quade heard Afganistan in Moss's voice. "Hop in. I'll take you out to Magnolia Alley."

It was Moss's turn to smile. "Thought you'd never ask."

They drove in silence through the meandering streets, lined with crepe myrtle trees in full blossom the color of raspberry sherbet. Combined with falling petals of white, they formed pink and white pools on either side of the streets.

Moss thought the land took over here, not the people. The people were just incidental, just caretakers carving out their little ode to civilization in buildings that would crumble, but the land was forever.

Moss was a city guy, uncomfortable with silence.

"So she's got another kid by this dirt bag? Kenya, I mean."

"No, no. She miscarried, fortunately. Her grandmother, we called her Root Woman because she was into native medicine, may have had something to do with it. At least, that's how the local scuttlebutt had it. Anyway, after a struggle with DFACS, she got custody of Kenya and Freddy. The other sisters got caught in the foster care grinder. Spit 'em out when they were eighteen."

Moss grunted in acknowledgement. "Hoo-doo. Native medicine combined with magic with some African traditions thrown in. My mama is from New Orleans. She believes in that stuff. Says I need a gris-gris bag to ward off evil. It would take a sack-full to stop some of the shit coming at me around Memphis these days. Go on. So how'd she end up singing with Shades of Grey?"

"Who?"

Moss had to laugh. "That's the gig she has now. Shades of Grey plays pretty much all the big time clubs. Vegas, included."

"Really?" Quade nodded. "I'm impressed."

"I'm sure she'd be glad to hear it. She's out to do that for sure."

"Seeing as you know her so well, I'd better let you hear it from her." Quade flashed a rare grin in Moss' direction. "I will tell you this. She got her start in the Glory Road Church choir, until arsonists burned it down. It took quite a while for the congregation to rebuild it, so the gospel choir had to go on the road to raise money. Some big-time music company heard them and signed them up for a couple of CDs. Kenya stood in for their lead singer in one recording session and I guess they thought she had something the others didn't. They signed her on as a solo artist, but I never heard anything she did. She was seventeen by then, and when Root Woman died of cancer,

Kenya left Julia Springs behind. Freddy was taken in by extended family. And here we are at Magnolia Alley."

As they turned into the tree-lined avenue, Moss whistled through his teeth. "Holy shit, Massa. We's home at last."

Chapter 12

After some coaxing, Faun agreed to meet Bjorn for a beer. She said she wasn't mad in her text, just upset with everything that was happening. The "everything" was vague. Bjorn couldn't help but think that was the polite Southern way to say "upset with you." He tempted her saying he had news, which he did, in a way, a very small bit of news. Still, it worked. *Why argue with success?*

She came in to the beer joint and, for a moment, something funny happened to Bjorn's usually steady heartbeat. Though he kept in shape, it skipped a couple of beats.

He stood up so she could see him. He was hard to miss, being so tall. Faun smiled and glided to the booth as only ballet-trained women can move. "Hi," was all she said, but it was enough. He could tell she was sorry for the scene she caused when her dad was there.

"Corona okay?"

No, she wanted an artisan beer. One of those microbrews. "They have it on tap here. Try it, why don't you? It's good."

They made small talk about beer—how up in Minnesota they had dozens of artisan beers and down here it was just catching on how it would make a great business, if all else failed.

Finally, she got down to the apology just as the waiter brought their beers. "Hi, Faun." It was Steve, her former lab tech. He had cleaned up his act, gotten a haircut, and cut his nails. "How's it going?" He nodded at Bjorn. "Bjorn. I hear you've about got that hacker whipped."

"Hardly. How are you, Steve? You moonlighting for the tech department still?"

Steve nodded. "And working here. I don't want to graduate owing my salary to the government. You about to get that doctorate?"

"Got to run my dissertation by the Committee. If it flies, I'm out of here next fall."

"Any leads on a job?"

"A few I'm considering. You know, the usual. The CDC, Dow. The biotech arm of the military or any of the above that will have me."

"Well, good luck, Chris. The manager is giving me the finger, so I'll see you around."

"Funny." Bjorn stared at Steve's retreating back. "That was one of the things I wanted to talk to you about."

Faun's eyes widened. "Steve? Why? What'd he do? I knew it!"

Bjorn held up his hand. "Wait, I didn't say he did anything—yet. But I'm really getting the feeling that someone that works with you did."

"In my lab crew?"

"Look, here's what I'm getting at. Someone visited the porn site that Holly was on and downloaded pictures of her."

"I'm not going to ask you how you know. I do want to know what creep knew about Holly enough to connect her with me and Julia Springs? And what's that got to with the virus?"

"Because this virus attaches itself to cookies on your computer—"

Trying to hide her exasperation, Faun tasted her beer. "I know that but I've got the university firewall plus virus protection and security of my own."

Bjorn took a sip of his beer. "That's good, actually. Doesn't matter to this hacker. He cut through it like melted butter. That's what I told your dad. It's coming from Europe, maybe even the States. They do a lot in the sex trade, these European guys."

They drank in silence. Then Faun looked him in the eyes. "Look, I appreciate what you're doing. I acted like a bitch in front of my dad and you when he was here the other day, and I'm really sorry. Just call me on it if I do that again, which I'll try not to. I don't want to be the Dragon Lady of the Lab, but so much has gone wrong. Holly's death, Kenya being threatened, this ALS thing. I guess I'm just burnt out."

Bjorn sat back against the booth. "I think I'm in love with you, even without sleeping with you. You think I'm not confused? I've gone along, head down, learning all this stuff, and I suddenly look up for a minute at the world around me and there you are. Beautiful and brilliant—a dream I never thought I'd find. Then, out of the blue, she says she's never going to get married, never have kids, thinks she's going to die young."

Faun laughed so hard, she got beer up her nose. There was this whole uncouth moment where she was choking, and blowing her nose in a napkin. "You make me sound like a nut case! Do I really come across like that? Oh, my god!"

"Not really. Beer up the nose is not fun." He looked at her red face and watering eyes. Even like this, she was beautiful. For the first time in his life, Chris Bjorn found he could love something else more than science.

Faun seemed unaware of such worship. "You know, before I inhaled my beer, I heard you say something about going along with your head down, learning all this stuff, and suddenly looking up and seeing the world around you. That's me, exactly, until Holly got killed and all this happened, then the bubble that I'd been living in just burst. It was like a curtain being drawn back and I saw the world around me in terms of black and white, good and bad, you know?"

Now their eyes locked in a long gaze across the table, blue into blue. "And that's all you heard me say?"

Faun wiped her eyes with his napkin. "I heard you say you loved me, and that you didn't want to sleep with me."

"I said that? I must have come across as some kind of monk! Of course, I want to sleep with you, but—"

People around them giggled, then guffawed as Bjorn slowly caught on. 'Oh, I get it. Joke. Wait 'til you get beer up your nose again. You won't get any help from me, sister. No napkins, no nada. Drool all you want." He paused, laughing at himself. "Will you, though?"

She caught her breath finally. "Sleep with you? Depends."

He leaned forward. "On what?"

"On what you've got to eat at your place. I assume you don't live on a park bench." She giggled, eyes sparkling, doing that thing girls with long hair do when they don't know what else to do with their hands.

Bjorn was not an impulsive man, but it took all the control he could muster not to grab her and kiss her. "I warn you, you may have to clean up the place first. I'll cook, you clean."

"Don't worry, I can't cook, but I've got a younger

brother. So I'm combat hardened. "She gathered her stuff while he fumbled for a tip.

"Let's get out of here." He slid out of the booth. "Maybe we'll have to cook and clean later—before you change your mind."

By the kitchen door, Steve watched them leave, Bjorn's arm protectively around her waist, as if he already owned her. A strange little grin crept along Steve's narrow lips.

Not for long, Bjorn, you bastard. Not for long you won't. Think you're such goddam smartass, don't you? Wait and see what happens tomorrow. Your whole world will come crashing down around you. Hers, too. So high and mighty.

No cushy job, no app, no girl. I'm going to destroy her, too. You bet I am. Treating me like shit. Like a slave. I'm a force to be reckoned with. I know as much as you two brains put together.

"Steve! You going to just stand there or you gonna wait on customers, huh?"

Steve sighed and stuck his pencil behind his ear. "Yeah, I'm on it."

෬෨෬෨

Big Earl was tired of listening to talk shows, rap, and the sports channel. Besides, between Memphis and where-the-hell-ever in Georgia Julia Springs was, there were dead spots where the country music stations bled through with their down home accents twanging like banjo strings out of tune. With a sigh of discontent, he turned the radio off, riding along in silence as Loquacious, in the passenger seat, spelled out the words in the book he was reading. Listening to the sibilant sound of Loquaious's mind working was almost as bad as country music.

"Learning anything about handling spoiled rotten brats, Lolo?"

"What does d-i-s-p-l-a-c-e-m-e-n-t spell? 'He will dis-something his rage on to you.' That might have been what he was doing when he went after my balls. You think, Earl?"

"Those psychology books are so full of shit. Give the kid a good smack, he won't bother you no more, believe me. My wife, she reads all the psychology stuff she can get her hands on. Loves it! Says I ought to use more of it in my business." Big Earl shook like a volcano getting ready to erupt. "I told her. I said, 'Baby, I just show them my gun. That's all the psychology they need.'" Big Earl shifted to take out his hanky, wiping tears of laughter from beneath his shades. "Hear that? All the psychology they need, Lolo."

Loquacious was unmoved by Big Earl's street-smart logic. "It says to get the kid on your side. Showing him a piece don't quite do that except maybe for scaring him shitless." He consulted the book some more. "Says 'for you to earn his trust, you must always tell him the truth.' My Pop lied to us kids all the time. We still thought he would do right 'til he ended up in the slammer. I don't want to be like him, no way."

Big Earl shifted in the seat of the Crown Victoria. It was a big car for a big man, but any seat got hard after sitting for five hours straight. "Look, Lolo, man, it's just a job. You use that stuff on your own kids, if you ever have any, okay? But this Sheldon kid is just a paycheck, get it? A paycheck. Think of it that way and you won't be confused by psychoanalyzing him, okay? See dollar signs when you look at him." He could not stop laughing. "Big, fucking dollar signs."

His companion wasn't convinced. "This could be a trap, you know."

"Now what you calling a trap? You don't make no sense sometimes, Lolo. No offense, but you don't, not when it comes down to logic. Just leave the thinking to me, okay?"

When Loquacious was extra wrought-up, he began to stutter, making several attempts at starting over before blurting the whole sentence out. "Well, Earl, they got Al and Squeak still in the slammer down there in Thing-a-ma-gummy, Georgia."

"Julia Springs." Big Earl sighed. The ride was getting longer every minute, no, every *second* he had to spend listening to Loquacious spell out words." I'm gonna pull off for a leak and some tea."

"Sheldon's mama's jumpy as hell and went into hiding. Boss could be sending us right into a nest of snakes, you know? Could be a security guard day and night wherever she's hiding. Already got word that Detective Moss is on it, going down to interview Al and the Squeaker. I'm saying it's a bad time to do another snatch, that's all."

"Get over it, ya hear, Lolo, would you? It's a job, okay? The Boss said do it this time or else."

"Or else what?"

"Or else we're back to holding up convenience stores and handing over to the Boss thirty percent of the take just to keep operating on the streets."

"I think that's a violation of our civil rights, don't you think, Earl?"

Instead of replying, Big Earl just shook his head. "Sweet Jesus, Lolo. You want sweet tea or half-and-half?"

"I heard tea ain't that healthy for you. Just a small coke, extra ice." Loquacious went back to his psych book. "What does es-stran-ge-ment spell?"

"Just that this is the trip from hell already, I can see

that now." The Crown Vic purred down the off-ramp toward clean toilets and loud country music.

Chapter 13

"Welcome to my little house of horrors." Kenya made a grand sweep of her arm, indicating the dust-filled parlor. "Come right in, gentlemen, you needn't look scared. Ghosts won't hurt you. Neither will robots. I've got both. And no car, so if I wanted to walk away or even drive away, I couldn't. So, you see? I'm stuck."

It was obvious she had found a liquor supply, had brought along a bottle, or cajoled Frederick, who had delivered their breakfast and was now playing a video game with Sheldon, into bringing along refreshments.

Either way, Moss had to admit she was beautifully drunk before noon. He made up his usually rigid mind to love this woman, no matter what she did, because everything she did he loved. He wanted to scoop her up in his arms, assure her everything would be all right—all the things that lovers said he would say…with his eyes. But that only happened in movies where a camera did everything, and Moss was a silent, careful man. Everything he did had the deliberation of a judge to it.

"Where's the restroom?"

Even Quade questioned that segue. "I don't know,

bro. The Phillips probably had an outhouse back then, and Ham was into the organic stuff."

"Oh, please, let's not be crude!" Kenya in her altered state of cushioned shock looked offended. "It's upstairs and to the left. And flush twice, the handle doesn't work."

"Just like home." Moss mounted the spiral staircase, two at a time, anxious to see where the mansion was vulnerable. When he got to the top, he turned to the left and then to the right. The boards groaned under his weight and he began to retreat on tiptoe.

But too late. Detective Grover Moss plunged down to his armpits through to the salon where, ages ago, ladies in bustierres and hoopskirts sipped tea from fine china cups. He had an awful vision of how they would react to a pair of black, skinny, hairy legs dangling above their heads in squeaky, pointy-toed shoes.

But he wasn't dangling over ladies' heads below. He had landed in a black hole somewhere in the dropped ceiling above one of the bedrooms. Anxious that Chantal wouldn't find him like a whale surfacing from a hole in the Arctic ice, he started to lift himself out of the pit.

Instead, the more he put his weight on it, the more the wood crumbled away under his hands, turned to saw dust over the years by generations of termites.

He remained suspended in the black hole until Sheldon reached him followed by the lurching, clanking Piglet. He bent over, examining Grover's bald spot as if it were a biology field specimen of a strange mushroom.

Then he straightened and, before Moss could plead with him to go get Quade Walker, he bawled. "Mama, the big, fat policeman has broken our floor! Look what he's doing to our beautiful floor!"

Moss decided then and there he didn't want any more kids.

ɔɛɔ

After searching himself below the waist for splinters in the downstairs powder room, Moss sat around fielding what seemed to be an endless supply of smart-ass remarks about his attempts at "instant renovation," references to using "the outhouse next time," and more pointed ones from Kenya about "staying in shape."

"I'll get it fixed, but until I do, the upstairs isn't safe."

"Never mind," said the lady of the house, "I don't want some do-it-yourself number, especially when the do-it-yourselfer doesn't know a wrench from a bong."

"You don't know it, but that term dates you, Miss West. On second thought, you just gave me an idea." Moss leaned forward with a look that made everyone get serious. "One that could be to our advantage."

Kenya's cell phone rang, spoiling the moment. It was Toya phoning from the motel. "Could you come pick me up? I have to say goodbye before we leave."

"You're going back already? But we really haven't had a visit yet. I've been so busy—"

"That's okay. We won't stay long."

Moss stood up. "I can go get them." Anything to get away from the continual smirks at the ceiling in the next room.

"No, you don't have to. Freddy's coming over with breakfast. He'll pick them up."

"Suit yourself." He sat down with a sigh. He was on his feet in an instant. He had found a splinter where he couldn't see it.

"Only don't go. Please stay awhile. I want to tell you something." Turning back to the phone, she told Toya Freddy would give them a ride. Then she phoned Freddy.

Moss headed toward the stairs. All this family drama

was making him feel slightly claustrophobic. "I'll make myself scarce, look around upstairs. I know what you're going to say. I'll be careful where I step this time, okay?"

Kenya drew a deep breath, preparing herself for what was bound to be a confrontation. "Okay. Just keep an eye on Sheldon if you're going to be up there. You never know what he's getting into."

"Oh, I plan to do just that." Something in his tone made Kenya look around, but the big man was climbing the stairs.

∽♡∽

Arriving in the hall, Toya teetered in on her platform heels, looking apprehensively at Moss who was checking out the second floor hall as if it had land mined.

"Who's that?"

"He's a police detective. But he's okay. He's a friend."

"A cop? In your house? After what you've done?" It was clear to Kenya that Toya hadn't come here just to say goodbye.

"What do you mean, after what I've done?"

"You know." Toya rocked back on her platform shoes, clearly enjoying Kenya's discomfort.

"No, I don't. Tell me, Toya."

"You killed our daddy. You and that woman you called Aya. Everybody else called her a witch. Root Woman, the one you called your granma. You're the reason we ended up in foster care." Toya addressed her using Pearlene's old accusatory stance, arms folded, hips at an angle, looking as though she was ready to grab any weapon handy and beat the tar out of the target of her anger.

"What you want, Toya? Pearl? I know you want

something, coming in here, copping an attitude like that."

"I'll speak for both of us when I'm saying you got to make it up to both of us. Five thousand dollars would about do it, won't it, Pearl?"

Pearl kept her eyes on the floor. "I guess."

Kenya went to her youngest sister and tilted her face up to hers. "I know you don't hold nothing against me, sugar. Toya has put you up to this, right?"

"Five thousand a piece," Toya repeated, tapping her blue iridescent toes, or I'll tell that cop all about it. That's all I'm going to say, then I'm going to the cops."

"What's the matter, Toya? Your pimp working you too hard? Want to take a break from turning tricks up in Five Points?" Kenya went on the offense now. Drawing herself up and clenching her fists by her sides, as if she was getting ready to do battle, she leaned forward on her toes.

Toya had to take a step back. "Bitch! You can't prove that." But her resolve was wavering. She looked at Pearl for backup.

"Oh, I did some checking. You not holding down some nine-to-five in an office. You being pimped out and you're getting Pearl used to the trade. That's procuring on top of two arrests for prostitution! Plus two for drug possession and three for shoplifting. You out to facing some hard time, but someone keeps bailing you out, your baby's daddy, I'll bet."

"Yeah, that's right and it's all because of you, Shekenya. Mama always said you killed Daddy and I'll get her to testify about what she saw."

"You think they'll take her testimony? Dream on, Toya, honey. She's a druggie, a prostitute, and a parolee. My word against hers, okay?"

Toya looked uncertain. "We'll see about that."

"She never saw anything because she turned me out

after whipping and burning me for letting my stepfather, your father, do me. And she was such a *good* mother to you two. I bet she put you up to this. You going to give her a cut for drugs? Let me tell you something. Your daddy was a rapist and a predator. He raped me over and over, and all the time Pearlene knew it. Even raped you, I bet money on it. Didn't he? Though you were only four years old. I don't even want to know. But if anyone ought to be put in jail, it's Pearlene. She didn't lift a finger to help me when she knew all along what he was doing to her own children. She left me scarred for life. It was Reverend Jeremiah paid for my first surgery, so he could stand to look at me while he did it."

Kenya was on a roll now, backing her sister up to the doorway. "Your daddy, he tried to kill me for telling my grandmother what happened. I hit him with a rock, and Grandma hit him with a shovel, then we threw him in the quarry so he wouldn't ever bother nobody again. There! And I'll say it for everybody in a courtroom to hear."

"I hope that won't be necessary." In the heat of battle, they had forgotten Moss was still standing there.

"Detective Moss." Toya sidestepped Kenya and confronted him. "You heard her confess. Aren't you going to arrest her?"

"I didn't hear her confess to anything more than hitting your father with a rock in an effort to defend herself, which a fourteen-year-old girl shouldn't have to do against a grown man. But I heard you trying to extort money from your sister, which carries at least ten years in the state of Georgia. And I believe drugs and prostitution carry ten more. So if we prosecute you, you'll be forty-four and past your prime for a pimp to run by the time you get out."

Toya was shaking, her thin body trembling in her ridiculous shoes. "You can't scare me."

"And I wouldn't count on your mother for a witness. She has a long history as a druggie. No, I think your sister Kenya saved you from a far worse life than the one you hold her responsible for. DFACS would have taken you and your sister away, anyway, once the word got about that your father was a pedophile."

Toya still mounted a shaky defense. "We'll see about that, won't we, Pearl?"

"I know what Daddy was like. The DFACS lady told me all about it. Daddy had a record for being a sex offender long before Mama married him. With children, even. And Mama knew about that and still married him." Pearl spoke with surprising firmness, even though her puppy eyes were filling with tears. "I love Kenya and Sheldon and Freddy. I just want to be a family again."

"C'mon, stupid. We're leaving." Toya turned her blazing eyes back on Kenya. "You'll be hearing from our lawyer. And Sheldon's not your son, he's Holly's. It's the truth. He's Holly's child and you took him away! I'll tell him the truth someday, you better believe it."

Pearl let go of Sheldon's hand and ran to Toya. Kenya held her breath, watching both her sisters retreat from the life she intended for them. "Toya, don't go. Please. Stay here with us. Let us be a family."

Seeing the expression on Kenya's face, Moss had to weigh in. 'You haven't got anything to worry about. She hasn't got a case." He longed to envelope her in his arms, instead his voice did. She gave him a grateful look that said it all.

"You shut up, cop. I'll tell the lawyer you said that." Twisting around on her high heels, Toya made for the front door. "Come on, Pearl."

Pearl dropped her arms which she had outstretched toward her sister. "Corry, it's gonna be Ashley now. New name, new start, right, Kenya?"

She smiled even though tears streaked her face.

"Oh, the hell with you, Pearl! I'm going! See you in court, Miss High and Mighty!" Making her exit, Toya tripped over the high wooden door jam and fell to one knee. As she got up, they could hear her cursing all the way down the driveway.

Moss grinned at Kenya. "She'll probably sue you for that, too."

"I better go after her." Kenya started across the foyer, but Pearl grabbed her arm.

"No, don't go out there, Kenya."

"But she can't walk to town from here."

"She's not going to." Pearl looked suddenly shy and fearful all at once. "Her boyfriend is waiting for her, that's why. He's got the baby and, if she don't get the money, he's going to take Zeb away."

"But I was going to give it to her, anyway. Oh, no! Oh, my Lord, that poor girl. Why didn't she tell me? I would have understood."

"No, I wouldn't give her anything if I were you." Moss put an arm around Kenya's shoulders, wanting to hold her to him, but she leaned against him, anyway. "Her boyfriend's a pimp, right, Ashley? He's not going to give up that easy. Even if you gave him the money, he'd just say it's not enough and demand more."

Pearl just nodded. "He tried to get me to...you know...go out with men I don't know, but I have a boyfriend. He goes to college and wants me to start going, too. And it's okay to call me Pearl. It's my name, whether I like it or not."

"I don't know. I kind of like Ashley." Moss grinned at the wispy girl whose eyelashes curled against her arched brows. "Let me check him out, see what I can find on him. I'm sure he's into a whole lot of things besides running prostitutes."

Sheldon had retreated to the top of the stairs. "Hey, Auntie Pearl, want to play Robot Swag with me?"

"Sure, Sheldon! I'm coming right up." Ashley Pearl looked over at Kenya, still leaning against Moss' big chest. "You make a real cute couple, you know that?"

Moss winked at Kenya. "I thought you were scared of robots, Ashley Pearl."

"I was, but if Sheldon's not scared, I can't be scared because I'm the adult, right? In fact, they kind of grow on you, like dolls on wheels."

"I'm not a toy!" cried Piglet. "I'm not! I'm not! I'm not!"

෩෩

Later, when they were sitting on the veranda with a drink, Moss asked, "Who's this Reverend Jeremiah anyway? And is Sheldon really Holly's son?"

Kenya moved just enough to look up at him. "You want to know everything? No secrets?"

"Yeah, I do."

"Why is that? You the IRS or something?" The whites of her eyes shone in the half light.

"You got something to hide from the feds?"

He tightened his arm around her as she chuckled. "Wish I did. Like millions in an off-shore account. But no dice—"

"So no dice about the Reverend or no dice about the millions?"

Kenya pulled away from and sat up on the old wooden bench, as if she was listening to something in the distance, beyond the Thicket, deep in the marshy woods. "You know what I want to do? I want to start all over again. Create a new life, a new family, a whole new me. And Moss, I can do that as long as you keep me from going back in the past any more. Just not remind me of all that's happened. Just let me go on."

"Sorry, I didn't mean to—"

She put a hand on his knee. "I know you didn't. If you want to know stuff about me, ask Freddy. But he probably won't tell you, so ask Quade or even Isis. Just don't ask me and expect me to tell you everything. It's not that I have anything to hide, it's just that I don't want to talk about it anymore, you know what I mean?"

"I know exactly. Shall we get something to eat? I hate like crazy to eat alone."

"Sure you want to eat with Sheldon? He's not the best dinner table companion."

"As long as he doesn't steal my biscuits, I'll be fine."

ℰ⁄ℐℰ⁄ℐ

The afterglow of love in the age of instant communication didn't last long. Neither did lust, at least for Bjorn and Faun. Rather, it was put aside for more pressing things like reading e-mails or making dinner that both vegans and gluten-free omnivores could eat.

"It reminds me of that old nursery rhyme that says something like 'she could eat no fat and he could eat no lean.'" Faun was peering into his refrigerator, Nordic sparse with things neatly wrapped in plastic.

"You read nursery rhymes often?"

"I used to read to my little brother, silly." She straightened up and found him looking at her, adoration shining in his eyes. "Don't look at me like that."

"Why? I can't look at someone prowling through my fridge?"

"I was just looking for the beer, not prowling. You're a neatnik, aren't you? Never seen such a neat refrigerator. Nothing touches."

"I bet yours is the same. Beer's clear in the back to the right."

Faun put her arms around him, in spite of the fact he was chopping onions. He dropped the knife and kissed her, the smell of onions enveloping them both. They made love standing up, in front of the open fridge, clothes haphazardly discarded, food forgotten for the moment.

Breathing heavily, they donned only some of their clothing and began cooking again, deciding on red wine, hummus, and organic blue corn chips because of the plethora of anti-oxidants, but even those had to be measured.

Life for both of them had to be objectified, analyzed to the point it was like a rare specimen under a microscope. With the world of empirical knowledge at their fingertips, the element of surprise was almost non-existent.

Almost. As always, love is full of surprises.

They found in each other mirror images, and since they had always considered themselves to be superior to the general population, they both were pleased with what they saw, to the point that to be separated brought them a kind of pain that was beyond their analysis.

"You know, don't you, that the chances were small and getting smaller that I'd find anyone like you before I turned thirty?" He was cooking a *frittata* for himself, while she made beans and rice for both of them.

"What happens when you hit the big three-oh? Cannons go off? Bells ring? It's all over." Faun rubbed up against his arm, making a purring sound. "I'll still love you when you're old."

"Even though you're a whole six years my junior?"

She snuggled against him like a cat. "I've always been a daddy's girl."

"You've got to quit that or our *frittata* will get cold."

"Your *frittata*. My beans." She stroked his groin, making him groan with pleasure.

Fortunately, it was a very compact apartment. The bed wasn't far from the kitchen. Shedding what they had just put back on, they fell the rest of way. Appetizer two. They began to wonder if they would ever actually eat.

လာ

Quade remembered the place as being bigger. The King's Own Children's Rehabilitation Hospital with its outbuildings, playgrounds, and pools had sprawled over at least ten acres of well-maintained grounds. Now, as he and Moss prepared to enter its wrought iron gates, it looked deserted.

"This the place? It don't look like anybody's home."

There wasn't anyone there, except for the caretaker who told them The Kings Own had moved after some snoop with the state pulled their license for tying children to their beds.

"You know where?"

Quade just let Moss ask all the questions. The place always cast a shadow over him that he couldn't shake, thinking how Isis used to fall apart whenever they came to visit Michael. Quade felt an inner shudder as he remembered the child he ought to have loved, but couldn't. A sandy-haired kid with an awful gleam in his pale eyes and pointed teeth that snapped at his caretakers like a spindly terrier gone mad.

His wife merely endured bites and bruises, trying to enfold Michael in her arms. More than once Quade had to lift the child away, snapping and spitting, after he drew blood on Isis's pale skin.

He often begged Isis not to go visit him anymore, especially when Faun and her brother Rudy were old enough to ask questions. "Where did you go, Mommy? The cemetery? Is that why you're sad?" or "Where did you get those bite marks, Mommy? Did the puppy freak out at the vet?"

The caretaker shrugged. "Out of state, that's all I know. They said Alabama, but that could be to throw the state snoops off. This place has been bought by a developer who wants to build upscale houses."

Since Quade was having some kind of flashback, Moss continued. "How long you been working here, sir?"

"Since I was fourteen years old. I'm seventy-two now. That's a long time in one place, now, ain't it?"

"So you must have seen a lot of folks come and go, right?" Moss had the style of a true detective, establishing a rapport before getting down to the nitty-gritty. Quade thought watching the Memphis policemen work was like watching a good rancher worry a steer into a corner, wearing it down little by little, coming ever closer to the point of contact.

"My friend here is looking for a kid who checked himself out when he was eighteen. What was his name again, Walker?" That was his cue. Moss was expecting him to take over, but the word stuck in Quade's throat.

"Michael. Michael Slade."

"Oh, yeah, we all knew Mr. Michael. I'll say we did." The caretaker, whose name was embroidered on his faded shirt pocket, allowed himself a wheezing laugh. "I'm Andy, by the way."

After one glance at Quade's sweating brow, Moss took over again. "I'm Grover and this is Quade. Nice meeting you, Andy. So you knew Michael?"

But Andy was studying Quade with narrowed eyes, squinting against the morning sun. "I'm bad at names, but I never forget a face. Your Michael's dad, ain't that right? I recall you and your pretty wife used to try and visit. Notice I said 'try.' Michael, now that boy was ornery as they come, no doubt about it. I hope you don't mind me saying, Mr. Walker."

"That's right, he was that. You've got a good memory." Clearly, Quade knew what the old man was trying to say. *I'd never forget that face if I lived to be a hundred.* "But I'm not Michael's dad."

"Oh, I see. Well, anyway, it was nice of you all to visit, is all I remember. Some people just dump their kids here and never see 'em again, even at Christmas or birthdays."

Moss kept everybody honest, now that he was on the hunt. "So, Andy, do you know what happened to Michael? We heard he just up and left when he was eighteen."

"Yeah, he did. Came as a big surprise 'cause I thought he was a lifer here at Kingdom House." Andy put aside his broom and produced a set of several dozen keys. "But I always thought those men were the real reason Michael just up and left like that. They, the doctors, shrinks like Doc Powell, said Michael would only get worse if they took him into the outside world, you know? I mean, Michael was bad enough while he was here."

Moss grabbed the hint and ran with it. "Was he, like, mean? Threatening to kill everybody? What?"

"All of the above and more. Threatened to blow us all up, feed us to the gators, all because he couldn't do what he wanted." Andy shook with silent laughter. "And he did it all, except the alligators part. Nearly blew us up a couple of times. I know he short-circuited all the computers, so many times they wouldn't let him near one finally. Eeewhee, he was somethin' else!"

Moss arched an eyebrow. "How'd he manage blowing you all up?"

Quade was silent, gazing fixedly at the trees beyond.

"Rigged up a propane tank with nitro glycerin and gelignite he ordered online. Then rigged up a cell phone signal that was going to set the thing off, but fortunately for us, the propane guy discovered the explosive package. The kid was a genius, all right. 'Cept he always left a trail, especially where girls were concerned."

"What was that?" Moss asked. He and Quade looked at each other.

Andy did this half-laugh, half-sigh thing. "He wanted to get together with a prostitute. Have one or two come live here, you know what I mean? Claimed his needs weren't being met."

"I remember the powers that be said 'no' to that request." Quade turned his attention back to the conversation as though he was just tuning in. "Called us about it."

Moss's next statement stopped Quade cold. "Not so he could have sex with them, I'll bet. So he could knock them off, one by one, right?"

"Yeah, sonofabitch wanted to kill the girls." Andy shook his head. "In ways don't bear repeating. And then he wanted to film it, and put out there for everybody to see. Oh, he was a sick one in more ways than one."

Their silence acknowledged the truth.

"We kind of lost track of him after I wouldn't let my wife come up to see him anymore." Quade looked more miserable by the minute and Moss could only guess why.

"Why? Because he threatened to kill her, too?"

Quade only nodded and turned away to look at the woods again.

Andy saw his discomfort and took up the narrative again. "Anyway, they give him some medicine to make him act normal, but I wouldn't call him normal, even then. Just made him less troublesome, you know what I mean? Come on, I'll show you his room and you'll see how he was, right up to the time he left."

"You said there were men who came to get Michael, Andy? Police, maybe?"

Moss caught up with the caretaker who crossed the manicured lawn with surprising speed in the direction of some small cabins. Quade lagged behind, looking behind him and all around for an unseen enemy, a habit he had developed during the war, on patrol. It only surfaced when his heightened sixth sense told there was somebody around who posed a threat.

"No, they wasn't police unless they got foreign police that spoke like they do on TV in those spy movies. Russian or French, maybe. Like that. See? Mike had this thing for computers."

"You said. This thing about screwing them up, as if they weren't screwed up enough. But tell us about these men that talked funny. Russians, maybe?"

Andy, the caretaker, was on a roll, describing Michael's penchant for chaos. He lapsed into a wheezing hee-hee-hee which ended, "Yeah, he did. Ol' Mike could screw 'em up real good. Made the whole system go down right regular. Them nurses would have a fit, I'm telling you. Over one night, he got rid of all the records of their hours—for good! Couldn't even get 'em back 'cause we had done away with punch clocks and sign-in sheets by then. There went all the patient records, everything. Whoosh! Damned staff—doctors and nurses—had to go back to writing every damned thing down on paper."

"I'll bet they were pissed, all right." Moss glanced over at Quade whose face had darkened with anger. He wished Andy would get on with it, but the man seemed to be enjoying the chaos of long ago.

"Pissed ain't even the word. An' when they asked little ol' Mikey to fix it, you know what he said? 'You can go take a flying fuck unless—'"

Andy stopped and turned to face them so as to deliver the punch line. He opened his mouth, but they never heard it because a bullet whizzed past Moss's arm and into Andy's heart. Moss and Quade hit the ground simultaneously and got out their guns.

"It came from that clump of trees." Quade fired a round at the pine grove and moved toward the fallen man on his elbows. "I'll cover you while you see how bad he's hit."

It was bad. Moss could see Andy's mouth hang open like a fish taking its last gasp of air. He crawled over to where the caretaker lay. "Stay with us, man. We're calling the EMTs right now. Hang in there, ya hear?"

The words emerged like puffs of cottonwood fuzz on the morning air. "Unless—you—give—me a girl to kill."

Then Andy closed his eyes to fight for his life as his embroidered cap said he'd done once before against the Viet Cong and survived.

This time, on home ground, he lost.

During the interim between the local police arriving with sirens blasting and the paramedics arriving with more sirens blasting, Quade and Moss winged out in opposite directions, covering the pine grove as they kept low to the ground. They needn't have bothered. The shooter was long gone, even leaving his shoe prints in the mud.

"A professional job, if there ever was one," Moss said.

"Except even professionals slip up occasionally, or the police do, one or the other." Quade squatted down over a partial footprint the killer had overlooked. "This guy was good, but not quite perfect, especially out of his territory, which, by the looks of things, was definitely not Georgia. European last, leather soles, guy was at least five-six to -ten, about 150 pounds." He looked up at Moss whose usual beat was all cement, hypodermic needles, and cigarette butts. "He was probably wearing suit trousers."

"How do you know all this stuff?"

Quade produced a nylon thread. "Because his cuff caught on the blackberry vines. Jeans don't catch. Too tough."

"You're saying somebody hired a hit man? To kill poor, old Andy there?"

Quade didn't answer. Instead, from his Levi's pocket he produced a plastic snack bag. "Isis always figures I won't get nothing to eat." He emptied out the trail mix, brushed out the left over salt, and put the thread in the baggie. "CSI don't have nothing on us."

☙❧

Faun didn't wake up as he crept out to teach his eight o'clock lab. Bjorn let her sleep, thinking how beautiful she looked as he closed the door softly behind him—silver-blonde hair spread out on the pillow like a night angel caught sleeping in the morning light.

From the corner of the graduate housing hallway, Steve took in the sickening look of the lover torn from the side of his beloved, as Bjorn dressed and softly closed the door to his apartment. Moving slowly, Bjorn exhibited all the lover's reluctance to leave a piece of a dream for a job teaching pimply freshmen rudimentary scientific principles. Steve could actually could relate to that feeling, having spent the night in the lab, seeing Faun come in, Starbucks in hand, so ephemeral he thought she was like the gene they were chasing.

When Bjorn took the stairs down, two at a time, Steve used his pass key to enter the apartment where Faun lay still vulnerable, still asleep, in nothing but a sheet. The smell of Bjorn's semen was surprisingly erotic.

Steve was in bed beside her in an instant. He took his time with her. She didn't wake up. That was due to her lack of tolerance for drugs of any sort. The two Quaaludes he'd put in her beer the night before had apparently synergized with the alcohol, causing a state of near toxicity.

But not quite.

He made sure both his cell phone's cameras were running as she responded to his lovemaking. When he was through and Faun was spread out like a starfish across the bed, he let Chuck in.

Tall, athletic Chuck looked at his former lover almost tenderly, the edge taken off his lust by a couple of shots of Jim Beam. For a moment, Steve thought the jerk was going to renege on his vow to avenge himself on the girl who had rejected him for, of all things, a comment about money. He stood looking down at her breathing with a snoring sound whistling out of her half-open mouth. "What did you give her, man? She's making a funny sound, kind of like an old drunk."

"I just made sure she wouldn't wake up and identify us, that's all. Are you going to do it or do I need to call somebody else."

"No, I said I would do it and I'm going to, okay? I just don't want her to die on me or something. That would be the pits, man." Chuck eased into bed alongside the sleeping girl. "Don't wake up, Faun baby. Please don't wakey-wakey. Let me make you feel good, okay? Just like I used to. Okay, baby?"

Steve couldn't listen to anymore slimy love talk. He had just left the room and gone to the end of the hall when he heard Faun's scream. "Get off me! Get off me, dammit!"

Chuck went flying out of the room, wearing only a T-shirt that said Columbia Athletic Department on it. He was down the stairs, pausing only to pull on his shorts. Clad only in his underwear, Chuckie baby went sprinting across the parking lot to his own room.

Steve edged down the hall to Bjorn's apartment door. All he knew was he had gotten what he wanted, a piece of the impossible dream. Now he had to retrieve his other cell phone and leave the geek, Chris, to take the blame without Faun seeing him.

He didn't have to worry. She had fallen out of bed, landing face down in her own vomit. He slipped in the open door, grabbed his cell phone, and left by the fire exit. When he hit the parking lot, he burst into an hysterical laugh that tripped up the scale like a hyena laughs after making off with a piece of some other animal's kill.

The flimsy construction of the gradate apartments came to Faun's rescue first. Alarmed by the sound of a body crashing to the floor, pulling the printer table over along with it, sent neighbors rushing towards the open door. Finding Faun comatose and choking on her own vomit, a medical student called 911 and campus security while he directed the first-aid trained among them to put a jacket under her head. Gently, he turned her head to the side to ease the choking and got the gunk out of her mouth that was interfering with her breathing.

The EMTs said she was a hairsbreadth away from choking to death.

It was then Bjorn arrived from class and was arrested by campus police for, among the list of charges, rape, possession of an illegal substance, and possible attempted murder.

Under the glare of adverse publicity, the university was coming down hard on cases of date rape, throwing everything against the wall, hoping something would stick.

The first person who came forward as a witness was

Steve. He told the police he had seen them together the night before at the pizza place where Faun had three beers to Chris's one, that Chris had wild parties that he, Steve, had to sometimes break up, and, most damning of all, Faun and Bjorn had just met. The lab techs could testify to that, he said. He'd had to deal with cases of date rape before, he assured the detective that interviewed him.

Chapter 14

Sheldon was exploring the top floor of the house when he saw the car gliding through the trees on the road past Magnolia Alley. He decided, right then, it was going to be like those African safari movies where the lions crept around through the jungle, figuring they were going to jump the hunters because they were dumb white men who used cheap after-shave that anybody with a nose could smell a mile away.

What they didn't know was that a fierce Hutu warrior was on their trail, crouching close to the ground, sniffing their dung.

Did he really have to do that?

Sheldon began to sharpen his spear, an old copper curtain rod with a do-lolly that stuck out at the end in kind of a point. His faithful bearer and, in case the lions attacked, backup-warrior Piglet waited at the bottom of the stairs. Not having feet could be a bummer sometimes, but Piglet had other talents such as reading bedtime stories from memory all about storms, floods, and strange creatures that threw bad guys up in trees. Stories which kept Sheldon wide awake, planning what he and Piglet would do in such cases.

Now, the moment of truth was at hand. The bad guys had arrived aboard a lion-colored Crown Victoria, crawling belly-to-the-ground, down the road at the end of the drive. The brave Hutu hunter assessed the situation: Uncle Freddy had gone back to work, the two policeman had gone, but the clumsy black one with eyes like boiled peanuts said he would be back. His mama had rolled her eyes and said she couldn't wait, which meant she was kidding.

"Piglet, I see lions out on the road." Sheldon waited for an alarmed response from his robot friend.

Instead, he got. "Excuse my ignorance but what is a lion, master?"

"Oh, zounds, Piglet." Sheldon thought Hutu warriors spoke like Englishmen educated at Cambridge since they always seemed to hang around together in movies. "Zounds and blast, you are ignorant, I must say." Sheldon left his post and slid down the banister to where Piglet stood, holding his latest comic book, a plate of cookies, and a can of pop. "Lions are furry things with teeth and claws that will tear you apart and shred you up like barbeque."

"Not a possibility, master." Piglets head swiveled around and he fixed his skewed vision on Sheldon. "In the first place, my parts don't shred, and I've been taken apart many times by my father, Dr. Phillips."

"How many times do I have to tell you, robots don't have fathers, only boys do."

"In that case, since you are a boy, where is your father? Is Uncle Freddy your father?" Piglet could sometimes be tedious. "Or the big one who tears up floors?"

"You always get off the subject by asking dumb questions, Piglet. What I am telling you is there is clear and present danger. You got that?"

Piglet rolled his mismatched eyes in opposite directions. "Excuse me, master, I almost forgot you know everything. What is this clear and present danger, please? Could it be you've got a splinter in your derriere?"

To which Sheldon let out a loud shriek, pulled down his shorts, took one look, and shrieked again. "Mamaaaaa!"

Piglet could hardly keep the satisfaction out of his programmed alarm. "Now hear this! Now hear this! Splinter in butt! Repeat! Splinter in butt! All hands on deck! Repeat! All hands on deck! Repeat! May Day! May Day!" He followed his shrieking master down the hall to the top of the stairs, repeating. "May Day! May Day! All hands on deck!" until Sheldon yelled at him to shut up.

"I must say, that's gratitude for you," Piglet grumbled, taking up his sentinel post at the top of the third floor stairs, There he loaded lions, clear and present danger, and zounds into his already scrambled database of trivia

ഒരുന്നു

On the tree-lined road, puddled with spring rain, the Victoria crept to a purring halt behind a cluster of oleander bushes.

"It sure is peaceful out here, ain't it, Earl? Just listen to those bugs a-chirping for rain or whatever. Sounds just like a Freddy Kreuger movie, don't it?""

"Peaceful, hell. Graveyards are peaceful. Besides, I got to pee again, and there's no place off this road except farms." Earl gripped his trousers, looking desperately in all directions.

"I think that's okay as long you don't aim for the collards, Earl. The cows and all got to go somewhere."

"You just don't get it, do you, Lolo? I meant not being seen, dufus. I don't want to be seen by anybody, especially taking a leak out in the open."

"I told you, you drink too much tea, Earl. Mama says it's hard on the kidneys. But go on, do what you got to do."

Big Earl was in the middle of relieving himself when Moss came along the road. He wasn't in a good mood, since his search for Michael Slade had ended in the Zebulon County Courthouse amid a clutter of yellowed documents. The sight of a flashily dressed man peeing in the bushes beside the road didn't do anything to cheer him up. The beat cop in him took precedence over the detective and he pulled his car up beside the Victoria.

"Hey, buddy, that ain't cool. There's a place in town that's got bathrooms called Saranji's. Do your business in there next time you got to go, okay?"

Big Earl looked less big as he zipped his fly. "Okay, sir. Sorry, I just didn't know how they treated us black folks, bro."

"They treat you just like anyone else if you act like you were raised with indoor plumbing, okay? Have a good one, ya hear?"

It wasn't until he got the Victoria in his rear view mirror that he saw the Tennessee plates. Moss was on the phone to Quade in a heartbeat. "Can you run some Tennessee plates for me? See what you get on a bronze Crown Victoria, about 2009?"

"Sure. I was gonna call you, anyway. Seems the county clerk at the Zebulon Courthouse remembered something after we left and gave me a call. He remembers Michael Slade wanted a copy of his birth certificate so he could get a passport. Seems the staff at the Kingdom Hall Children's Home either lost it or never got it so he had to send to Macon to get it. He remembers Michael coming to the courthouse with a couple of foreign guys, German he thinks. Nicely dressed in three-piece suits. Reason he remembers is, Michael threw a fit when he saw his mother's name and tried to scribble it out with a pen. But one of the Germans grabbed it before he could do any damage. Said in all his born days he had never seen anyone try to do that. Said the look on the kid's face was downright scary."

Moss paused before answering, taking it all in. "Geez. That must be where he is, then. Figures with the Biopharma lead and the ALS license plates and what poor ol' Andy said."

Quade made a negative sound that came across to Moss as defeated. "I don't know. Sounds like a dead end to me. How we going to get any information out of an international conglomerate? Anyway, I doubt that Michael's still alive. Doctors only gave him ten years at most and he was eighteen then."

"If he isn't, then someone just like him is carrying on for him. Run those plates for me, will you? Talk to you later." Moss ended the call, thinking white folks got themselves into some kind of weird.

Chapter 15

Kenya had finished getting the splinters out of Sheldon's behind when Moss pulled up in the driveway, next to the loaner car the Cadillac dealer had delivered earlier in the day. The shiny sleek convertible made his serviceable sedan look mundane and dusty. He wished he could say it was paid for, but he still owed a year's worth on it.

Moss noticed the electrician's truck around back. Apparently Dr. Phillips had tried going solar, but once he was dead, so was green energy. Nobody within 100 miles knew anything about repairing the solar panels and the team at Lesbos were certified electricians, so it was back to the power grid for the new owner.

He heard Sheldon's voice in the living room. "Mommy, it's the clumsy, lumpy man again."

"Well, let him in, baby—and tell him to take a seat. I'll be right down."

Sheldon opened the door. "I got splinters in my butt, only Piglet calls it my derriere. That's butt in Piglet language."

"I'm sorry to hear that. Does it hurt much?"

Sheldon's voice rose to a squeak. "That's a dumb

question! It hurts so much I can't even sit down, you silly, lumpy, clumsy man who tears up floors. Hear that, Piglet! The lumpy man asked me if it hurt. Is that stupid or what?"

Moss took a deep breath. It had been a long day and he needed a cold beer, and to watch the sports channel. "You know what, son? I don't care how much you're hurting, you got to be polite to people. That's the rules of the game. Be polite no matter what your problem is."

"I don't have to do what you say, lumpy man. Go 'way!" Sheldon slammed the front door in Moss's face.

Moss thought about kicking it in, as with anyone who defied the law, but then, since that defiant person was only seven years old, he resisted the temptation. Moss was about to go get that beer when the door opened and Kenya stuck her head out.

"Why, Detective Moss, leaving so soon? Come on in and have something cold and tell me what you've been doing all day. I got air-conditioning now and a new refrigerator." She smiled and all the problems of the day vanished as Kenya did her magic act. "And an ice maker, too."

"Sounds good."

It sounded more than good, to be treated cordially, even welcomed by someone as gorgeous as Kenya, especially tonight. She had on red shorts and a loose, filmy top that let you know she had a matching bra on underneath in case you thought you were going to sneak a peek. Her hair fell in relaxed curls to her shoulders, the art of a local hair dresser, and she had teeny strappy sandals on her feet that revealed a diamond piggy toe ring on each foot.

"Sheldon, come and say hello to Detective Moss, please, son." Kenya made a pretense of looking around, although she knew right where Sheldon was. "That's funny, he was just here a minute ago. Probably playing with that robot of his."

He stood inside the marble foyer, marveling at the transformation to the house that had taken place in twenty-four hours. The Lesbos team had been at work, changing the walls from mildewed yellow to chocolate. The ornate molding in the living room was tricked out in bright white, contrasting sharply with the chocolate walls and the gold leaf frames of the turn-of-century paintings, which had suddenly appeared.

Kenya followed his eyes. "Found those in the creepy basement. Guess they came with the house. Kind of the 'Rent-An-Ancestor' look, don't you think?" She handed the stunned detective a tall glass. "And just kind of guessed what you like."

He tasted the frosted glass. Vodka Collins just the way he liked them. It was perfect like the living room, *like her*. Moss stood looking around as though he was in a museum. Chantal West had created another world *just like her*.

He realized he was one conversation behind because she was standing, looking as though he should say something. "I'm sorry, say what, now?"

"You were looking at the paintings just now." Kenya smiled and his pulse started to climb as she sidled over to stand beside him in a cloud of perfume. "I know what you're thinking."

"Is it that obvious?" His voice suddenly had a mysterious crack in it.

"You were thinking how those people in the paintings are white so they couldn't be my ancestors, right?"

"Well, you know how it was back in the day." Moss took a large gulp of the vodka. "My mother's Creole, as mixed as gumbo, she says."

"I'm going to make sure to get some black artists up

there as well. In fact, I was thinking about opening a gallery someday."

"A gallery here? In the boonies? If you don't mind me saying, you'd probably be better off betting on the greyhound races across the river in Alabama. You have better odds of getting your money back."

"You sure are cynical, but I suppose being a detective makes you that way."

Like the evil dwarf in a fairy tale, Sheldon suddenly stuck his head out from a closet under the stairs. "He dumb, too. And fat and lumpy!" He shut the door again, like a malevolent cuckoo clock.

"So that's where you've been hiding! Mind your manners, mister!" she yelled at the closet. "Believe me, I wasn't raised to be rude." She looked as though she was waiting for his approval before dragging the kid out in the hall.

"Sheldon? That's okay, we've had our run-in for today," Moss changed the subject before he dealt with the brat himself. "Anyway, you and I've got to talk. Looks like you've been a busy girl today." He nodded at the fireplace which was no longer a refuge for mice and cockroaches. "Doing a little painting and plastering? Looks good."

"You don't know the half of it." Chantal rolled her luminous eyes. "These white people still act like taking orders from a black woman is taking away their civil rights."

He looked around for some place to sit. "I see you got a sweet ride now."

"That's a loaner from the agency until they fix mine." She made it sound like driving a red Caddy convertible was slumming as she gave him a tour of the downstairs. "Come on to the dining room. That's the only chairs I've got for now. You think this place will make a recording studio, Mr. Moss?"

"Grover, please. Do I take it you're planning on staying here then?"

"Only the summer. You know, 'til this thing settles down. Grover." She stuck her head around the kitchen door where she had gone to refresh his drink. "That doesn't suit you except when you're being all detective-like. What'd your mama call you? C'mon, tell me."

In the back of his detective's mind, Moss made a mental note that, for electricians rewiring a place, the crew in the kitchen had gone quiet. If he were paying for it, he would see what they were up to, but Chantal came back with his refill and worked her magic again.

She smiled so teasingly, so softly he would have told her that he loved her right then. Except his phone rang giving him an excuse not to make a fool of himself. It was Quade Walker. The usual taciturn drawl had a strange urgency to it.

"Something's happened to Faun. I'm on the road to go get her now. I've got Isis with me. I want you to go over and make sure Lois is okay. I'll fill you in later, okay? I'll get back tomorrow sometime. I've already called the station and the two part-timers are filling in."

" You got it. Anything you need."

"Thanks, Moss. And I checked the Interstate files on the plates you gave me. Nothing. I'll call you if anything comes up. Andy's autopsy is set for Friday week. Pretty straightforward, except the make of the bullet. I'd love to see what this guy uses. Hold the fort, Moss. Got to go."

Moss found himself holding a dead phone.

"What's wrong? " Kenya dropped the act and came over to peer up into his face. "What's happened?"

He dodged the question. "Do you know where Walker's mother-in-law lives?"

"Sure, but why? Is she in danger?"

"What makes you think that?"

"The look on your face, for one thing, and because I felt something cold-like come over me a minute ago." She didn't add that phrase had popped into her mind again that warned her of Holly's impending death. '*You never know what life is going to bring. Listen, baby girl!*'

"I just want to check on her. Quade asked me to. Can you show me where it is? I can get there by myself. I'm a big boy now, Mama."

He tried to play it cool, but something in Quade's voice told him to hurry. As usual, he figured, the chief had understated the situation.

Kenya was all action, grabbing her sweater, changing her shoes to an old pair of loafers she kept by the door. "I'll do more than show you. I'll put her up in a motel if you think she's in danger. Sheldon! Sheldon!"

Just then Freddy's truck pulled up in the driveway and the young man bounded into the foyer, his arms full of takeout boxes.

He got out the bill and started ticking off the orders. "I've got the subs and sides, salad for you, pulled pork barbeque for whoever and the hot dog for his nibs." He stopped short, seeing their grim faces. "Did I miss something? Drinks? I left those in the truck. Be back in a jif! Hey, where'er you going?"

Kenya stood on tiptoe to drop a kiss on Freddy's cheek as she went out the door. "You didn't miss a thing, sweetie. We got to run out to Auntie Lois's place a minute. Keep an eye on Sheldon while we're gone, will you? You know, he's upstairs somewhere playing with that machine of his. They're like Frankenstein and that mad scientist, I swear."

Moss resisted the temptation to say something snarky—like, it was hard to tell which one was Frankenstein. "We'll be back in a few. That's the electricians in the kitchen, in case you're wondering. Ghosts usually aren't that noisy."

"Wait a sec. Just hold the phone." Freddy looked from one tense face to the other. "Besides the fact that I have to go back to work, all kinds of what-if's come to mind."

"I'll call Saranji and explain the problem. She'll understand. We'll make it up to you, sweetie. I promise." With that, Kenya was dancing out the door.

Freddy set the boxes down on the window seat by the front door. "If you're worried about Auntie Lois, I just saw her at the post office mailing some packages."

"When was that?" Moss looked longingly at the sub sandwiches, knowing he hadn't been invited to join them. It was turning out to be one of those days when he'd had more alcohol than food.

Freddy screwed up his handsome face in an effort to be accurate. "I guess about five. An hour ago, maybe."

Moss said a longing goodbye to a lot of calories he didn't need anyway. "A lot can happen in an hour. Let's go, Miss West."

Kenya looked at Freddy, a warning in her eyes, but he only grinned. He knew something was up. "She could be on her way home by now, in that case. I give her a fifteen minute head start, allowing for a stop at the Winn-Dixie. Look. One of the kids got a cell phone 'cause they call in orders all the time. Why don't you just call her, KK, if you want to check on her? Why run all the way out there to Lesbos? Your food will get cold and I really got to get back to Saranjii's. What about it, Detective?"

Freddy looks a bit desperate, Moss thought. *Probably at the thought of staying with the kid and the robot. That would be enough to scare anybody.* But he only grabbed Kenya's arm and pulled her out the door.

"'Cause the chief told me to check her place out, that's why. Fred, give the house a call, see if she got home okay, and tell her to lock up 'til we get there."

Moss kept his voice flat and quiet, as though it was just a suggestion. It was like playing catch with Jell-O, getting anything done around this one-horse berg. Had it been Memphis, he would have already dispatched a patrol car to check on the old lady and headed for the bar.

Kenya got to the convertible first. Easing into the driver's seat, she said, "Let's take this baby for a spin. I haven't even seen what it can do."

Moss sighed, wishing for a Scotch on the rocks to drive the Vodka home about now. "Oh, no. I've seen how you drive, sister. Forget it. I haven't got that much insurance."

She gunned the motor. "You want to find Lois? Hop in, hold on, and shut up."

He was on the leather seat beside her, trying to fasten his seatbelt, as the back wheels spit gravel.

Heading for the gates, Kenya put her foot down on the accelerator, her wicked laugh floating back behind them like a silk scarf on the warm breeze. "Now let's play chicken. Tell me what your Mama calls you and I'll slow down."

They tore down the line of magnolia trees and spun out on to the road. Moss looked at the speedometer. They were doing seventy-five on a road made for mule carts and logging trucks. "Promise?"

"You know, you're kind of conservative for a police detective." Her perfume, anything but conservative, drifted over him, fueled by the air conditioner.

"Abraham. That's what Mama calls me. Abraham. Now, you tell me yours. I bet you weren't born Chantal, right? What is that, anyway? French or something?"

He expected wild, wicked laughter from this crazy

woman. Nope. She didn't even take her eyes from the road. He waited for the inevitable derision. It never came. After a long few minutes, she pronounced it like a verdict. "I like it. She was into presidents, wasn't she? Abe. That's what I'm gonna call you. Honest Abe. That suits you." That said, she slowed to sixty. "And my real name is Shekenya, only I shortened it to Kenya."

Moss grinned. "I like it much better than Chantal. That's sounds kind of…I don't know." She glanced over at him. *Even more beautiful in the shadows. She's a dream,* he thought. *A freaking fantasy.*

"Kind of phony?"

He ducked the question. "For that matter, I could be taking kickbacks off the street for all you know, could cheat on my time sheets, doctor my expense accounts, hand in the till, or all of the above. Honest Abe don't cut it in my profession. Bending the rules is just part of staying alive."

"But you don't, do you? I have to be kind of phony," she said. "People like and glitz is phony. Just part of staying alive, like you say."

Her profile etched in gold by the setting sun, lashes so long they touched the curve of her brow, eyes that dominated the rest of her face, full lips that begged to be kissed, a nose inherited from some Caucasian ancestor— straight and then curved down to her upper lip—she could have decorated the wall of a pharaoh's tomb and yet, here she was beside him. His mind wandered…

"But I'll bet you aren't, Abe. Never have been."

"What's that?" It suddenly became important to Moss what she thought of him.

Then the smile. *I bet they didn't show that on old Pharaoh's tomb.* "Phony, because you're too poor to be crooked, that's why." Kenya indulged in a wicked laugh.

It wasn't what he'd hoped for, but it was better than

nothing. Why did he expect her to care, anyway? She was right—he was just a poor, honest, lumpy-looking cop. They never put people like him on a pharaoh's wall. "I guess. What you see is what you got."

But she slowed down, just to please him, saying softly. "Abe," then started to sing something about loving a man. In his wildest dreams, he couldn't imagine she was singing about him.

 භංඏ

Freddy was trying to multi-task—text with his thumbs, look in the takeout orders for Sheldon's hot dog, and get the kid to eat. "Shellfish! Your dinner is here. Come out, come out, wherever you are."

He was used to doing three things at once, sometimes four, which was why he didn't hear the peculiar bumping noise coming from the stairs. "Okay, I'm coming up there! One...two...three...here I come."

He took the winding stairs two at a time, until he arrived at the third floor landing, where he found Piglet head down, wheels in the air. Turning the little robot upright, he adjusted a few knobs and fixed the golf ball eyes so they didn't roll in opposite directions.

"What happened, little brother? Sheldon do this to you?"

"Not the little master. He would never hurt Piglet, no sirree. I heard him cry out when he was looking for something in the kitchen, where he had gone to make garbage soup for the cat and I to eat. He just yelled once and then was quiet. I was trying to come to his rescue when I took a tumble."

Just then, the sound of an engine caught Freddy's attention. Hoping Kenya had changed her mind and was back already, he raced back down the stairs to the front door and saw truck tail lights disappearing into the growing darkness. Silhouetted against the Spring sky, he could still make out the shape of a white van with a rack on top. Slamming the door, he raced back to the kitchen. Wires jutted out of the fuse boxes like twisting serpents. He tried to turn the lights off and on in vain.

"Sheldon! Sheldon! Come on, this is no joke. Your fries are getting cold and I know how much you hate cold fries." Ordinarily, that line worked. Now, it was met with the noisy silence only old houses have.

In an instant, Kenya and Moss's urgency took on a new meaning. Though they hadn't said anything about Sheldon being the one in danger, Kenya had told him about the foiled abduction attempt in Memphis and why she had come back to Julia Springs.

It took Freddy a split second to decide what his next move would be, then he was out the door and in his truck, following the trail of dust the van had left to the road.

Chapter 16

Big Earl and Loquacious were just finishing the last lick of pulled pork barbeque off their fingers when the white van tore past them, swinging wide to avoid hitting them, screeching on two wheels as it nearly hit a tree.

Earl was the first to recover. "Would you look at that redneck fool? I mean, what kind of brains does it take to know a truck like that can't be driven over sixty? Chassis ain't built for it. Now, looka here!"

A pair of headlights lit up Earl's greasy face. "Here comes another country cousin, probably thinkin' he's gonna catch up to the first one." Earl pulled on to the shoulder as Fred's truck sped by. "And I just had to get a detail package just before I came down here because the wife made me. Waste of good money. Look at this shit-load of red dust covering up my wax job. Hot double damn!"

Loquacious mumbled something around a mouthful of chili cheese fries.

"What'd you say, pinhead?" Earl wasn't in the mood for jokes. He took out a perfectly clean hanky and wiped off the side-view mirror. It did him good to know his mother-in-law would complain when she did the wash, "Earl's been polishing his shoes again with them hankies." *Serves her right, eating her weight in groceries.*

"Said those looked like Tennessee plates."

"Where? On the pickup? Not on your life, Lolo. No, they were redneck Georgia peaches from the peach state. That's a lie. Best peaches come from Carolina and Tennessee, everybody knows that."

"No, on that white van with the ladder." Loquacious shook his head and swallowed a gulp of sweet tea. "They was Tennessee plates, I'm telling you."

"Naw, man,. Peach State rednecks, that's what I saw. Finish your fries or dump the rest of them. We got to check on the house again."

He eased the Crown Vic down the road toward Magnolia Alley while Loquacious gobbled down the rest of the fries.

"I know I saw Tennessee plates. That van was from home! I'm telling you as Jesus is my savior."

Big Earl's chins shook with convulsive laughter. "Only thing's gonna save you tonight is Alka Seltzer, my man. One fart and you're outta the bed and on the sofa."

Earl slowed as they drove past. "Looks like nobody's home at the big house. I'll go turn around up the road and come back. If it's still clear by then, we'll take a closer look."

"Maybe it's a trap-like." Loquacious wiped the grease from his chin with a napkin. "Maybe they're just all in there waitin' for us, Earl."

"You know, Lolo, for once you may be right. Tell you what. When we get up there, you go up to the door and yell. 'Anybody home?' If nobody answers, then you try the door. If it's unlocked, go inside and yell again. Like, 'Hello, is anybody home?' Then you give me a signal and I'll hide the car in that barn back there. You lock and bolt the front door and come let me in. Got it?"

Loqucious nodded. "Hey, Earl…"

"Yeah, what, Lolo?" Earl steeled himself for the inevitable non-sequitur.

"Why can't I just ring the doorbell?"

☙❦❧

Following the white van on the road into town, Freddy dialed Saranjii's first, knowing the two part-time deputies were there eating. The white van had a good head start and was being driven by a crazy man with a death wish. In three minutes, it would arrive at Julia Springs only stoplight, just outside of town. Depending which way it turned, he could either lose the chase, and Sheldon with it, or cause a crash the likes of which Julia Springs had never seen.

Either way, it wouldn't turn out well for his little cousin trapped inside the van.

"Hey, it's Freddy. Are the deputies still eating there? Give the phone to them, please."

One of the deputies answered, his mouth full. "Fred, what's up, man?"

"I'm chasing a white van with Tennessee plates, roof rack with a ladder coming up to the four-way light.

The chewing stopped. "Why in hell are you doing that, Freddy?"

It was all Freddy could do to keep from yelling into the phone. "'Cause I'm pretty sure they've kidnapped my cousin, that's why I want you to block the main drag."

The deputy started chewing again. Can't do that, Freddy."

"What? Why not?"

"The chief's got the SUV."

"Gimmee back to Saranjii." Under his breath, Freddy

said something about cops not wanting to get off their asses.

"Freddy, what's wrong?" Saranjii's voice cut into that thought.

"Some guys in a white van've got Sheldon, and Kenya's gone to see if Lois is all right. Can you send everybody with a pickup out to block the road to town? Hurry it up and tell 'em to make a citizen's arrest of the driver and whoever's riding shotgun." He could count on Saranjii to rally the troops—the usual loafers who gathered in the cool evening to drink beer on her porch.

The van reached the light ahead of him. A line of pick-up trucks greeted them including a backhoe and Amos Perkin's hay bailer which took up most of the street. The rest were lining up across the road to the Interstate, leaving the van no choice, except to turn around.

After doing a U-turn, they found Freddy was blocking both lanes with his pickup.

The two deputies got out of their police cruiser, and with officious importance, strolled toward the van's driver and passenger, two frightened white men in paint-spattered coveralls.

"What the hell is this, a Klan rally?" The driver indicated the barricade of vehicles and men cradling their rifles, trying to look casual.

"Put your hands against the truck, sir. And spread 'em," said the deputy. "If you wouldn't mind, that is."

"Sure, I mind, but I'm doing it because you're the law. I just don't know what I've done." The driver muttered something about the sticks to his cohort who looked ready to burst into tears.

"That's talking back to an officer of the law," said one of the deputies. "That constitutes…what does it constitute now, Kenny?"

Freddy was trying to open the back of the truck.

"Unlock it will you, Marv? I've got to see if Sheldon is in there. Hold on, Sheldon! I'll get you out in a minute."

"Who's he yelling at?" The irate driver looked from one suspicious face to another. "There ain't nobody in there. Hey, buddy, nobody's in there, okay? Wait a minute, are you the idiot chasing me down the road?"

The deputies weren't buying it. "Just shut up, friend. Now, get out of there and release the back door. And don't get any funny ideas, ya hear? Unless you want to leave here in itty-bitty pieces."

Grumbling under his breath about asshole cops, the driver climbed from behind the wheel and released the door lock. Freddy pulled the door open and looked inside. It was empty except for their tool belts, a paint-spattered generator, and trash.

No Sheldon.

Chapter 17

He hadn't planned to find a theme park in this dump of a town. The stranger checked his GPS for the location. Unless he had been given the wrong directions, this castle with its high walls and guard towers housed his second target for the job. It wouldn't be his mistake, of course. He never made mistakes. You couldn't survive in the business of killing people and get a reputation for sloppy work.

No, it would be some nitwit at the other end who gave him his orders. It would be that person's mistake, and the last one he would make. One thing about working for this client was for sure—this client, whoever he was, didn't tolerate people who made mistakes. The killer would have a bonus job when he returned to Munich, or maybe he would just eliminate the idiot for free for causing him to lose time.

He was crouched behind some bushes, figuring how to get into the place, when he heard the sound of marching footsteps approaching. He wasn't dressed for this wretched climate.

Mosquitoes were feasting on every exposed patch of skin. Bugs of every sort were crawling on him, but he didn't dare move to retrieve his repellent from his pocket.

What's this coming? The changing of the guard, perhaps, he mused, smiling in the dark. A man for whom surprise had been one of his victims early in life, he wasn't prepared for the Amazonian Guard, all of whom towered at six feet or more, with feathered helmets, breastplates, and short tunics coming at quick-step in perfect unison around the castle walls. They each carried power crossbows, side arms on each hip, and a sheath of steel arrows.

Better and better. He hadn't expected a show, only to do the job and get out. Here he was, getting to see Las Vegas showgirls who could do him some damage, if they were only smart enough. A couple of well-placed shots and he would collect an easy million just for taking out an old lady. He was beginning to enjoy himself.

The killer loved fantasy of all sorts. He had never been allowed to indulge in make-believe as a child. But as an adult, he could carry out his innermost desires without feeling that he was compromising his dignified public persona.

In perfect unison, the troop halted before the guard towers, shouldered their bows, and saluted. He waited, something that proved to be a fatal mistake.

Then, on a signal from their leader, they turned on their heels, facing forward, and drew their bows. From the guard towers came a loud voice. "Man in the bushes, rise to standing position with your hands in the air."

The killer's blood froze. He stayed crouched as though he was suddenly exposed naked. The authoritative voice repeated. "Man in the bushes, rise to standing position with your hands in the air. This is your second warning. On the third, we will shoot."

Ridiculous as it was, he had no choice. Though his Glock still had the silencer on, he rose firing deliberately at the one to the left of the haughty leader. He would save that beauty until last. The girl fell, but by the time she hit the ground, the killer was bristling with arrows. His face still retained an expression of surprise, as though he was trying to figure out where he had made his first, last, and only mistake.

In the command center, at the heart of the Lesbos compound, Lois switched off the microphone, watching the monitors as the Amazon guard administered first aid to their comrade, ignoring the bristling man in the bushes.

"This is Michael's work," she said aloud. "I know his trademarks. He never does the dirty work himself. He's watching somewhere. I know he is."

But no one heard her. The boys and girls at the monitors were watching their siblings and cousins deal with the death of one of their own. It was the first time they had seen death, as if reality had materialized before their eyes. The walls of Lesbos kept them safe. Outside its walls was death. They had seen it with their own eyes. The name Michael meant nothing to them, Lois had made sure of that.

e/ɔe/ɔ

Moss got nervous when other people drove, regardless of the expertise of the driver. When it was a crazy, beautiful woman who laughed with the wind in her hair, his blood pressure reached overload.

When she screeched to a stop at edge of what looked like the jungle and said, "We have to run from here," it was like relief gone bad. He'd heard stories of gators thirteen feet long, just aching to get their chops on some pork fat. And snakes—*Oh, lord, don't even bring up the subject of snakes.* Just the very thought made him long for the drunks and druggies of Beale Street.

Moss felt positively faint, but he'd be damned if he'd show it.

So when this jungle princess leads the way, you best follow, looking like you do this on a regular basis, and do your best to look at home in this reptile, mosquito-bitten, oh-what-is-that-crawling-on-me place in a citified suit.

As he followed in Kenya's somewhat erratic wake, the first thing to go was the tie, then the jacket. He was thinking he would just strip down to his undershirt when they came upon a clearing in the godawful jungle. *Oh, Sweet Jesus, give me Beale Street any time of night! I won't ever complain again.*

He came up, wheezing like an old horse, beside Kenya who had hardly broken a sweat. Moss was bent over, sucking in the fetid air, when he connected with what was in front of him. There was what looked like a pro basketball team in drag. They lifted up a body on their shoulders and, moving like a presidential funeral at slow march, went into the huge double doors of a gated community. The double doors slammed shut behind them. For a lost moment, Moss thought someone had slipped something into that last iced tea he'd had back there at Saranjii's. Or he could be hallucinating from hyperthermia.

What was that?

He was about to question his guide, but at that moment, they heard a slight rustle in the bushes beside them. Kenya, the fearless, was in his arms in a New York second, right up against his sweating self. It was time to act like a cop instead a city-bred fool lost in the forest, and he did the best job he could.

Flinging her behind him, like in the movies, so his body shielded hers, he yelled. "All right, show yourself, you there in the bushes! Hands up, no funny business now."

All they heard was a kind of a sigh like someone letting the air out of a tire. Cautiously, not knowing what he
would find, Moss stepped over toward the sound and
drew the bushes aside. There, almost prone but not quite,
was a man with a bunch of arrows sticking out of his
chest.

He was being slowly lowered to the ground by the
weight of his body pressing on the arrows. As they
passed through his lungs up to the haft, he kind of sighed
like he was thinking something over. Fortunately for him,
he was quite dead.

Behind him, there was a thump as fearless Kenya
fainted dead away. After checking to see if she was all
right, he approached the body. Moss noted that the dead
man was wearing trousers, tailor-made with pleats in
front in the European style. Quade's earlier remark echoed in his mind. *He wasn't wearing jeans like an American would have worn, knowing he had to go into rough
country.*

A stranger in a strange land. The hit man sent from
somewhere overseas by someone who didn't want to be
found. But the human dart board himself, sighing in the
bushes, was the real clue, Moss realized. The body of the
assassin would lead to whoever sent him.

Kenya moaned. In an instant, he was bending over
her, thinking how much he loved her, when the double
doors opened and a tall, striking woman in a kind of mu-
mu and turban stood there, assessing the situation. He
froze when she was followed by two of the guards.

It was the same voice that he had had heard booming
orders through the forest as he and Kenya had run
through the woods. He certainly didn't want to die like
the dart board in the bushes.

"Evening, ma'am." She was evidently a person of
some authority because she ignored Moss who greeted

her, invisible hat in hand. "I'm Detective Moss and this lady here is—"

The woman waved his explanation away like the mosquitoes and midges swarming around him. "Save your breath. I know who you are." She regarded the dead man with a desultory glance, as if his death were an everyday occurrence in her front yard, and advanced to where Kenya lay stretched out as though she was asleep. "She always was a cream puff. Had her scars covered up, has she?" She looked at Moss with the probing eyes of one who has lived too long and seen every evil under the sun. "Let me guess. You're the man Quade said would protect me, aren't you? Well, I guess you see how that ended up. Let me instruct you, Mr. Detective from the big city, on one thing: we women have survived by our wits. He, on the other hand—" she said, gesturing toward the wheezing corpse. "—he thought he would survive by his balls. I guess you thought so, too. Men always do."

"No, ma'am, I—" Before Moss could choke out a reply, the woman again cut him off with a swat of her hand.

"Never mind, I'll get the guards to carry her inside. When my son-in-law gets back from rescuing my grand-daughter from a sexual assault of the foulest kind, he will attend to that human garbage out there. You, on the other hand, can spend the night in the gatehouse, or you can come back in the morning, it's up to you. Goodnight."

Dismissing him, Queen Sappho gave rapid instructions on the two-way radio.

Ignoring white, female domination, Moss bent down and gathered Kenya up in his arms.

But the imperious woman was still barking orders. "I said leave her, Detective. And goodnight."

"Excuse me, but—"

The gates opened and the guards came marching out

again six deep. Not wanting to be used for target practice like the killer, he meekly handed Kenya over to the first two guards who towered over him by a foot. They might have been taking Kenya off a tree limb, or from a gurney, so little did they acknowledge him.

But as she leaned over, tickling his cheek with her feathers, the tallest guard whispered. "Don't worry, sweet cheeks. Spend the night in the gatehouse, and I'll be over to tuck you in."

Then, carrying Kenya between them, they went at quick step back into the mighty gates of Lesbos and the double doors slammed shut.

Chapter 18

I want to speak to him."

"Sorry, Chief, I haven't received authorization yet, allowing any other law enforcement agency in on the investigation, you know how that is." The campus police chief knew a distraught father when he saw one. This one looked like he could do some damage and the campus police chief wasn't taking any chances on what might happen if he let Quade Walker near the rape suspect. He didn't even want to think about it.

But Quade was not taking no for an answer. "My daughter is the victim. I've met the young man before. I just want to talk to him. Not officially, just as a concerned father. As a favor of one law enforcement officer to another."

The campus police chief shifted his weight from one foot to the other, as if his shoes pinched him. "Okay, but I'm going to have to be present when you're talking to him, Chief. You know how it is. And leave your service pistol at the desk, please. I know how touchy these things can be."

Quade took off his side arm belt and handed it over to the sergeant. His scarred face looked even grimmer in the neon-lit station house of Campus Security. "Anything else?" she asked, eyes sliding sideways to her superior. In cases like this, of date rape and sexual assault, they'd had to deal with irate fathers before.

The chief shook his head slightly. They had a metal detector at the door and Quade had put his phone and car keys in the basket, but had been allowed to keep his badge as a courtesy.

The campus police officer led the way to a room with a two-way mirror, a table, and four wooden chairs. "It isn't much but it's home," he said, trying to lighten the mood. These sexual assaults were hell to deal with. Give him a good robbery any day. "Have a seat, Chief Walker. What's-his-name will be brought in shortly."

"Bjorn. Chris Bjorn. And just call me Quade. I appreciate this. I really do."

"Bjorn? What kind of name is that? He an immigrant?" The campus officer professed ignorance, trying to assess Chief Walker's mood. He looked like the type of guy who could kill with his bare hands, given the motive. And he certainly had one.

"Norwegian, I think he said. From Minnesota, I believe."

"We get all kinds here at the university. I've got two daughters and two boys, and I tell them all, just know who you're going out with before you start anything serious. You never know these days. Could be a terrorist for all they know. How's your girl doing, Quade?"

"Wife's with her at the hospital. The DNA test, semen test, and blood test are being done."

"Tough for a young girl. Traumatic. She's not hurt otherwise? Bruises?"

Quade shuddered at the thought. "I haven't seen her. She was at the hospital when we got here. Wife's just got there now."

Just then, the door opened and Chris Bjorn came in with a burly sergeant. When he saw Quade, he blurted. "I didn't hurt Faun. I never would do anything—"

"Shut up, Born, or whatever your name is. Don't talk unless someone talks to you first, understand? Sit down!"

The sergeant shoved Chris roughly into a chair. His hands were cuffed. Bjorn went silent, but his blue eyes were begging Quade to ask him to explain what happened. Quade did just that in a minimum of words in a gentle voice that brought tears to the young man's eyes.

"All right, we spent the night together at my place." Quade's jaw tightened making the scars stand out. "Then in the morning, I had an eight o'clock class to teach and I left about seven forty-five. Faun was still sleeping, so I didn't wake her up. I came back at nine fifteen, nine-thirty to find the place in an uproar, cops all over the place, and they just slapped on the handcuffs and brought me here. I haven't seen Faun, but they said she filed a sexual-assault charge against me. Not only that, they said I drugged her with some pills they found in my apartment. Mr. Walker, I don't take pills of any kind. I don't know where they came from, honestly. And I wouldn't do anything to hurt Faun. I love her! I want to marry her just as soon as I get a job." Bjorn shook his crew cut head in bewilderment. "This is some kind of nightmare."

"For everybody, most of all for Faun." Quade studied the young man. "I know my daughter. She wouldn't say something like that if it weren't true, Chris."

Bjorn raised his head, looking Walker straight in the eyes. "My class will tell you I didn't leave the building until after nine. I got back to my apartment about nine-twenty. I'm sure you can find somebody to verify that. I passed some neighbors in the parking lot. I said hello or something."

"What about the pills?"

"The prescribing doctor's got to be on the label. I know it doesn't have my name on it. I don't take pills."

Quade looked at the other police officer. The pills were found in a baggie on the kitchen counter in plain sight. "You could have bought them on the street."

"I could have, but I didn't. You can't use drugs and do what I do. Please believe me. I love Faun. I wouldn't hurt her for the world."

"You got a lawyer, Bjorn?"

"My fellowship covers legal defense. I've already spoken to him. He'll go before the judge tomorrow morning and find out what the bail is."

"Okay, if that's all, Quade…"

"That's all for now."

"Take him back to his cell, sergeant." When the door was closed, the security chief studied Quade's face. He was a hard man to read, especially when something touched him deeply. "Well, what do you think?"

"We'll just have to wait and see what the test results are. That'll take a few days. His lawyer will make him take a sperm test, and all the other stuff. If he's exonerated, that just leaves the drug charge. He'll get off with a fine and community service."

"Funny what he said about them being in a bottle. They were in a baggie on the kitchen counter right out in the open. Kind of like a setup." The corpulent law officer picked at his ear until a little drop of blood appeared. "If Born has an alibi like he says, and people can substantiate it, then maybe it was a set up to get him out of the way. A jealous classmate, even someone on the faculty who feels he's a threat. A former boyfriend, someone who knew your girl maybe. I've seen it all in my time here at college: videos, one kid blackmailing another, the whole nine yards. By the way, at the scene, we grabbed another guy running like hell across the parking lot in his shorts."

Quade seemed to snap out of a fog. "What?"

"We're charging this kid with attempted assault, somebody bailed him. His dad's a big Atlanta attorney and making false arrest noises. I'll see what I can learn from him though. Could be Bjorn was just a patsy."

They got up to leave.

"You'll keep me updated?"

"Off the cuff, if it's all right with you."

They exchanged private phone numbers and shook hands. Quade stepped out into the heavy night air. After all his years in law enforcement, he thought he could spot an innocent man. Until now. He had liked Chris Bjorn on sight. Something about him—whether it was his Midwestern directness, his teasing, affectionate way with Faun after she brushed him off like dust, or his quick mind—something about the guy reminded him of his younger brother, killed in Afghanistan more than twenty years ago. Maybe that was why he was inclined to believe Bjorn's story. In that case, someone had it in for Bjorn, like the security chief said, or Faun, or both. Could it be whoever had Holly killed, hired a professional hit man, and hacked in to Faun's research were one and the same person? A person who had an entire global organization at his command?

Quade took a deep breath, his old wounds reminding him, as they did every day, that his body had taken a beating. He was almost immune to pain, but someone had managed to hurt him through his child. And his first instinct was to find that person and make him suffer.

He called Moss's phone. The detective sounded out of breath. "How's it going? Everything okay down there?"

Moss tripped over a root in the primal dark and swore.

"Moss?"

"Fine, just dandy. Except for the guy in the bushes stuck full of arrows. Looks like he's had a rotten day. Somebody must've mistaken him for a sixteen-point buck in the dark."

Quade chuckled. "Damn poachers, and it's not even deer season. Tell me, is he wearing pleated trousers."

"Tailor-made. Some dude thought he had to dress up to hunt, I guess." Moss let out a yell as he slid down a muddy embankment.

"Moss, where in hell are you?"

There was the sound of splashing, cursing, and finally Moss was back. "That's what I don't know. I'm lost as hell and just fell into a creek or something. Are there snakes around here? Oh, lord, I just saw red eyes coming at me."

Quade's voice lost none of its laconic drawl. "Just move away from there in the other direction as fast as you can go."

"Don't worry, I got that figured out."

"Okay, there's a little path." Quade visualized what Moss was seeing. "It leads back the other way. You're bound to see lights pretty soon if you just keep walking. Listen, I'm going to hang up and call Lois, okay? She'll let you sleep in the Gatehouse. You'll be safe there."

"No, no. don't call her. She's the one in the mu-mu who threw me out here to the gators in the first place. Got something against men, I take it. I'll make it on my own. Piece of cake, really."

Quade had to put his hand over the phone to blot out a chuckle. "That's Lois. That's her, all right. Queen Sappho rules. Okay, let me call one of the girls I know in the guard tower."

"How 'bout that seven-foot beauty with the feathers? I think she digs me, but I don't have time to take her up on her offer. I got to make sure Sheldon's all right and hasn't destroyed the place with that machine he's got."

"Kenya's there, right? At her Magnolia Alley?"

"No, she came with me, but we left Freddy with the boy. She passed out when she saw the man with the arrows and the basketball team took her inside and shut the door."

Quade silently nodded. "I know, no men allowed. Moss, stay where you are. I'll call the guard and get right back to you, okay?"

"I may be alligator bait by that time, but okay."

Quade made the call and called Moss right back. His voice mail came on saying to leave a message.

Chapter 19

Sheldon crawled out of the utility cupboard where he had been hiding since he overheard the two men posing as electricians say something about snatching the brat. Knowing that the term "brat" used in his vicinity always referred to him, Sheldon took refuge in the closet behind the buckets and mops.

The two bogus electricians had frantically searched for him, but when they heard Uncle Freddy, they had bolted out the back door without even bothering to pick up their tools.

Before Sheldon could climb over all the junk and stop him, Freddy had gone after them, leaving him all alone in this spooky old house except for Piglet.

Now Sheldon made his way over the debris the two kidnapers had left behind—spools of copper wire, a tool box with some kind of cutters, screwdrivers, and tape measures—to the front room. The house was eerily silent. His voice was only a little louder than the squeak of the old floorboards underfoot.

The boxes of food were still on the window seat where Freddy had left them, and Sheldon rummaged among them until he found his hot dog and fries. He took a bite of the hot dog, and crammed a few fries in his mouth after it.

"Hello? Is there anybody here?" he called, spitting out bits of food as he wandered into the foyer.

"Nobody except me, Piglet, master," came the reply, three landings up.

"You're no help at all!" The hapless Piglet became the target of all his frustration and fear at being deserted to face the enemy alone. "You're only a useless piece of old vacuum cleaner and a hair dryer, and your eyes don't match." Sheldon got louder and louder until he was at tantrum volume. "I don't care if I ever see you again, Piglet, so put that in your pipe and smoke it, ya hear? I don't care if you fell on your head and smashed your brains out. What am I saying? You don't even have brains. You're just stupid. A stupid old piece of junk! Okay? Huh?"

By now, Sheldon was yelling so loud he didn't hear the car coming up the gravel drive with its lights off. A car the color of a mountain lion, a car on the prowl, its motor growling softly as it neared its prey.

"Master," came Piglet's voice from upstairs. "I detect a strange vehicle coming around to the back of the house. There are two humans in it. Maybe you ought to come upstairs forthwith."

Sheldon was about to say that, besides being a piece of junk, Piglet didn't make good sense either, when the sound of car doors slamming sent the Hutu warrior-in-training up the stairs on all fours with fries still dangling from his mouth.

cɔɛɔ

Alone in a mysterious, green world alive with the throbbing sound of countless night life, Moss put his useless phone away and struck out along a faint path through the thick underbrush away from the creek as Quade had instructed. Mosquitoes sucked their fill on every patch of his exposed flesh, undeterred by the ooze of perspiration that suffused every pore. Briars scratched him, sticky vines ensnared his feet. More than once, the bushes beside him rattled as if he had startled some creature into flight.

Still, he was making good time when a voice halted Moss in the middle of crossing a marshy ditch. Something about the icy tone and foreign accent stabbed through the thick air like a bayonet. This was not someone Quade had sent to rescue him.

"Ah, Detective Moss. Going somewhere?"

The voice had a faint clipped cadence like Nazis in the WWII movies. His hand moved slowly toward his gun which he had stuck in the belt of his pants and now threatened to slide down to his crotch on a rivulet of sweat.

He didn't answer in case the killer—because instinct told him that's who it was—and got a fix on his voice. Moss wasn't a fan of fiction, but the edges of his mind toyed with the thought of the *Walking Dead. How else could the man lying in the bushes be alive unless, unless he wasn't really?*

Slowly, Moss began to lower his body down in the marshy ditch. His hand touched the little pistol he kept hidden for just such occasions as this. It had saved his life more times than a melon has seeds.

Only the killer seemed to see in the dark like some jungle predator.

"Oh, really, Detective, don't think you can hide." The clipped voice was caustically derisive. "Night vision glasses have been around for fifty years, although I doubt if you can access such technology where you come from."

There was a crunch of twigs as the killer took a step. Obviously, they didn't have twigs underfoot where the killer came from. That footstep gave Moss a direction to aim for, and he shielded the glint of metal with his hand as he leveled it toward the voice.

"At least stand up and die like a man, not crouched like a toad in the marsh. One clean shot and it's over. Oh, I see you very clearly. Crouching down there." Moss made a mental note that the killer pronounced the word 'there' like zere. "I believe in some circles, people of your race and skin color are known as night fighters, yes? Because they blend so well with the darkness." A slithering, mirthless chuckle followed. Another crunch of underbrush. "Jungle bunnies, eh?"

Moss knew the killer was trying to get him to react by baiting him with racial slurs. *That's an old game to us, Kraut, but we know how to play it back.*

The killer was advancing toward him, and Moss was prepared to shoot it out, when what sounded like a strangled laugh, a *thunk*, and then a gurgle followed in rapid succession. Moss fell backward, sending a single pistol shot zinging through the night like a deadly bat circling toward the moon.

Then something crashed heavily to the ground.

A voice all liquid chocolate said, "Fool must've thought we can't order those night vision glasses off the Net."

Then a flashlight burned through the muddy night, light footsteps came toward him at quickstep, and above the aura of light, Moss saw tall feather tips waving above the tall brush. The Amazon guard had found him.

He still kept his hand on his gun, thinking they might use him for target practice, too, him being male and a stranger and all. But apparently, he had an added attraction.

The flashlight suddenly had him blinking in its glare. "Come on now, Sweet Cheeks, show me some of that Memphis loving you promised me. Your girlfriend's still with the Queen having a fit of hysterics. Diva all the way, if you ask me. So we got some time to get it on."

Moss felt himself shrivel down there at the mere thought. "We?"

"Oh, no, I meant the two of us, honey baby. Just you and me, Hippolyta—just call me Lyta, not Hippo. And the whole troop didn't come along, not unless you're Superman, and I don't think even he could do them all."

He was too miserable to pledge fidelity to Kenya who had sought safety while leaving him to the mercies of the night. "But I need a bath before—"

"Oh, never fear, Lyta is here to do all that little stuff that puts you in the mood. That includes a bath for two. After all, I been tracking that killer all the way from the time she entered the property—"

"She?" On the path back to Lesbos, Moss stopped mid-step.

"Yes, sir, that's a roger, Sweet Cheeks. You was being chased by a butch woman assassin and a real woman done assassinated her. That just goes to show you we're ready for combat, us girls."

"But how did you know? She sounded like a man when she was calling me out."

"I pulled off her hood after she was dead and she had her hair up in a knot, but she was not a dude. She was a she all right. I checked it out just to make sure." Hippolyta put her slender arm around his shoulder and gave him a cheek-to-cheek hug. In the early June heat, she smelled of feminine musk and designer perfume. The aura was intoxicating. "Anyway, you can check for yourself in the morning. Right now, let's get some boogie time in."

☙☙☙

They were sitting in the copper tub in the Gate House buck-naked and up to their respective chests in bubbles when Kenya burst in.

"Moss?" She took in Hippolyta's bare breasts, Moss's pile of clothes on the chair beside the tub, and pressed her hand to her heart as if she was going to collapse again.

To make matters worse, Hippolyta said. "Hey, girl, would you mind shutting the door? We're taking a bath."

Instead, Kenya the crazy woman, came back to life. "Moss, is this how you protect Sheldon? Is it? Because if it is, you're fired!"

Before he could say anything about not being hired in the first place, Hippolyta stood up to her full six foot-seven height, resembling a black Venus rising from the sea, except where Botticelli had strategically placed a scarf, this version was wearing a thong. Despite the tension, Moss played with the idea it probably doubled as a slingshot when things got down and dirty.

"Okay, you've just now fired him, Hoochie Mama, so just back off and leave us alone. And shut the door behind you. You're letting the mosquitoes in."

"Don't you talk to me like that, Miss Snakebutt! And your bikini-wax job needs a redo, so I would sit back down if I were you, especially if you don't want your ass mosquito-bit."

"Ladies!"

They both ignored him, continuing to glare at each other like rival cats.

"Who you calling Snakebutt, Pillow-Ass?" Hippolyta put her hands down by her hips like a gun fighter getting ready to draw.

"Pillow Ass!" An outraged Kenya turned on Moss, cowering in the tub. "You listening, Moss? You just going to sit there and let her insult me?"

He opened his mouth to say he was sitting because his clothes were just out of reach on the stool when the action began. The cat fight was on when Kenya, wielding his trousers like a battle axe, knocked Hippolyta back down in the tub.

Next, as Hippolyta re-emerged from the tub, coming at Kenya with the back brush, Kenya grabbed his shorts, slapping the girl across the face. Hippolyta retaliated by grabbing a jar of oil and dousing Kenya with the contents. The younger girl went to pursue her, stepped in the spilled oil as she got out of the tub, and fell on her back.

With Hippolyta now down on the cement floor, Kenya grabbed her by her long braid, apparently intending to do an Achilles number on the fallen warrior, only it turned out to be mostly weaves. They broke off in Kenya's hand as Hippolyta grabbed her ankles, causing Kenya herself to slip and fall beside her opponent. As she went down, Moss winced. The love of his life, her once carefully-straightened locks, lashing like snakes around Medusa's head, her designer outfit now shredded, had never looked more fascinating,

Seeing his chance, he grabbed his dripping, oil soaked trousers out of the bathtub and fled naked out the door. His last glimpse of the two women was like a frame of female mud wrestlers glimpsed through the window of a sleazy bar. Had he looked back, he would have seen both women suspend their fighting for an eighth of a second as they appreciatively watched his retreat. Then they resumed battle again, deciding what they had seen was worth fighting for.

Chapter 20

Big Earl went first, tiptoeing through the dark kitchen, only to trip over a tool box and land on his knees with a thump accompanied by an echoing squeak of the old floorboards. He wanted to howl with pain, those being his bad knees, the most painful joints in his entire body. But he held it in, exhaling an agonized hiss through his teeth that evolved into a shrill whistle.

"I thought you said be quiet, Earl. I don't call that whistlin' quiet. Sure don't." Coming up to him, Lolo stepped on Earl's hand which crunched under his considerable weight. "Sorry, I don't see so good in the dark. Don't eat enough carrots, heh-heh."

I am going to have to kill him. I really am. Earl used his good hand to pull himself upright again. He felt a hammer in his hand that the electricians had left behind. They worked for the same mob he and Lolo did and they were supposed to have doused all the lights in the house so he and dumb ass Lolo could pull off the snatch.

But like the sorry-ass white druggies they were, they had let down their end and bailed before the job was done. Now, he and Dumb Ass were on the spot.

"There must be nobody home because if there were, the D-Day invasion we just made would have woke them up." Earl confidently walked through the dining room into the living room. "Looks like they were just getting ready to eat. Hope they believe in leftovers."

"I could have sworn I saw a kid in the window as we drove up." Loquacious checked under the dust covers shrouding the furniture. "Whaddya think they've got these sheets on everything for?"

"Are you crazy? Nobody would leave a kid like that alone for one minute in a great big house like this. He'd destroy it in a heartbeat." Earl took in the freshly painted rooms, the luxurious curtains at the windows, the flowers in tall vases. "Man, the wife would love to have a place like this. Must've cost a pile of happy cabbage, I bet. The staircase, this marble foyer, the walnut banister. Must have cost a pile of green stuff, man, I'll testify to that."

"Hey, somebody else likes chili fries besides me." Loquacious began opening the various carryout boxes. "And pulled-pork barbeque. Now, that's a person after my own heart. Let's put it to the taste test and see if it comes from that place in town where we ate."

"Hey, that's mine! Keep your filthy mitts off, okay, Fat Ass?" came from somewhere above them.

Loquacious paused, a barbeque sandwich halfway to his mouth. "Who said that? Who's calling me Fat Ass?"

Sheldon briefly appeared on the second floor landing. "I said that, Mr. Fatso. So what are you going to do about it, huh, bro?"

"Why, you little bas—?"

"Who you calling names?" Sheldon stood in full sight as Loquacious barreled up the stairs. "Your mama so ugly, your daddy had to wear a blindfold while they was doing it."

"Oh, that's mean talk, you little shit! You can't talk

about my mama that way. Wait till I get ahold of you, you brat!"

"Lolo," Big Earl called. "Hold on! It might be a—"

But Loquacious fell for it.

Sheldon backed down the second floor hall. In his rush to get to his tormentor, Loquacious followed him to the very place where, earlier, Moss had crashed through the rotten floorboards. The gaping hole was now covered by a worn Persian carpet and, to Sheldon's delight, with a yodeling wail, Lolo plunged through the trap, and through the first floor ceiling. There he stopped as Moss had before him. Lolo shook himself off, made sure he was still alive and not in hell where his mama always said he'd end up, took a few tentative steps in the dark and crashed down into the pantry. The hapless Lolo ended up bringing down an entire rack of shelves containing jars of ancient strawberry jam. On regaining consciousness in the dark, he mistook the sticky jam for blood and clotted flesh, shouting his lungs out for 911.

By then, Big Earl had deserted the scene, rushing out the kitchen to the safety of the Crown Victoria. He started down the driveway, but seeing a pair of headlights coming through the gates, took off over the fields in panic. The shocks did their job, bouncing over old furrows, although Earl's head tapped clear to the brougham roof. He was searching for an entrance to the road, checking his rear view mirror to see if he was being pursued, when he found a large tree barring his path. His last thought as the Crown Vic wrapped around it was, it was a good thing his wife kept up the insurance.

⁕⁕⁕

Freddy had found Moss walking down the road shirtless and barefoot. Pulling up beside him, he could resist teasing the big man. "I thought you Memphis boys knew all about playing strip poker! Hop in, sucker."

Moss was in no mood for jokes. "Just drive me up to the house, will you? Just to make sure the boy is okay. I'll call a cab back to the motel."

Freddy looked at the detective in alarm. "You mean Kenya's not there? Where is she, then? You left him alone?"

"Look, you forget you were supposed to stay with the kid, right? I don't know what goes on around this crazy damn place. I just came down to find out who killed Holly Simpson, understand? Not to babysit some looney woman's kid."

Freddy shifted into second gear and tore down the dark road. "Kenya's not crazy. She's had a rough life, that's all."

But Moss wasn't feeling sympathetic. "Yeah, who hasn't?"

Freddy was yelling over the whine of the motor. "There was that thing with her stepfather, then her mother almost blinding her and throwing her out and, on top of all that, Root Woman went off and died, leaving us in foster care. Why are you mad at her, you mind my asking?"

"Yeah, I do mind, kid." Being mosquito-bit and fighting a poison ivy rash didn't help reduce the snarl in Moss' voice. "Wait, who's that coming?"

They saw headlights come around the house, then abruptly swerve off the driveway, heading across the field. "I don't know but that way ends in a gulley big enough to swallow a jumbo jet." Freddy wasn't buying into any more speculation after the electrician fiasco. It would take him twenty years to live that blunder down and that might not even be enough. They'd probably put it on his tombstone.

"Get on up to the house and let's see if the boy is what that guy's running from. Twenty bucks says it is. No, fifty, and throw in that robot for sweeteners."

"You think you're the man, don't you? Okay, I'll take all the money you can throw around." Freddy's grin shone in the light from the dash as he floored the pickup. "Moss, you are seriously jaded, you know? You really got it wrong about Sheldon. He's a good kid. Just needs a firm hand, that's all."

"Applied to his behind, you mean. That kid could empty a cinderblock jail faster than a green prosecutor." Moss almost conjured up a laugh. "Hell, fastern' somebody yelling fire. Naw, my money's on the boy."

Moss won the bet. Sheldon was standing in the foyer of the great house holding his blankie to his cheek and sucking his thumb. "The man fattern and dumber than you just fell down the hole in the second floor hall. He made a big crashing noise. You can hear him hollering for the police right through the wall. Where's my mama? What'd you do with her? What'd you do with my mama?"

Just then Freddy came through the front door. "Shellfish, you okay?"

Whereupon the Hutu warrior burst in tears. Moss decided all bets were off.

Chapter 21

Bjorn was out of jail the next morning. He posted bail with money gathered by friends. He didn't want to bother his family in Wisconsin. They wouldn't understand. His mother would only say he had disappointed them. His father would carefully avoid meeting his eyes, not wanting Chris to read his unspoken rebuke in them.

The whole thing was absurd, anyway. He had an alibi, at least for the time he had spent working with a dozen or so sleep-deprived graduate students. If the district attorney decided there was enough evidence to prosecute him for pandering, he would eventually have to face a grand jury, but so far he was free on bail.

He had to find something, some kind of impartial irrefutable evidence that put him in the parking lot that last few minutes before Faun had screamed. Maybe the management had a surveillance camera that would catch him parking his car.

Then he remembered something so petty, something that had been swept away in the events of yesterday. As he had gotten out of his car, there had been a couple taking a selfie standing in the entrance to Building Four.

Married or just roomies, it didn't matter. He thought he had seen the guy around campus a few times. Maybe, just maybe, the camera had picked up him in the background. It was worth a try. Anything was worth trying.

Bjorn went back to his room. The moment he opened the door, he felt his entire life change as if something integral to existence—his private world—had been violated. It had been ransacked, his papers scattered, textbooks splayed face down in heaps, as though someone had been looking for something between the pages. The bedding had been taken by police as evidence. His computer was gone. Thank God he had the flash drives on separate key rings. All the vital information especially his doctoral thesis, was safe in the university's online storage.

There was a note in a plastic bag hanging from the door knob from the Management to vacate premises. It was the only clean piece of paper in the room. The reasons were vague. He, Christopher Bjorn, had broken the terms of his lease. He had seven days to vacate the premises.

"What was it, a drug bust?"

Bjorn was so intent on salvaging his notes, he didn't look up at first. "No, the cops did it." When he did look up, he saw Steve, the building manager, leaning in the doorway, surveying the ruins of an academic life.

"Anything I can do to help?" Steve flipped his greasy hair out of his eyes. "How's Faun taking all this?"

"Don't know. I'm the last person in the world she wants to talk to."

"Sorry. I imagine that's pretty hard. I heard some guy raped her, right? I wasn't here, just scuttlebutt, you know."

Something about the acne-scarred face with the permanent sneer triggered an association in Bjorn's numbed mind. "Hey, you worked in her lab, right? I remember you from last night. At the pizza place."

"Correction. Did work in Faun's lab. Got to get to class, buddy. Need some boxes to pack your stuff? Got plenty downstairs. Just let me know." The manager backed out of the ransacked room, leaving Bjorn standing helplessly in the ruins, wondering what to do next.

It was a full minute before Bjorn remembered why Faun had said she had fired Steve. By that time, Steve was on his way down the stairs. "Wait! Is there a security camera in the building?"

"Yeah, but it's on the fritz. Sorry about that. Just let me know when you're leaving and I'll see what I can do about getting your deposit back." *Like the management's going to give it back.* "See ya around." He almost added *sucker.* Steve went on down the stairs.

There was a main number for an agency managing the graduate housing complex. Bjorn dialed it and got a pre-recorded menu listing all the apartment complexes they managed, twelve in all. Each development was broken down into separate buildings. At last, he got the manager of Building Four's number. Janet Goodlaw. He left a message to call him back.

෬෨෬

Quade found half the tree the next morning. The other half was in the Victoria, its branches having punctured one of its air bags. The air bag had saved the driver. The all-night gas station on the main highway had a security video of two men who looked like they'd been in a fight, though the shorter one said he'd collided with a tree.

The other man was in worse shape, his clothes covered with white plaster dust and he smelled like strawberry jam. The short one could be heard talking to his wife, trying to convince her to come pick him up. Apparently, he had gone off with some girl named Victoria, then left her out in field somewhere. The security camera provided close-up shots of Big Earl with two black eyes and what looked like a busted nose. Lolo was only recognizable by his ears, which, though covered with plaster dust, stuck out from his head like flaps on a crop-duster.

Quade almost felt sorry for the pair when he slapped the cuffs on them at the truck stop where they were hitching a ride to Memphis. Their makeshift sign on a piece of cardboard read *Please help us reach civilizashun.*

Chapter 22

Moss had already put his suitcase in the car and was just going to leave his room key in the motel office when Quade arrived.

"Had breakfast yet?"

Moss suspected this display of Southern hospitality was just a ploy to get him to stay. He played it cool. "Thought I'd stop on the road somewhere. Breaks up the driving."

"Bet you won't find anything worth eating along the road, though. My treat for all you've had to put up with while I was up in Athens."

Moss stopped himself short of swearing. After all, Quade had been through hell in the last week, too. "You mean getting shot at, almost eaten by gators, and jumped on by a bunch of girls dressed up like Indians? No amount of breakfast's going to fix that, Walker. But that doesn't mean I'm going to skip an offer of a free breakfast. 'Cause you know you got that right, there's nothing to eat from here to Memphis 'cept chicken biscuits."

Quade stifled a chuckle, knowing the detective couldn't take humor without coffee first. "Sounds like more fun than I had, that's for sure."

Moss softened, then a grin broke across his face.

"You win, bubba. Let's go to Saranjii's. I want to show Freddy what I look like with clothes on."

"That sounds interesting."

e/sc/s

Freddy gave them a quiet table in back. "You find those two guys yet?"

"Yeah, just not the same guys. Just bring us a pot of coffee for starters, huh, Freddy? No questions yet, okay?" Quade let fly an unusual number of words before he had his coffee, Freddy noted.

The young man beckoned a passing waitress. "Kenya's asking, that's all."

"Oh, I'm sure we'll be hearing from her. Got to have our coffee first." Quade stretched out his long legs, checking his phone with a frown.

"Surprised that woman needs phone service. I think I can hear her yelling right now." Moss knew enough about people to know that Quade would tell him what happened yesterday when he was ready.

A smiling girl came with two mugs and a pot of coffee. "Freddy said not to bother you all 'til you finished the first pot. I'll be back."

Moss doctored the first cup lovingly. "Think I'll take Freddy back to Memphis with me. Places up there could use somebody like him. Service with a smile like you mean it, not like how big a tip you'll leave. That's the way it used to be." Tamping the acid brew down with sugar and a dose of half-and-half, Moss tentatively tasted the result. If he got it wrong, it would explode in his gut like a bomb.

Watching him, Quade observed, "You don't want coffee, you want a milkshake."

"Oh, god," replied Moss. "I knew it was too good to

last." He slumped down in his seat like a teenager who hasn't done his homework.

Before Quade could figure out what was going on, Kenya came in from the kitchen behind him and sat down. Concentrating entirely on Quade, she ignored Moss.

"I was at Lois's when Faun came home. I know what happened, Quade, honey, and I'm going to cut off somebody's balls. Don't know whose it going to be yet. That's y'all's job." She cut her eyes in Moss's direction. "But when you find out, just let me know first. That booger will never make it to trial."

"Thanks for the offer, Kenya, but that's my job." A smile broke across Quade's dark face. "But I appreciate your volunteering. I really do."

She poured another round of coffee. They both watched as Moss began the doctoring routine.

That was her cue. Quade sat back and watched the show unfold. "Something wrong with the coffee, Detective Moss?"

It sounded like she wanted a fight. Moss kept his eyes down, knowing if he looked at her his resolve to leave would melt like butter on the biscuits the waitress brought to the table. "No, ma'am."

She had made an effort to look perfect just for him, skinny jeans and a flimsy top, casual, but her heels were worth the whole outfit. Expensive scent mingled with the smell of frying bacon, is an odor no man can resist.

"Tell me what you want," Kenya said, her sultry voice heavy with innuendo. "For breakfast, I mean. I'll have Freddy do it himself, Saranjii's style."

"You helping him out today?" Moss couldn't resist the temptation to have one last look at her and, like the biblical tale of Lot's wife, it was his undoing.

She batted those incredible lashes. "Just taking orders. Baby, I own this place, got to make it profitable now, don't I? Mary, bring these gentlemen a short stack just for starters. Syrup's on the table." Gliding away on her outrageous shoes, Kenya looked back over one shoulder to watch the effect on Moss. He was satisfactorily pole-axed.

"So you staying, after all." The worried look on Quade's face had been replaced by a grin. It was more a statement than a question.

"Just 'til the weekend, then I got to get back." But nobody believed Moss, least of all himself.

☽☯☾

For the first time since the railroad had come to town in 1853, and the murders in '39 and '99, Julia Springs actually made the news—TV, radio and print. The town was a flash in the pan on social media, but that was something, at least.

The FBI got involved, posting perspiring agents who didn't like grits in the same motel where Moss was staying. Interpol even sent a man with a French accent down to identify the bodies of the two foreign assassins. He was bemused by the feathered arrows used to kill them and wondered if there were still natives around these parts.

Quade got a kick out of that. When he introduced Lois, Queen Sappho of Lesbos, the FBI agents traded guarded looks, but the Interpol agent kissed her hand. "Extraordinaire!"

But when he saw Hazel, the Amazonian guard who knocked off the second of the assassins, the Frenchman was speechless. He immediately got in touch with his brother who knew the manager of an all-female basketball team in France. Within a month, Hazel was in Paris, posing for the *paperazzi* and inspiring a new trend in Paris couture—the "Amazon" look.

🙢🙠

As the late Spring ripened into June, Bjorn's future rotted like fruit left too long on the tree. He was suspended from the university while he was a suspect in Faun's sexual assault case. His scholarship was withdrawn and his grant money dried up because he wasn't allowed to finish his research. He made a frugal living tutoring and got a job at a bank. The social media vigilantes crucified him.

He had at least a hundred texts a day from women saying what they would do to him if they got hold of him. He felt hunted, condemned by a society that believed in guilty until proved innocent.

The manager of Building Four hadn't answered his phone calls and texts so he figured Steve had been talking to her. Until late one night when he had a message from a Janet Goodlaw on his phone. It was the manager, saying for him to come by her office next afternoon.

"Chris?" She opened the door before he could knock, adjusting her thick glasses. No loaded gun, no pepper spray, only a tentative smile on her plain face. A slender, brown girl cradled a cat in one corner of the little office. She hummed a little tune into its quivering ear.

"I'm sorry about the clutter, but I'd be lying if I were to say I'm going to clean it up." said the manager, who was a blonder version of the one holding the cat. "That's Irene, my partner. Hope you don't mind cats. Mr. Muggs lives here, too."

Bjorn agonized through the small talk, refused a soda or tea.

At last Janet said, "Oh, yeah, I made a digital copy of

the security tape you asked for. So it's backed up just in case you lose it."

He tried to hide unbidden tears and quickly ducked his head. Janet shoved an envelope over the desk and went on, never making eye contact. "Sorry it took so long. And one other thing you ought to know, that creep Steve came over next day after you called back in May and wanted *me* to give *him* the tape. I told him it was screwed up and ya-da-ya-da. You don't have to say anything. Just wanted to let you know that Irene and I are on your side. The camera plainly shows you in the parking lot talking to a couple of students and the time you arrived. And Irene was walking home from class. She recognized you from the year before. You were her instructor in Biochemistry, wasn't he, honey?"

Plain brown girl nodded, stroking the cat. She looked up, and so did the cat, as if it were her alter ego. "Hi, Dr. Bjorn. I was in your eight o'clock section first semester last year. It was a big class. Guess you don't know one of us from the other, huh—"

Janet cut her short. "If you need a statement or anything, just let us know. Everybody knows that Steve is a creep. He hates us, you know. Complained to the management about Mr. Muggs. Complained I wasn't doing my job, I was incompetent, yada-yada-yada. Refers to us to other tenants as those lesbians. One tenant told us he knocked on Steve's door one night when he was locked out and Stevie boy was watching hard core porn and invited the guy to join him. No, I'm *sure* he had something to do with your girlfriend getting raped." As she walked him to the door, Janet drew in her breath. "And one more thing," she said, holding up a sentinel finger. "I almost forgot. The tape shows a guy running across the edge of the parking lot in his shorts as you chatted with the students. He's got something written on his T-shirt but you can't see it clearly. You had your back to him so you didn't notice."

Bjorn was outside on the steps in the soft June dark, just breathing in the soft air. His life taken shape again, handed back to him in the space of fifteen minutes. He didn't believe in miracles, only the emergence of right, however long that took. But to Chris Bjorn on that sultry, early June evening, *that* emergence of right had suddenly come from two people he had hardly noticed before—two people who were willing to bear witness for him, two people who were just as maligned and despised as he was. On his way to his truck, he looked up at the scattering of stars and patted his jacket pocket to make sure the envelope was safe. Then he headed for Julia Springs, the face of Faun illuminating the road before him.

ᘓᕠᘓᕠ

The reporters descended on the hamlet like swarms of mosquitoes rising from the swamp. They could be seen on Main Street, talking on their phones, in Pop's Place and Saranjii's Café on their laptops describing the town—its retro charm, its quaint people. The whole place was made for feature stories. When the motels were full, the locals began renting rooms in their houses, complete with family meals and parking for TV vans.

The big story was not the brother and sister assassins—shootouts and even hit teams were old news. It was Lesbos—a colony of women and their children entirely defended by women. And what women they were! Everyone six feet or more, skilled archers! There was such a run on hunting crossbows that gun dealers were sold out within hours.

A New Amazonian Kingdom, one headline read. Lesbian groups wanted to interview Queen Sappho about holding weddings there and Lois's herb business exploded, boosted by all the publicity.

It was into this chaotic scene that Chris Bjorn pulled up in his overheated truck. All his belongings, those that weren't confiscated by the police, behind him under tarp, his life in his pocket. When he saw the police cars, he almost got back on the highway.

There were signs all over Julia Springs for Help Wanted. The first place he went hired him on the spot. The manager's name was Fred, a young guy about his age. Between fielding orders from the packed tables, he gave Bjorn the application to fill out. "Just a formality, you're hired anyway. You're from up North, right?"

"Minnesota." *Here it comes. Surely this guy reads the papers, describing the potential suspect in Faun's sexual assault as coming from Minnesota.*

But whirlwind Freddy hardly slowed down between pouring coffee and cleaning off tables. "Then maybe you can figure out what all these out-of-town customers are ordering. I don't want to tell you what it sounds like they're saying."

Bjorn slept in his truck that night, ate a salami and cheese sandwich, and read by flashlight. Somewhere, in this little town, Faun was hurting and he had the video that could clear him of any wrongdoing. But that wouldn't make her hurt less, only vindicate him.

Though he dreaded encountering Faun's father, Chief Walker didn't come to the café for the following week. Freddy noticed his anxious glances toward the door each time the bell rang announcing a new customer.

"Cool it, Minnesota man, you don't have to jump on people as soon as they come in the door. Let 'em mellow awhile. It's not like a drive-through."

"Sorry. I was just—just my OCD showing, I guess."

"That's okay, you're doing great. Just smile sometimes. You look like Igor, the executioner, sometimes. You sleeping rough?"

Caught out of excuses by Freddy's directness, Bjorn blurted the truth. "Couldn't find a place that I could afford. What's going on, anyway? Who're all these cops and reporters after?"

He busied himself scrubbing tables, although he had scrubbed them twice already.

"Forgive me for snooping into things not my business, but aren't you here because of what's going on? And go easy on the furniture, okay? So far no cases of Ebola in the vicinity if that's what you're thinking."

"I don't know what you mean. I'm not here because of anything to do with the police, if that's what you mean." Did he look as guilty as he felt, but for entirely different reasons than Freddy had intimated.

"Okay, I'm going to level with you. An educated, intelligent guy like yourself waiting tables is either on the run or here to do a story, in my humble opinion. That's it." Freddy slung a dish towel over his shoulder and leaned against the counter with arms folded. There was a lull in the hectic morning and he was glad to take a breather.

"Is that what an educated, intelligent guy like you is doing here running a restaurant? Doing a story or on the lam?"

Freddy flipped a dish towel at Bjorn, who returned a wet dish cloth at his accuser.

"Okay, touché, buddie. Look, I know a lady who's got a house big as Graceland but funkier. She's kind of like my aunt, but not, you dig? Anyway, I'll ask if she's willing to put you up 'til this dies down. Oh, and it will. Give it two months and it will be as dead as a doornail around here."

"If I'm waiting for something to die down, might as well know what it is, don't you think?"

At that moment, the door opened and Quade came in followed by Moss. "Here's the very gentlemen that can answer that question better that I can." Freddy straightened up with a grin. "Big Chief Walker."

Freddy turned to find Chris Bjorn had retreated to the kitchen.

He had planned to give Janet's flashdrive to Quade as soon as he saw the sheriff. But when he saw the dark, scarred face of Faun's father, Bjorn lost his nerve and bolted for the kitchen, head down like a kicked dog.

There, cursing himself for being a miserable coward, he busied himself scraping plates and loading the dishwasher while Mary took over waiting on tables.

"Well, I call that a nice pair of muffins, myself."

At the sound of the sultry voice behind him, Bjorn who was squatting to load the bottom rack, leaped to his feet. A jazz addict, he had heard about Cajun Queens all his life, but he thought they had faded with the last century. But the beautiful woman standing behind him in a dress made of stars, and not much else, was either a ghost or their reincarnation.

When she saw he was a complete stranger, Kenya burst into a giggle. "Sorry, honey. I can't help saying what I admire. Didn't scare you, did I?"

"Chris Bjorn at your service, and at your feet." He stuck out a grimy hand and then withdrew it, wiping it on his jeans. "I wish the rest of me was so admired," he added, thinking about Faun. She was always lurking at the back of his mind.

Freddy burst through the kitchen door, carrying a tray loaded with plates. "Chris, if you're going to work here—"

Kenya took the tray and put it on the sink. 'Oh, he

works here, does he? Since when? I'm sorry, Chris. I'm Kenya West. I own this place."

Mary came in with a batch of fresh orders and Kenya and Freddy got busy filling them. Figuring Kenya was going to fire him, Bjorn snagged Mary as she passed by with a fresh pot of coffee.

"Can you give this to Sheriff Walker?" From his pocket, he produced the envelope with Janet's flashdrive.

"Why don't you? He's right out there." The petite waitress nodded toward the tables.

"Too much to do." He indicated the loaded tray Freddy brought in. Opening the door for Mary, Bjorn took care to stand behind it. "I'd appreciate it."

It worked. "Sure. Shall I tell him who it's from?"

"He'll know." And Quade did, taking one look at the flashdrive and the note with it. Without a word, he walked back to the kitchen, boots rattling the plates and glasses on the shelves behind the counter.

Kenya looked up from the griddle. "Hang on, it's coming, Quade. I'll wrap it to go if you're in a hurry."

"Where is he?" Quade paced the small kitchen and opened the back door. "Must've gone out here."

"Okay, man of few words." Kenya sighed and rolled her eyes. "Where's who, Quade?"

"Chris!" he shouted. He shook the envelope at the ceiling "The one who gave me this!"

"Okay, chill, he's right—"

The kitchen was empty. Chris Bjorn was gone.

Plying a zigzag path among the tables out front, the waitress Mary discovered Moss was gone as well, although she had just filled his coffee cup. "If that don't beat all," she said to no one in particular. "Waste of good coffee." As Mary picked up the cup, Moss came back in the door followed by an apprehensive Bjorn. "You busted, Chris?"

Moss shrugged and motioned Bjorn into a chair. "No, he just didn't bring my coffee in time—or my side of bacon either."

Mary went scampering back to the kitchen to tell them the detective from Memphis was fixing to arrest Bjorn for holding up his order. "Freddy, you're going to be next if you don't hurry up."

Quade joined the two back at the table. "How did you recognize him?" he asked Moss who was busy doctoring his cooling coffee.

"Oh, I thought you knew he was here. We passed his truck when you were going on about parks and pools on the way through town. I saw the university sticker and license plate matched the one I had run through when you first told me about your daughter."

Quade's jaw tightened. "I didn't tell you yet."

Moss wasn't the least rattled. He tasted his coffee, adding more sugar. "Well, man, I'm a detective who watches the news, okay? So what's in the flashdrive, Christian? Mind sharing?"

Bjorn made it quick, telling about Janet, the manager of Building Four, who gave him the flashdrive, about Steve the creepy manager of his building, who Faun had fired from her lab for downloading porn.

"And that's where Holly comes in," Moss said, taking a chicken biscuit from the pile. "Along with the porn, came pictures of Holly and the virus that shut down Fawn's research as well as the whole university system."

Bjorn looked as though his heart had started pumping again. "That's right. Except for the fact Faun had everything backed up, it would have destroyed everything. The company she worked so hard to build, all of it."

"You're a computer tech, right?" Quade trusted his voice for the first time, torn between strangling this boy or hugging him.

"I try to be."

"Wasn't there something about this hacker's signature that you said was unique to someplace in Europe? I remember Faun said that."

"Yeah, some international configurations, symbols, and patterns we don't use in our codes here in the US. They're used by particular groups of hackers."

"Switzerland one of 'em?" Moss said through a mouthful of biscuit and fig jam.

"More like the Stans. Even Turkey. That was the rumor in the tech department at the university security office, anyway. I had to turn it over to them. They turned it over to the police."

"And this guy Steve, he's the manager of your apartment building, right? I remember when Faun said she fired him for downloading porn. Furious doesn't describe it." Quade leaned back in his chair, sipping the steaming cup. He met Moss's eyes across the table. Moss was thinking what he was thinking. It was all coming together in kind of a crazy quilt pattern.

"I had to move out after—you know, so I don't know if he's still there." Bjorn didn't go into all the ways he'd suffered since that night in June. He didn't have to. The two detectives exchanged looks again. Bjorn slid back his chair. "If you'll just look at the recording on that flash-drive, Chief Walker—And tell Faun I didn't—I wouldn't—" He stopped and looked away, agony written on his face.

"You ought to tell her yourself, Chris. I don't have to look at no camera recording to tell you didn't know anything about what happened. Now, man up to her. She'll listen, I know my girl." Quade motioned Bjorn back down in his chair.

"But I have to clear my name first. Then she'll believe me."

"Leave that to us, son." Moss sent an explosion of biscuit crumbs at the other two. "Sorry, never could eat neat. That's our job. Yours is done, except for telling your girl the truth. Even if she won't believe you now, let it kind of sink in. She'll come around."

Quade saw Kenya coming toward them, coffee pot in hand. "Whoa, Grover, looks like you better take some of your own advice."

At that point, Moss looked up and saw Kenya weaving through the tables. He got up, still chewing. "I got to go do some shake, rattle, and roll with those two clowns you got in your lockup, Quade. I think they're working for the same outfit that killed Holly, Biopharma—only on the ground floor. More like the basement."

"Leaving so soon, Detective?" Leaning over to refill their cups. Kenya made a point of showing her generous décolletage. "I thought you liked it in our little town. You certainly were having a good time last time I saw you."

"If getting shot at is your idea of a good time, then yeah, I was." Moss threw some bills on the table like he couldn't wait to get out of her sight.

Quade covered his cup. "No more for me, beautiful. Got to borrow this boy for a little while. I promise to bring him back in good shape."

"He's already in the right kind of shape." Kenya flashed the smile that beckoned Moss like a road sign to heaven. "Don't keep him too long now. We need a lot of help with all these strangers here in town."

Quade nodded at Bjorn. "Guess you've still got a job. Kenya, I'll have to get you to come down to the office to make a statement, okay? About what went on at Lois's place?"

Her wicked eyes slid to Moss who made a point of fumbling for a tip. "All of it?"

Moss took a deep breath. When his voice came out,

it was like a football sailing across the goalpost. "Miss West, Holly was your friend, right?"

Kenya bristled, her coquettish looks cooling to hostility. "What about her?"

"Because whoever killed her also sent that brother-and-sister hit team who tried to take me out, *and* paid those two bozos that Sheldon gave a nervous breakdown to, to try and kidnap him. So I'm gonna find the bastard that did all that and put him away. Do I make myself clear?"

Quade pushed his chair back, anticipating Kenya's reaction.

"So should I do a happy dance?"

"No, I'd just appreciate it if you'd quit calling me to come babysit."

Doing a graceful pivot as if she was headed to the kitchen, Kenya made a tiny "peeping" sound, then turned back, coffee-pot in hand, and splashed the contents on Moss's clean shirt.

Then she skittered off to the kitchen while Moss calmly sponged off his shirt with a wad of napkins dipped in ice water.

"Way to go, brother," said one of the locals at one the nearby tables.

"Praise Jesus! First time I ever saw Kenya shut down," a voice said in the corner.

"See, I told you Moss needed to take his own advice." Quade punched Bjorn in the arm. "Don't worry. You can wear my bullet-proof vest when you talk to Faun."

Chapter 23

Faun didn't want to see Bjorn. She hadn't left her room upstairs in the spacious attic for a week. When Quade tried the door, he found it locked.

"Tell him to go away, please. And don't try to call. I've blocked his number."

Bjorn who waiting on the porch heard the whole conversation through the screen door. "I told you, I've got to clear my name, before she'll believe me," he said when Quade came downstairs again. "It's the only way."

"I'm sorry, man. She'll get better."

"I know, it just takes time." Bjorn echoed the platitude as it had been said to him a thousand times over the course of the past month. "Thank you just the same for trying." He turned to go, keeping his head down so they wouldn't see the tears of frustration and loss in his eyes.

"Keep in touch, ya hear?" Quade knew better than to go after him. He had been in the same spot before in a place no one could reach him. Only love could do that.

As the hours passed, Quade would knock on the door periodically, asking if she was okay. A faint voice said she was, not to worry.

"I'm worried she might do something to herself," Isis

said in a whisper that night on the porch of their Crafts-
man bungalow nestled in an old pecan grove. "I've tried
to get her to talk about it but she says she's okay. I know
she's not. She seems to resent me for some reason. See if
you can get anything out of her, Quade."

But Quade just walked into her room and gave his
daughter a hug. "Phew, you need a bath. You stink like a
billy goat, darling." Her long hair was matted as if running a brush were too much effort. It wasn't so much her
hygiene as the dead look in her eyes that alarmed him.

"C'mon," he said, scooping her in his arms, "into the
shower."

Despite Faun's weak protests, Isis was waiting with
the shower running. After she had dried off, still in the
terry cloth robe, Quade escorted his daughter down to the
kitchen where he made her soup from a can. He sat at the
kitchen table, watching her slurp and blow the way he
had when she was small. When the bowl was empty, he
spread his arms wide and Faun rested against him. They
swayed together as one body, as if they were dancing out
their heartache.

Quade kissed the wet head leaning against his chest.
"It's going to be all right, baby girl. It's gonna take me a
while, but I'm gonna find the bastard who set this whole
thing up. And it wasn't your friend Chris. Far as I'm concerned, he's in the clear."

眈眈眈

Moss was on the way back to Memphis when Quade
got through to him. "Where the hell are you going,
Grover? I thought you were going to question those two
that tried to kidnap Sheldon."

"Let those boys go, Walker. They're not worth wasting a pro bono on."

Quade's voice practically melted Moss's Bluetooth. "Maybe where you come from it's okay to break into peoples' houses and scare their kids, but not here."

"Oh, save me the righteous bullshit, Quade. Look, they gave me something I can use, okay? Let 'em go on probation after a week or so. I promised them."

"That was good of you, Moss. Kind. Merciful, even. Mind telling me who died and made you God?"

"I thought you'd see it my way. Listen, I'm going to meet their contact—the clowns, that is. The guy who they say shells out the beans."

"Why don't I think that's a positive thing? For one thing, you could end up like Holly, in a dumpster somewhere in a dark alley."

"Yeah. That's a strong possibility." Moss acknowledged Quade's prediction with a chuckle. "If it's all right with you though, I'd rather go out that way instead of ending up in a gator's gullet."

His attempt to be funny was lost on Quade. "So, why the hell won't you tell me where you were going? I want to come with you, Moss. It's my daughter that's been hurt. I want to bash some heads, too."

"That's exactly why you're not along, Walker. Because you're mad as hell and want to kill whoever is responsible. Not good for business. Cool head, cool heart, cool hands."

"That why I saw smoke coming out your ears at Saranjii's this morning?"

"Look, Quade, get real, man. Stay with your wife and daughter. They need you now and I'm gonna see what this Skoot can offer me in exchange for taking his liquor license away. Holly's dead because nobody gives a damn. Kenya was right when she cussed me out the night I told her Holly was dead. What's one more black girl turning tricks for drugs? Your daughter's still alive, white

with a boyfriend and a loving family. Got everything going for her. Somebody gotta play for the losing team. I
win the toss-up, I guess."

The wire crackled again. "Cut the shit, Sherlock. I'm
eighty miles behind you and coming up the fast lane.
First blue light you see, that'll be me."

"Hi, ho, Silver," sad Moss and hung up.

Skoot wasn't hard to find. He was operating out of a
bar off Beale Street in a part of town that gave sleaze a
new dimension. The bar advertised "The World's Hottest
Babes" to attract tourists walking on the wild side, but the
stiffs inside were there to feed their addictions, ignoring
the bump and grind. Moss sauntered in, staggering a little
to catch the pimp's attention.

"Where're the girls? When they coming out?" *Don't
overdo the loaded routine.* He might just end up on the
sidewalk with the guys who drank anti-freeze.

He saw that he was interrupting a deal, so the bald,
wispy man behind the bar ignored him as he put a wad of
bills in his apron pocket, but his fellow customers on the
bar stools turned in his direction.

"That's what we want to know. If you find out, buddy, tell us. We've been waiting here for an hour soaking
up a bar tab like the national debt."

Moss tried to get the bartender's attention by waving
a twenty at him. "Hey, my main man, give me a vodka on
the rocks when you got the time, okay? I don't want to
rush you or nothing."

"Don't worry, Scoot's not going to do anything in a
hurry," said a man on a neighboring stool.

He wasn't from Memphis or Tennessee or anywhere
in the States that had a non-accent. That was the first
thing Moss noticed about the stranger, dressed in new
designer jeans to look casual. The second thing was the
gun. It was a small, deadly weapon designed to look like

a phone, and the stranger was pointing it straight at Moss's heart.

Moss knew his plan had worked. "Have we met before, sir?"

"No, but I know who you are, Detective Moss. Now we are going to take a ride. You don't have objection, I take it?"

"As long as there's a girl in it for me, I'm game."

"Ach, the blacks!" Moss caught the man at his back saying under his breath. "Can't keep their minds off of sex."

Moss couldn't resist zinging back. "Do they clone you guys over there or are you and the twins really triplets?"

The man moved closer so Moss could feel the hard edge of the gun against his arm. "I said shut up."

"Look, I was just trying to find some female company, man. What's wrong with that, huh?"

"Nice try, Detective Moss." The man tapped his phone and Moss heard his voice saying, "...and when I find the one that did all that, I'm gonna charge him with two murders and one attempted murder."

The man gave a nasty cackle. "Correction, three. Yours will make three. Now, walk toward the door."

Moss looked over his shoulder. In the crowded bar, only Skoot took notice of their leaving. The detective he had ordered to shadow him was nowhere to be seen. "Anyway, I know where we're headed, Hans."

"Oh, and where is that?"

"Biopharma headquarters in South Carolina. Did my homework, see. Right below Greenville going East on state highway—"

"I said shut up," his captor hissed.

They were outside where the night mist from the river swirled in ghostly shapes around them. A long sleek car came out of nowhere, its headlights snapping on as it pulled up in front of them.

Moss felt the gun pressing in his back. "Get in back and don't try anything heroic. Your partner won't come to your rescue."

"Either you've paid him off or he's in a dumpster somewhere."

"To my organization, they are one and the same," said his captor with a snarky smile twisting his thin lips. "And watch your head. Wouldn't want you to get hurt. Yet."

Moss got in the back seat of the car. It smelled new, brand new like they had just bought it for the occasion. No doubt it had a temporary license plate, too.

The ride took two and a half hours. Moss figured they were going east and heading toward Chattanooga, then South Carolina. He hoped the GPS device in his shoe would keep emitting his location to headquarters. He had let Donovan with the FBI know before he had even ventured into downtown in search of Skoot, just in case his partner was on the take or dead. Like the man in the new jeans had said either one meant the same thing.

Donovan had introduced himself while his team had been at Lesbos. "Guess you dodged the bullet that time, Moss. This was the brother and sister team out of Switzerland every country has been trying to nail for political assassinations from Argentina to Canada. They were interchangeable, transgender to be politically correct, both appearing as men, then women. Couldn't tell the difference between 'em, they say."

Moss chuckled. "They must have been slumming to end up down here."

"They would have gone any place if the money was right. Somebody paid them enough to fight these damned mosquitoes, that's for sure." Donovan put on his rimless glasses and pulled out two photographs. "What's interesting is they both had identical tattoos. Ever seen this before?" He shoved one at Moss.

"Yeah, I have. Hey, Walker!" He flagged the tall Georgian who was squatting in the tall grass, studying the ground intently. 'Come look at this."

It was the same tattoo had been on Holly Simpson's arm and the image Faun had described as appearing on her computer screen just before the virus struck. It was the same hunched figure with his mouth wide open, showing a double row of shark's teeth, in some kind of wheeled rocket chair. Now, in the back seat of the car, hurtling through the night, Moss heard a siren. The man beside him put the gun to his ribs and barked instructions to the driver. "It's only a state patrol car. Just get the ticket and go on."

The tall trooper took his time getting out of his patrol car. He strolled over to the limo. *Smokey-style,* Moss thought.

"Evening. Can I see your license, please?"

The driver willingly handed it over, knowing it was faked.

"You know you were doing ninety and the legal limit is seventy?"

"Sorry, sir. You know how it is, get on the open highway—I promise to be more careful from now on."

The patrolman glanced in the backseat where Moss sat rigidly upright. "Evening," he said. "How're y'all?"

His captor's accent grew even more clipped. "We are in a hurry, sir. Would you please write the ticket and let us get on our way."

"Just doing my job, sir. No ticket, just a warning to slow down. Those South Carolina troopers, now they won't be as nice as we are here in Georgia. Night."

Moss relaxed in relief. The terse words in the sorghum syrup drawl and the dark eyes under the wide brim of the Georgia trooper's hat belonged to Quade Walker.

"Stupid oaf!" said the man beside him. "Must have an IQ of twelve."

The Biopharma complex sat on vast acres of good Carolina bottom land, so far off the road that its lights weren't visible through the thick forest that bordered the rural highway. A guard at the gate kiosk waved them through the automatic steel gate that had opened the width of the limo with only inches to spare. From there, Moss estimated they drove at least another mile until they reached a huge building with smoked windows. The driver parked in an underground garage beneath the building. Holding the gun at his back, his captor took Moss up to a room two floors up in an elevator.

Two men who looked like professional wrestlers were waiting to grab Moss and put him in what looked like a dentist chair. They took off his jacket and shoved a needle in his arm.

"He'll squawk like a jaybird now, Mr. Reed."

"He better 'cause singing is the only thing that's keeping this Nubian alive. I'm going to see if he can dance, too." Through their laughter, Moss recognized the voice. It was the FBI agent Donovan.

For the first time in his life, Moss was thankful he was a caffeine addict. On the way up from the sticks in Georgia, he had OD'd on those barista creations like the something-something lattes, so the sodium pentothal injection they had given him had just taken the edge off the caffeine jitters, leaving him fully awake and feeling slightly high.

"All right, put him on the table." The one that sounded like Count Dracula seemed to be doing something with an instrument that looked like a cattle prod. Moss had a good idea of where Dracula was planning to put it once he was on the table. While the Count was occupied with his joy toy, Donovan, aka Reed, was on the phone with someone he kept saying "sir" to.

When the two goons undid the straps binding him to the chair, Moss decided it was time to make a move. He kicked out and up, catching the man in the crotch, simultaneously bringing his left fist under the chin of the second one. As he charged up out of the chair, he head-butted Dracula, sending him crashing into Reed. He gave Reed a kick in the head just for fun and, as he went out the door, stomped like a mad bull on both men.

He was midway to the stairs when an alarm sounded and a voice came over the intercom, nasal with a hint of twang. "Don't worry, boys, he won't get very far. I've got him in my sights." The doors that weren't already closed were closing and Moss barely squeezed through the Exit door to the stairs by sucking in his gut.

He reached the ground floor and tried the door to the lobby. Locked! The next door down led to the garage but he heard voices shouting, "Try the stairs! I'll take the elevator!" echoing within its concrete walls. Moss took the stairs three at a time, passing what looked like a closet. He paused midflight. It was marked *FACILITIES ONLY* and housed the plumbing supplies, what looked like breaker boxes, and, beside them, thick plumbing pipes for that end of the building. All could be used as weapons, if it came down to that.

Moss stepped in, closing the door softly behind him.

With seconds remaining until they found him, Moss spotted a pipe wrench lying on the floor beside the water pipes and smashed at one of the pipes until it cracked and water gushed out. The noise would certainly attract his pursuers. Throwing all the breakers to OFF, he flattened his body behind the door just as it opened letting a flood of water out.

"What the bloody hell? Detective Moss, I know you're in here. Won't do you a bit of good to hide from us." It was the count who whispered to someone behind him. "Go turn the lights back on."

Whoever the flunkie was, he was cautiously advancing toward the breaker box, when Moss brought down the wrench on his head, throwing all his weight against the door. Two pistol shots played off the other side of the steel door followed by an "Uh, uh" sound. Moss listened and heard nothing but the rushing water.

Opening the door, he stepped over the body of the count who had received his own bullets back, one had entered his body about the waistline, but the other had deflected upward through his jaw to his brain. Moss relieved him of his pistol and picked off another guard coming up the stairs.

Now that the breakers were off, the doors to the hall would open, letting water flood the stairs. Moss took the first floor at full speed. He hadn't run like this since he played for Alabama, but the opposition wasn't packing heat then either. He headed toward the main entrance just as the lights came back on.

"Hello, Mr. Moss. Going somewhere?" It was the same nasal voice with the slight twang Georgians inherit with their DNA coming over the intercom.

Moss squinted down the dim hall. He could make out a hunched figure sitting in a chair, the head rest rising far above the tilted head. The slumped figure in the chair came slowly toward the lobby, hovering slightly above the floor but not touching it. As the little man in the chair came nearer, Moss could see his head was unusually large for his crumpled body. Spindly legs rested at odd angles, his torso like Humpty Dumpty of the children's nursery rhyme. Moss immediately realized this man was the creator of the shark tattoo.

"You've just about worn out your welcome and your usefulness, too. By the way, I'm Michael Slade. I think you and that monkey my mother is married to have been trying to find me. Did you like my little video I sent my step-sister the whore? The one with pictures of that black slut, Holly, or whatever she called herself. Your girlfriend will be next, Mr. Moss. But you won't see it because you'll be dead."

Moss had kept moving around the lobby keeping the furniture between them in case Slade had a gun—a moving target was harder to hit especially since Slade hardly looked capable of marksmanship. There was a slight whirring sound and suddenly the chair rose higher in the air, spraying bullets where Moss had been standing a second ago.

Slade had counted on the element of surprise to claim his victim as, no doubt, he had claimed many others. But he wasn't counting on having a veteran of Iraq and Afghanistan for his prey.

Moss was always prepared for anything and everything to explode without warning. He dove behind the leather couch that formed a conversation pit in the huge lobby of Biopharma headquarters. Using the couch for cover, Moss crept around the padded arm. The whine of the chair's engine told him Slade was making a move. Moss gripped the pipe wrench, counting the seconds he had to live.

Slade's chair was coming closer. Moss could hear the decreased whine of the RPMs as it lowered to put out its scythe wheels, ripping the back of the leather couch wide open as Slade got too close.

"You can run, but there's no hiding from me, Moss. I'm way smarter than you, and besides this building is airtight. You're locked in and your help is locked out."

As Slade rounded the corner, scythe wheels were

ready to dig into his prone body. In desperation, Moss stuck the pipe wrench around the protruding metal blades and heaved upward. The chair flipped over on its side. Slade however didn't fall out as he was strapped in his chair like a kayak racer. Moss scrambled to his feet, vaulted over the couch, and made for the long corridor just as Slade maneuvered the controls to bring the chair upright again.

"I'll get you, Moss, and when I do, I'll chop you up and feed you to my cats. Better yet, I'll let them do it. Bring on the cats! I said bring the cats!" That was followed by a burst of automatic weapon fire from the chair. Slade's voice rose to a shrill scream, sounding like a mad Roman emperor. "I want the damned cats!"

Moss hunched down as a hail of bullets whizzed by his left shoulder. Despite everything he could do, Slade was now matching his speed, getting closer by the second. He was rounding the corner of the corridor, belting down the long hall when another miracle happened. Slade overcorrected for the corner, knocking his chair sideways. The spray of bullets punctured a wide arc along the walls.

Just as Moss thought he had a chance to make it, a translucent panel in the hall slid open as he ran past. There were three panels which served as rotating screens touting Biopharma's numerous products.

Behind him, Moss heard a deep cough which only a large animal can make when it feels apprehensive. He glanced behind him to see a tiger cautiously step into the hall.

The animal was so frightened by the bullets and Slade shrieking curses in his flying chair that it fled back inside its cage in the wall, cowering there.

"Godammit!" Slade shouted through his voice box. "Can't anybody stop this nigger for me?"

As if on cue, a car crashed through the plate glass window and landed in the hall. Quade jumped out, gun drawn, bringing down Slade's chair with two shots. The speeding chair crashed on its side in the hall floor, but its occupant remained strapped to the seat. The shrieks were now replaced with moans.

In a flash of black and orange, the terrified tiger sprang out of the wall and plunged through the gaping hole in the window into the night.

Moss finally stopped running, afraid his heart was going to burst. He bent over, hands on knees, hauling in air.

"You okay, Moss?" Quade was beside him. "What are you? Suicidal? Tracking down Michael all alone?"

"I thought you were right behind me, what with the Smokey act and all. What took you so long? Nearly became cat food."

"Stopped to pick up those guys," Quade nodded at several men in SWAT team gear trying to right Michael Slade's chair. "Speaking of cats, was that a tiger I just saw go by?"

"Yeah, I was gonna be his dinner." Before he could warn Quade about Slade's lethal chair, with a sudden jolt, the chair rose abruptly, tearing it from the men's grasp.

"Hit the floor!" Moss yelled. Those that didn't move fast enough were hit by a spray of bullets as Slade retreated down the hall in reverse, holding on to the trigger. Two men were caught in the line of fire as the rest hit the floor.

Quade couldn't get a clear shot off, but Moss followed, running at a crouch, and using the desk for cover, nicked Slade somewhere in the upper body. "Lord, forgive me for missing the bastard," he said and spat.

The hail of bullets stopped for a few brief seconds, and Moss was about to pursue the careening chair, but at that moment, four men in Biopharma uniforms appeared at the far end of the hall. Two held off the arriving SWAT team with AK 47s, as the other two guided Slade's chair to a bank of elevators. The guards then vanished through the exit door leading to the roof.

A voice echoed down the hallway in the silence that followed. "Damn, if that dude don't look like a witch on a broom."

"I dunno, got mighty good coverage for a witch," someone answered.

The men penned down on the first floor were tending the wounded when they heard a helicopter landing on the roof. That meant Slade was gone. They waited, listening. Satisfied the building was empty, their captain called in reinforcements to secure it. The two men they had left outside were found unconscious, coldcocked from behind.

By the time they were able to get to the roof of the Biopharma building, Michael Slade had left the country in his private jet, from his private airport somewhere offshore, on his private island.

Chapter 24

Bjorn waited in the alley behind Corleono's Pizza until two o'clock on a drizzly night when Steve came out, saying "so long" to a person, who like him, was disappearing into the humid dark.

Following Steve to the Vespa he had locked in the restaurant's bike rack, Bjorn grabbed the wispy computer tech in a choke hold from behind. Pressing a key in Steve's ribs, he said, "Tell me why you did it, you worthless piece of shit. What'd you have against that girl? What did she ever do to you?"

Steve's voice shook with fear. "Always acting like she was just too good for me. Too high and mighty. Too perfect. Jesus, you're hurting me!"

"Trust me, not like I'm going to hurt you if you don't spill your guts to the police. If that doesn't happen soon, I'll kill you very slowly." Bjorn tightened his arm, sudden fury sweeping through his brain.

Steve's voice rose to a squeak. "Please let me go. If it's money you want, I got paid today."

"Just tell me how and why you did it, you little turd. Start with the camera." Bjorn had made sure he had the mike chord attached to his phone so he could pick up every sound.

"Okay, okay, I did it all. When she was here with you that night, I slipped two Quaaludes in her beer. Watched her have sex with you, then when you went out, I had her, then invited that guy Chuck—you're strangling me! I can't breathe!"

Bjorn let Steve drop to the alley pavement like a broken toy. He gave him a kick in the ribs as he walked away into the night. Steve raised his head to look at his attacker.

"You tried to kill me! I'll get you for this, Bjorn!"

Bjorn whipped around and came at him. "You ruined her life, do you know that? Of course you know, you faggot! I should kill you here and now."

"Please. Please. I'll say I was the one who did it to the police. Only please don't kill me." Like an injured snake, Steve writhed on the ground.

"Want your photograph all over the world as you die slowly?" Bjorn couldn't believe the words coming out of his mouth, but he knew the power of social media and knew what it would mean to Steve.

"No, no, please! I couldn't breathe! I'll confess everything!"

"You already have." Bjorn patted his jeans where the phone rested in its holder.

"But confessions under force won't stand up in court."

"It'll be enough to sway a jury. But let's just say Faun's dad will hear it first. You've met Chief Walker, I take it?"

Steve's head dropped back down. "Okay, what else do you want to know? I've told you everything."

Bjorn squatted beside him, pulling him up by his greasy hair. "Who is Michael Slade?"

"Okay, I had a check from him. Or his company. Bio-something. I forgot."

Bjorn punched him with his fist.

"Biopharma."

"What for?"

"For just what I did. Setting up Faun Walker."

Bjorn let Steve fall hard to the ground, gasping for breath.

"You," Steve said turning his head painfully toward Bjorn. "I hate you, too. You and her both. I put you both out of business for good. And the icing on the cake is Biopharma's going to fund the rest of my research."

"From prison? You're out of your mind." Bjorn walked back down the alley.

Steve got up on his knees. His jeans were wet where he had pissed his pants. "Slade says he's gonna get me away from here." In a sobbing voice, he muttered, "I'm going to be famous. So long, sucker."

ℰ∽ℰ∽

Quade spent a couple of days in Greenville, SC, explaining his part in the shootout at Biopharma Industries to a mystified circuit court judge. Biopharma, it turned out, was one of the state's largest employers of locals, a big contributor to political campaigns and sponsor of their local baseball team.

"I guess it doesn't matter how many people they kidnap or kill, in that case, your honor." Moss didn't do any better when it was his turn on the stand. "As long as they sponsor a ball team."

"Don't get smart with me, son, or I'll bind this case over to the grand jury to decide on whether to indict you and your Georgia friend here for invading private property, killing several guards in the process."

"What about the tiger, your honor?" That was the FBI agent who, along with Quade and the SWAT team, had crashed the SUV into the Biopharma building. "Is it okay to hunt people down with wild animals like the Romans did two thousand years ago? Tigers, for example. "

"Tigers? Are you playing with me?"

"No, sir, Judge, we have it all on camera—kidnapping Detective Moss here, taking him across state lines, turning a tiger loose on him when he tried to escape—everything we need to close Biopharma down as a shell corporation for illegal drugs, money laundering, extortion, human trafficking, just about anything you can think of. And, oh, yeah, possession of rare, endangered, and exotic animals like Bengal tigers. The animal rights people would love that."

He didn't mention that the tiger in question had meekly returned to its cage after trying to eat an outraged Carolina raccoon in the wilds. The raccoon put up such resistance that the tiger, gave up in despair and limped back to his mate for solace.

❧❧❧

When Quade got back to Julia Springs, Isis was waiting for him on the front porch. He hadn't even stretched his legs from the long drive home before she was in his arms, smelling of sandalwood and hibiscus.

"Hey, I'll have to go away more often if this is the welcome committee. You said she's gone?"

Isis nodded, her eyes filling with tears. "What's worse, I don't know where. I tried her phone. She didn't answer." She quickly wiped the tears away and smiled. "You know how I get when you leave. I can't really function outside. I tried to find our girl, even asked Freddy to try. You know how they are, so tight. He said what you said. She'd probably left to go see Chris Bjorn. But I tried his phone, it's cut off."

They walked arms entwined up the steps into the

comfortable living room. "I take it hers is working, though. And she's not at Lesbos with her grandmother, right? Did you call Lois to see if she was there?"

"Of course! That was the first place I looked. Lois told me she was out there to put something under The Mama Tree. "

He untangled himself from her arms long enough to pour himself a drink. "Go on, I'm listening. So what was it? A clue as to where she was going, I hope."

Isis curled up in a chair. "It was a gris-gris bag."

Quade parked himself on the arm of her chair. After taking a large belt of Jack Daniels, he resisted the urge to laugh outright. This whole thing with Michael was surreal—the tigers, the flying chair, Moss acting like Super Cop. He took another drink before he answered. "That's probably your mom's way of giving her somewhere to go with all her grief."

"Quade, Mom didn't make the gris-gris bag for her. I asked Freddy and Saranjii who makes them now that Root Woman is gone and they both said Kedzia."

"You lost me there. Say who?"

"Kedzia. I've heard of her. But Mom says she's bringing the Glory Road tradition back, including the old customs."

"Tell me what's that got to do with Faun? I'm getting hungry in more ways than one." He regretted saying that the moment Isis raised her tearstained face. "Hey, beautiful ladies shouldn't cry. I'll find her. You know Faun, she's her own girl, always has been."

"I'm just so glad you're back. I hate it when you're away. I can't sleep. You know how I am. I can't function without you."

His wife clung to him as if she was afraid to lose connection with his body. She had always needed him more than either of their children had.

He knew then she would follow him in no time if he died tomorrow.

∽∾∽

The Atlanta Police, when Quade contacted them, said Chris Bjorn had been cleared of any wrong doing in the sexual assault case. He might be called as a witness for the district attorney's case against the other two defendants Charles Hawthorne Howard III who had already confessed but had made a plea bargain to witness against the apartment manager. They didn't mention the digital recording the district attorney's office had received with Steve's confession on it. They didn't have to. Quade had received a duplicate copy from Bjorn.

Quade put down the phone and stared into nothingness. They said Bjorn had left town, wasn't answering his phone. Parents said when they last heard from him, he said he was going to visit an aunt and uncle in Switzerland. They'd look for Faun if she showed up at school.

From her computer, Quade learned that Faun had applied for a patent for her chronic disease application through a patent attorney named James A. Bradford in Atlanta. Bradford hadn't heard from her either, but the leading contender for the application, a company called Biopharma Corporation, showed signs of pulling out of the patent race, putting Faun's company in the lead.

The attorney asked how Faun was doing—that's when Quade finally came to grips with his daughter's disappearance. "I don't know," he said in a hollow voice." We can't find her."

∽∾∽

Freddy had seen her number on his phone at 6:30 in the morning, but seeing as it was the busiest time at

Saranjii's, he answered it an hour later. There was no message, just that missed call.

He texted back, saying he was sorry he missed her call, to call back. That was it. She never called. Faun had disappeared. Her parents tried not to panic, but the unspoken fear was suicide.

ℰℐℰℐ

When Bjorn arrived at Zurich Airport, he took the shuttle into the city. He had been there several times to visit his aunt Clara, once as a high school graduation gift from his parents, another as an undergrad, then briefly during grad school, so he knew the ropes.

His uncle Lorenz was at the shuttle stop to meet him, looking like the Swiss banker stereotype—dark gray overcoat, matching leather gloves, smartly-shined Italian shoes.

They hugged without touching bodies, just shoulders the way men do. Uncle Lorenz smelled of expensive cologne. Bjorn was aware he had slept in his clothes for two days. Lorenz drew back and surveyed his nephew. "Ugh, is that Minnesota I smell? Cow manure? We have to do something about that, now don't we, Christian?"

Bjorn had forgotten how his uncle always stated everything as a question, no doubt as a by-product of his trade. "It's 6:30 in the morning and about 0 degrees. Who cares how I smell?"

"That depends on who is driving you home, which is me." They got in Lorenz's Mercedes and made their way through the city that looked much as his uncle did—neat, gray, and bankerish.

Aunt Clara was waiting in the hallway of their townhouse as though she was part of the scenery and not an alien from Minnesota. Slim, blonde, and perfect, she had the same reaction as Lorenz when she hugged him. "What a splendid young man you've turned into! So handsome! Now upstairs to your room and take a bath. You smell like a goat herder from the Alps."

His intention was to start looking for Biopharma's headquarters right away and track down Michael Slade. He hoped to get some inside information from his uncle, but when he started inquiring about the company's assets, his uncle raised an eyebrow and a silent alarm. Leaning forward, Lorenz said, "Biopharma? What exactly is your interest in Biopharma, Chris? Have they offered you a job?"

He made up some story about scoping out career prospects. Biopharma's representatives had been at a job fair at the university. He thought he would take a look, that's all.

Lorenz zeroed in on the truth. "Do you have an interview with Biopharma or not?"

Aunt Clara intervened. "Let the boy eat his dinner, Lorenz. It's getting cold while you are cross-examining him."

They were eating at a cozy little place where the food was pricey and sparse, served on china plates with wines from four countries. Bjorn found himself drinking more than he ate, filling up on bread and good Alpine cheese. She wasn't much of a cook, his aunt said. That was strange, he thought.

His mother often said Clara was a better cook than she was growing up. That was saying something, considering his mother had won prizes at state fairs every year for her baked goods.

Chris had heard his mother say the real reason they ate out so often was because Clara didn't wanted to be tempted by food. Lorenz confirmed what Bjorn had always suspected was just a sister's envious remark.

"Puts on the pounds, then she has to go to the spa to take them off," his uncle said with conspiratorial wink.

Bjorn noticed the subject of Biopharma had been expertly side-stepped as the acid banter between the couple escalated.

"No, the reason we eat at restaurants is because he has to get back to his mistress at the office." Clara leaned toward Bjorn. "Does that shock you, American boy?"

With a sharp look at Clara, Lorenz took a sip of wine. "She's just teasing, Chris. She means my mistress is my work."

But he knew by Clara's sour expression, she had meant just what she said. She was his mother's youngest sister who had gone to Switzerland to study cheese making. His grandfather kept dairy goats and Clara wanted to carry on the tradition. She had majored in animal husbandry in college and planned to run the goat cheese business herself after her father retired.

But she and Lorenz, the Oxford-trained son of a Swiss businessman, met at a party. The pretty artisan and the handsome banker married, and she became a sort of ornament in his fine townhouse. Clara worked hard at being a trophy wise. They had no children and Lorenz devoted himself to banking, food, and sex—in that order—while Clara devoted herself solely to pleasing Lorenz.

Bjorn felt his aunt's excruciating loneliness, having been there himself. Instinctively, he felt Lorenz's eyes on his face, searching for signs of having grasped their unhappy situation.

Seeing that it had, his uncle sighed as if it pained him to acknowledge loyalty to his wife's family. "All right, Chris, I will make some inquiries about Biopharma, if you'll remind me. All I know is you should stay away from that company. I have heard things I don't like. How about one of the other big international ones? Have you any offers from them?"

When Bjorn shook his head, making sure his mouth was full as an excuse not to answer his uncle, Lorenz took another sip of wine and sat back in his chair. "I'll see what I can arrange. See me your CV. Let me distribute it to some of my customers and we'll see what turns up, shall we, hmmm?"

❧❧❧

The first lead on Faun came from a most unlikely source—Angela. Angela was the least friendly of the FFs—Faun's Friends—as the group of cronies called themselves. The few times Quade had met her, he thought the girl seemed out of place among the outgoing, twenty-words-a-minute, driven group of mostly science majors.

"Mr. Walker?" The call came late in the day as he was just leaving the station. "You probably don't remember me. My name is Angela Morris. I had a hard time getting your number until I remembered you were the police chief."

What Angela told him sent Quade out the door, telling Isis goodbye over the phone and not to worry as he went. Isis sounded as if she was used to it. Angela said she had phoned Faun to see how she was doing. That was when Faun had told her she was going to kill herself.

"I didn't believe her. I tried to say she would get over it, that she was too strong to let one incident stand in her way. I don't think she heard a thing I was saying. She kept repeating over and over 'I don't want to live anymore. I'm just tired of feeling dirty.' Then she just hung up. Mr. Quade, you have to find her because she's going to try. To kill herself I mean."

"How? Did she say how or where? Think back to

what she said, Angela. She give any hints?"

There was a long silence, after which Angela's voice had a different tone in it. A sadness that reached out to Quade over the miles. "It doesn't work like that. Nobody knows when or even how sometimes. It's always in the back of your mind, waiting for the opportunity to strike."

"Sounds like you know something about it, Angela."

"I do. I had something like what happened to Faun happen to me. I tried to commit suicide at fifteen, then again at eighteen. Luckily, I just messed up my body, not my mind. I've still got that, and it's saved my life. And I told Faun that, but like I said, I don't think she heard a word I was saying. You just sort of close your mind at that stage."

"You're a brave girl. Keep up the good fight and call me again if you want to talk. Or if you think of any place Faun might have gone."

"You know I made up my mind not to trust anybody ever again, especially a man, but you changed my mind, Mr. Quade."

"How's that, Angela?"

"You're the only one who ever called me pretty since I was thirteen when he did that to me—my stepfather."

He was on the road to Athens when the university police called. Faun's car had been found near a lake outside of town. Her phone was in the car on the floor. The last call she had made was to Angela Morris at three that afternoon.

The police divers scoured the bottom of the lake for Faun's body while Quade looked on, a growing dread at what they would find as each diver emerged. As dusk fell, the divers turned on their underwater lights, appearing like prehistoric amphibians as they waded out of the murky water.

At one point Quade was aware of cars driving up be-

hind him, illuminating the beach and the emergency vehicles parked on the sand. He looked around to see Isis
running toward him, Freddy and Kenya standing back,
arms around each other. The other car had Tennessee
plates and Moss, a phone stuck to his ear, got out still
talking in grunts.

Isis nestled close to him. "I have this funny feeling
they're wasting their time," she said. "Faun's still alive, I
can feel it."

"That's good." Quade held his wife closer. "'Cause I
can't feel anything."

When it grew dark, the police left the lake, calling
off the search for Faun Walker.

"We'll call you if we hear anything." The officer
gripped Quade's shoulder. "Hang in there, buddy. She's
not in that lake, we're pretty sure."

"Quade, read this." Kenya and Freddy came up after
the police had left. "Lois found this in the gris-gris bag
Faun left on The Mama Tree. You'll see why I couldn't
call you. Read it."

The crumpled note was in Faun's neat handwriting.
"You read it, honey. I can't."

But Isis only shook her head. "Let's get a motel. All
of us. I think she's all right, my darling. I feel good about
it."

"Will you read the damned letter? What exactly does
it say?" He rarely spoke to her like that, but Isis knew it
was because his nerves were completely frayed.

"I'll tell you on the way to the motel," she said firmly. "You're going to see why in a minute, you big dope."

He had no choice but to do as she said, following her
like a whipped dog to the car, where Moss was still on
the phone, this time speaking in yelps. He flagged Quade
to hold the questions until he finished yelping and hung
up.

"She's left for Germany about an hour ago." When Quade looked like he hadn't spoken English, Moss enunciated clearly. "Your girl, Faun, left Atlanta for Germany an hour ago. She's alive, Quade. Let's get a drink. You and me could use one. Drinking ought to be in our job description."

They all had Jack Daniels over ice, except Quade who belted a couple of straight shots.

Moss took over. "According to her note, Chris has gone to Switzerland to kill her brother Michael, or at least beat the crap out of him, and she's going to save Chris and, at the same time, put her brother in prison, which you know they will never do because he's bat shit crazy. Who does this girl think she is, Super Woman? I mean, come on, the dude has a flying chair that shoots rounds like an AK47. And tigers for pets. Why do those two think they have a snowball-in-hell's chance of catching him? We sure couldn't manage it, that's for sure."

"That's because you two are old and slow and got no ideals," Kenya said, laying it on the line. "They're young, smart and believe they are invincible. That's the difference. They're going to put that bastard away, 'scuse me, Isis, I know he's your son, but a bastard all the same."

Isis put down her glass, her shaking hand making the ice rattle. "I know Michael. He's full of hate. You can almost feel it from a distance, radiating toward you, killing everything it touches. But it won't kill Chris and Faun. Love will conquer hate. Love is life. Hate is death. I believe it. I have seen it."

There was a long silence when she finished. Moss looked at Kenya who was looking straight at him with glowing amber eyes.

Quade suddenly erupted, surfacing from a pool of thought. "Goddammit, I don't get why she put everybody through this! That's just like her, thinking about herself, not what she does to people around her. She called this poor girl, Angela, saying she was going to kill herself. The girl frantically called me, which sent me on this wild goose chase, getting the local law enforcement and you all involved. Everything. When she had this planned all along. It's typical Faun. Not thinking of the way she treats others."

"Because that was part of her plan to throw them off her trail, don't you get it?" Freddy said, veiled fury in his voice. Everybody looked at him, slack-jawed. "I told you she called me and didn't leave a message. I lied. She called me from a pay phone at the airport. Like she says in the note, she thought her phone, and your phone, Chief, was tapped. Don't look so skeptical. If Ham Phillips could do it twenty years ago in the Swamp, Michael can sure do it now."

"He's got a point," Moss said. He could see a fight looming between generations: one who got it, the other holding fast to norms like confiding in your parents. "Go on, son."

"So she had to make it look like she committed suicide to throw Michael off. That was what he was aiming for, anyhow, her suicide after setting up this whole thing with the apartment manager/dumped lab tech Steve. So she called Angela Morris, told her what she was going to do, figuring she'd get the message to you, Quade, then drove to the lake, left her cell phone in the car, took a taxi back to Atlanta and caught the night flight to Germany. Pretty smart. Oh, yeah, wore a wig just in case. That long blonde hair attracts attention."

Moss frowned. "But she had to use her real name on the passenger list. To match her ID."

"She bought two tickets—one to Puerto Rico and the one to Germany. Under her first name—Ariel. Ariel Walker. By the time they figure that out, she'll be in Michael's back yard. You forget, she's a genius, too." Freddy sat back on the itchy motel chairs. "I should be a lawyer."

"You should be something else besides slinging hash, baby." Interrupting the intense conversation, Kenya did a Scarlett O'Hara number with the motel brochure. "You know, I just can't stand these hot, humid days of summer. I'd like to go to someplace cool myself. What'd you say you and me take a trip to Switzerland, Isis? My treat. And that invite includes anybody else that wants to go." She directed a glance at Moss who looked apprehensive.

"Is Sheldon going?"

"Yes, but Ashley Pearl will watch him. Freddy?"

Normally Freddy was up for any adventure, so Kenya was surprised when he declined the invitation. "Not me. One, I hate flying, and two, I need to sling that hash, remember? Do you want the town to riot, or worse yet, all go over to Pop's Place for his chicken biscuits? I'll pass."

Quade was passed out by now, but Isis answered for both of them. "I've never been on a plane or even out of Georgia, but I know Quade will go anyway, so I might as well go with him." Isis made a face. "Even if it's straight down."

"That's settled then. I'll call the travel agent in the morning and book the tickets. And I'll call my agent to find me some bookings in …where'd you say we were going?"

A chorus of voices let her know. "For god's sake, don't land us in the wrong place!"

Casting an alluring glance at Moss, Kenya yawned. Even he could tell she faking it "I guess I'll turn in now. Won't get much sleep with those cicadas singing like that. No big bugs in Switzerland, just those cute guys in the suspender shorts yodeling in the mountains."

Moss and Kenya got two rooms next door, but spent the night in only one. Freddy, who had gone to see a couple of fraternity brothers now in medical school at UGA, returned around midnight. Peeking through the door adjoining his room and Kenya's, he saw she was asleep beside Moss in the oversized king-sized bed, her head on Moss's shoulder. Moss was dead to the world, snoring like a man who's every desire had been satisfied. Freddy chuckled to himself. Kenya had got her man.

Chapter 25

Bjorn was at the Zurich airport a little early the next morning. By pre-arrangement, he went straight to the Lufthansa gates, walking along, pretending to talk on a prepaid phone. Ducking into the men's bathroom, he got in a stall and switched phones.

Dialing the airline's ticket counter, he asked for Information to page Celeste Bjorn to the kiosk. He waited by the kiosk for over an hour, after all the flights from Germany were in their arrival gates and had deposited their passengers.

Faun was not among them.

He went back in the bathroom and dialed her hotel in Mannheim. Indeed, the desk clerk said, Mrs. Bjorn had arrived last night around ten o'clock and checked out about 7:30 a.m. the next morning. The desk had called a cab to the airport at that time to give her plenty of time to catch her Lufthansa flight.

"Do you know the flight number?"

The clerk consulted his call log. "Flight 1332 to Zurich." Bjorn felt a stab of fear spread through his chest. That flight had come in two hours ago.

For some reason maybe she had missed it. He knew

238 Trisha O'Keefe

Faun had traveled in Europe before, had studied German, spoke it fluently. Maybe she didn't hear her flight being called. But that wasn't like Faun. She'd have been waiting at the gate before the plane even got there.

He checked with the ticket agent at the airline counter. "Yes, there was a Mrs. Bjorn listed, but she had not boarded, so they had given her seat to someone flying standby. Sorry, Mr. Bjorn, may I page her for you?" The girl behind the ticket counter smiled at him, despite the line of customers behind him.

"I've tried that already, thanks."

"No harm to try again. I'll give a call to the Information kiosk to keep paging her, all right?"

He was on his way back to the Information kiosk when two men came up to him, dressed too smartly to be travelers. "Mr. Bjorn?"

He took two steps back. "Who wants to know?" he answered in German.

"It won't do you any good to run away," the one closest to him said. "If you do, you won't see the American girl alive again, understand? I have a gun pointed at your heart with a silencer. Get moving."

At the ticket counter, the agent was keeping an eye on the handsome American, just in case his wife showed up. Hardly his wife, most likely his lover, since the good looking Mr. Bjorn wasn't wearing a wedding ring. She particularly noticed those things when a handsome customer came to her. Single life in Zurich was trendy, but nobody wanted to marry before thirty or even later. Nobody could afford to. When she looked over at the Information kiosk, she saw him walking away escorted by two men dressed up like narcs. One was carrying something in his pocket, something he kept his hand on.

The two men escorted him to a stretch Mercedes parked at the terminal curb. Poking Bjorn in the back with something metal, the man who spoke better English of the two, ordered him to get in the back seat of the car. "Don't try anything funny, Mr. Bjorn. I will just shoot you and pretend you had too much to drink as you fall into the back seat, okay? And I will take your phone, please."

❧❧❧

After what felt like hours, Bjorn was pushed through the doorway of a sprawling alpine chalet. He briefly got a glimpse of Faun sitting at the end of a long table in the front room before he was shoved down a long hall. At the other end was a wheelchair with adaptions. Without seeing who was sitting in it, he knew who it was. He could hear Faun calling out his name when one of the men behind him pushed him into a room and slammed the door behind them.

In the front room, Faun sank down in the chair to which her ankle was shackled.

"Don't get up, my dear." The dwarfed figure in front of her raised his chair to be on the same level as his captive. "Those men are my security guards. They'll take good care of your lover. They have orders not to touch him until I say so."

Through his voice box, Michael Slade's voice sounded artificially loud and robotic. It did nothing to reassure her anxiety.

"Please let us go, Mr. Slade. Mother doesn't know where I am. She thinks I might have done something stupid to myself."

"Isn't that just like her, now? But you brought that on yourself, my dear Faun. Calling that girl Angela. Leaving that note under the tree for Lois to find." He sat at the other end of the table with a large white screen behind him. "Let me just look at you. So pretty! You look like an angel sitting there. Don't look at me. I'm a mess. Like a balloon with a leak in it, somebody said before I killed him. Like a melted toy, like a toad,...words fail me. But you, you are beautiful. You know that, don't you? Yes, you know you are. People must have said, 'Oh look at that beautiful child' when you were growing up, didn't they, Sister? How nice that must be, to know you're pleasurable to look at, not ugly, like me."

"Why do you keep calling me that? Sister? I have a little brother but—"

Slade pressed a button and in an instant he was hovering close to Faun. She tried not to show fear, but she could see death in the pair slits that served Michael Slade for eyes. Like a cobra's, she thought, mesmerizing its victim before it strikes.

She fought back. "Is that why you want to hurt people, Michael? Because you are jealous of those who look better than you do?"

"What? What?" he said, "What did you say?" A robotic arm grabbed a handful of her long hair and jerked her head toward his. "Say that again."

Faun strained her head around to meet his eyes, red and askew in the head too large for his collapsed body. "You know what I mean. You hurt Holly who never did anything to you. And you are hurting my mother right now. Why did you do that, Mr. Slade? Why?"

There passed a long moment as the arm gripped her hair in its steel fist, his eyes sliding down at last to gaze at the golden strands breaking away from the strain. Though she was shaking, Faun remained as upright as she could, locking eyes with her tormenter—his own glistening with rage, hers cold as the snow-capped peaks flung out along the horizon.

"I see the whore hasn't told you," came the robotic

voice. "I'm your brother." Then Michael Slade started to cry, a long wail at first, then hoarse sobbing like Arab mourners at a funeral.

The two men standing in the shadows cast by the candlelight stepped forward. "Come, Michael, you're very, very tired," one of them said. "Come sleep a little. You will feel better after a little sleep. We are having a very special dinner tonight. Lobster and shrimps, your favorite."

A long, lithe shadow slid out from under the table, turning its yellow eyes up at Faun, who froze under its gaze. Then it looked toward Michael as if the panther were deciding if she'd hurt him or not.

Still shouting guttural cries of pain, Slade was wheeled away, the robotic fist still clutching strands of Faun's bright hair. "Come, Max." The man pushing Michael's chair gave an order in German and the panther followed at his heels, coughing and looking back at Faun as if it were thinking about doing something else.

The other man was by her side as Faun pushed her chair back from the table. "You're to come this way, miss." He unlocked the shackle holding her to the chair and put his hand under her elbow, supporting as she stood up. "Please follow me. Don't mind the cat. Mr. Slade likes cats, big ones as you can see, but Max is still a wild animal. Very unpredictable sometimes. Remember that."

She could only nod in reply. Her teeth were still clinched so tightly, her jaw ached.

The man called Remi took Faun to a room down the hall in the opposite direction Slade had gone. When he opened the door, she saw it, too, had the same panoramic view of the alpine valley below. There was a woman with a towel over her arm standing by an oversized sleigh bed on which were piled clothes of all sorts—ski outfits to evening gowns.

"*Willkommen, Frauline*. Sit please. I must cut your hair."

"What? No, you damn well won't!"

"It's the master's orders, my dear." Implacably, the woman nodded and Remi grabbed her arms, sitting her roughly down in a chair beside the panoramic window. "Please, be still. I don't want to hurt you."

The more she struggled, the tighter he pinned her arms back until she screamed.

After trimming off the length of her hair, the woman started to shave her head. By way of apology, she said. "Your brother wants you to look like him, and we have to follow his orders. But it is a shame, such beautiful hair."

Faun looked around wildly, seeking an escape route. "My brother is crazy. You're following orders from a crazy man!"

"We must be crazy, too, in that case." The man and woman seemed to find humor in the situation as if Faun's words had struck home.

When she had finished shaving Faun's head, the woman said. "Mmm, this would fetch a big price on the market. They pay top US dollars for naturally blonde hair."

The man replied. "Woman, you *are* crazy. Besides, that's not what he wants to do with her hair, believe me." He glanced over his shoulder as if he was afraid of being heard.

"I know. He told me." The woman turned to Faun. "Please, my dear, now you will select what you would like to wear and I will take the rest away."

Faun's arms ached from being pinned behind her for so long, but Remi released her to go sort through the clothes on the bed. She pretended to look at them, throwing them aside as she went through the pile. In the Swiss longing for order, the woman got busy folding the discards into boxes lined with tissue paper. Remi had swept up the short pieces of shorn hair and was putting the broom and dustpan away when Faun made her move.

Hurling a thick fur coat at the woman bending over a box, she leaped onto the bed and, using it like a trampoline, bounced down to other side where the sliding glass door led out to the balcony. Opening the door just enough to slip through, she vaulted over the railing, falling almost ten feet to the ground below. Almost immediately, she found herself hurtling over and over toward the valley floor.

Halfway down the slope, a tree stopped her headlong spiral, cracking several ribs as she smashed into it. Getting to her feet, she felt dizzy, and one of her legs buckled under when she tried to put weight on it. The pain caused her to black out and she fell again, down the nearly perpendicular embankment.

Fear woke her up a minute later. Her downward plunge had been halted by a rocky outcrop. Somewhere below she thought she heard the sound of a motorcycle and even farther away, the sound of a truck. There was a road below. She recognized it as they one they had taken to reach Michael's villa.

Through the thick fog that began to cloud her mind, she knew she had to reach the road before Michael's thugs caught up with her. She had no doubt her brother would eventually kill her and Chris, too. Her only chance to save them both was to reach the road that wound along the base of the mountain, where perhaps some passerby would take her for a fallen climber. She was incapable of walking so, with her last ounce of strength, Faun plunged down the mountainside.

She lost consciousness before reaching the road, landing in a high patch of grass and alpine wild flowers where a herd of goats was grazing. As the unconscious girl rolled to a stop, scattering the animals, their sudden movement attracted the attention of a busload of tourists coming up the road from the valley.

"Look at that, the perfect alpine scene!" They all took up the cry. "Stop the bus! I want a video of that to show the relatives back home in Iowa." They clamored for a photo-op of the pastoral scene, and the beleaguered guide instructed the driver to park on the emergency shoulder.

"Only five minutes," he shouted in three languages as the tourists poured out of the bus, all intent on getting the best vantage point to shoot the prize-winning photograph. They were seeing who could take the best selfie with alpine goats, when they discovered what had scattered the picturesque flock.

Remi and Gottlieb ran down the steep hillside as far as they could go. They didn't get very far before they spotted cars coming up the road from the valley.

Gottlieb was the first to turn around. He was wanted in three countries on a variety of charges, one for murder. "Someone will see us. She is dead anyway. Nobody could survive a fall like that, from the balcony to the ground. If it didn't kill her, the rest of the way to the valley would. Let's just tell Slade she died when she fell."

"He'll want a body. How'll we produce a body? You know how he is. He'll want to gloat." Remi followed his partner's footsteps, trying not to look down.

Gottlieb's retort surprised him. "Yeah, well, I'm sick of what Michael wants, I'll tell you that. Screw him. I'll tell him his sister's dead. That's what he wanted to do, anyway. I could think of a lot of better things to do with a girl like that. I know guys that pay a cool million euros for a blonde like her."

☙❧

The paramedics, who brought her into the nearby

hospital, thought Faun was a young man at first because her head was shaved. "Probably some skinhead high on acid thought he could fly," remarked one. But when the doctor admitted her, the triage nurse had the final word. As the techs crowded up to her desk to get their orders signed, she was shaking with laughter. "Your guy turned out to be a girl. Probably trans. You know, they're all over the place these days. It's not uncommon for them to come in all beaten up like this one, though. Looks like this was a really bad date."

❦❦❦

Bjorn had trouble seeing the two men asking him questions. There seemed to four of them, sometimes three.

They kept asking him about programming codes, what patterns he used, symbols, language. When he shook his head, to clear away the confusion, one of them punched him hard in the stomach. "I don't know what you mean," he kept saying, or thought he was saying.

They slapped him around some more, but it didn't really hurt. He was numb all over.

"Give him another injection," one said in German.

"It might kill him. His pulse is practically racing now."

"Never mind that. He's only a kid, anyway. We can toss him down the mountain like his girlfriend, say they were hiking together or some such thing."

Gottlieb made no effort to hide his dislike of Americans. He grown up in fractured Bosnia where the Yanks had come across as ignorant cowboys or gangsters from Chicago and Montana.

The woman opened the door. "Someone's coming up the drive. Black Mercedes limo. Diplomatic flag, plates. American."

"Damn! What in hell are they doing here, sticking their nose in everybody's business?"

He went to look in the mirror, smoothing his hair and washing his hands in the dressing room sink. "No matter. See who it is first, Remi, will you? Tell them Slade is indisposed, but if they will wait in the salon, I will talk to them, or Pyiet will. One of us. That will give this kid time to recover his memory." He gave Bjorn another sock in the jaw. "Until then, sleep well, Yank."

When they were gone, Bjorn waited a few minutes before opening his eyes, aware there was the single eye of a camera staring from the ceiling above him. He gambled on the guard at the door to be momentarily distracted by the visitors' arrival. *Whoever they are, they will buy me a few seconds of valuable time.*

His heart was pounding so hard, he was afraid it would burst from the exertion of struggling out of his bonds. His captors had been so sure he was incapacitated by the injections, they had neglected to check his restraints before leaving. The leather straps on the chair were loose, as if they were meant to restrain someone far larger than himself.

Bjorn lurched out of the chair, his legs turned to butter, and he fell with a crash to the floor, bringing the table and syringe in the enamel pan clattering down with it. He lay on the cool floor, trying to figure out why his legs didn't work.

In the foyer, the noise was audible. The two diplomats suspended their conversation with the security guards at the door.

"What was that?" The shorter, broad-shouldered man took a step toward in the direction of the sound. "It sounded as if someone fell."

The two guards looked at each other. What if they had let another one get away? "Only that clumsy maid.

Go check on her, will you, Pyiet? Gentlemen, this way to the salon, please."

But Pyiet was tired of being ordered around. "No, Remi. You check on the maid, I will show guests the way to salon. You want a drink, gentlemen?"

Just then, as Bjorn tried to get to his feet, his hands blindly clawing at the only stable thing in the room, he fell over the table again. The enamel pan skidded across the floor, clattering against the wall.

By that time, the guards had decided who would show the guests the salon and who would check on their captive. Pyiet was just starting back to the room when the powerfully built guest passed him running like a soccer forward making toward the goalie.

"Chris, Christian Bjorn, is that you? Answer me! It's Lorenz! Where are you?"

Bjorn had managed to pull himself to his feet and, using every available piece of furniture as a crutch, made his way to the door, moving as if he was 200 feet under water. "Here!" he said in a whisper. Then gathering all his strength, he called "Lorenz! Here!" It came like a moan but Lorenz heard it and barreled into the room, knocking Bjorn back down.

Bjorn was vaguely aware of a scuffle. His uncle was engaged in fighting off the guard who had chased him down the corridor.

For every martial art move, Pyiet countered with the defensive one, until for a moment, it seemed they were just in a sparring match at the gym.

Then after countering Pyiet's effort at a choke hold, a thought occurred to Lorenz.

Maybe Pyiet could be bribed like any other man who worked for someone else. "Hey, Russke. You fight well. How much does Slade pay you?"

His fist still in defensive mode, Pyiet took a moment

to consider the joke. "Nothing. He pays nothing. I am like slave. That is truth."

"I'll pay you 1000 Euros a month to come be my bodyguard." Lorenz had his hand on his gun by that time, hoping he wouldn't have to use it on this peasant boy.

Just then, Gottlieb came hurrying down the hall, gun drawn. "What is it, Pyiet? This man giving you a hard time?"

That forced Lorenz to draw his pistol and stop the bullet-headed thug in his tracks. "Put the gun down or I'll shoot your friend here."

The German guard shrugged and took another step toward Lorenz. "He's not my friend. Shoot him, I don't care. There are plenty more where he came from."

A voice behind him said in crisp German. "Exactly my sentiment, too. Put your weapon on the floor and your hands up unless you want a bullet in the back."

Seeing his American friend in the doorway, Lorenz said. "About time, Andy. I do all the work while you sip sherry in the salon." He put down his gun and knelt beside Bjorn. "No telling what they've given him."

The American diplomat was on the phone, calling the ambulance when a reedy, querulous voice said. "Put the phone down."

The voice was quavering, high-pitched as a girl's. The men turned to see Michael Slade coming toward them. Max padded beside him, his yellow eyes on the men.

Lorenz divided his attention between the man in the wheelchair and the panther beside him, trying to decide which was the most lethal and which was the most bizarre.

Slade was wearing a flowing blonde wig and a red satin evening gown which covered his withered legs. Max crouched beside his master's chair, waiting for his command. "Johan, I'm surprised at you, letting these two get the upper hand. You must be past your prime. I'll have to replace you." With his robotic arm, Slade stroked the animal at his side. Before the man could answer, Michael shrilled. "Attack!"

For a millisecond, the cat looked uncomfortable, as though he had something to say, then took a few steps toward Gottlieb.

At that point, there was a commotion outside as several men burst in the front door. Startled, the panther turned from Gottlieb and rushed toward the front door. The lead policeman felled him with a single shot between the eyes.

"Politzei! Drop weapons! Hands up!"

In the commotion, overlooked by the storming policemen, Michael Slade glided away down the hall in the opposite direction.

Lorenz, who was showing his credentials to the police, saw Slade's retreat. "Stop that man! He is the mastermind of an international crime syndicate!"

But the policeman only exchanged derisive looks among themselves. "Sure. And I'm the bloody Godfather."

Lorenz's tall companion spoke up then. "Well, I'm Andrew Brown, the Assistant Under-Secretary of the American Consul. You've no doubt passed my car outside with diplomatic plates. We had reason to believe Mr. Slade had two American citizens here being held against their will. In fact, that's this man's nephew your men are trying to revive right now. I suggest you let him go to the boy and look for the other captive, a young girl. It appears Michael Slade does human trafficking as one of his enterprises."

Lorenz went to kneel down beside Chris, whom the emergency technicians were giving oxygen. "Foolish kid," he said fondly. "Why didn't you tell us that's what you were here for?"

Bjorn didn't open his eyes. "Find her," he whispered. "Before he kills her."

At that point the gurney arrived and they wheeled him away.

Chapter 26

Quade was in the shower when Isis brought him the phone. "I think you had better talk to her. It's Chris Bjorn's aunt calling from Zurich, Switzerland."

Quade only dried one side of his head before he snatched the phone from his wife's hand. "Hello! Quade Walker. How are you this evening?" It was nearly one o'clock in the morning, but that was beside the point. The point was, Faun had been missing for three days, and he was so glad to hear from anybody that he lapsed into platitudes.

The woman introduced herself as Clara Verli, Bjorn's aunt. "I have news of your daughter," a woman's voice said. "Not so good, I'm afraid, but could be worse."

She spoke perfect English with a clipped accent. She said Faun was in hospital, that she had sustained injuries when she fell, including a concussion, broken arm, broken left leg, broken right ankle, and numerous ribs.

"What was she doing, mountain-climbing?"

There was a long pause at the other end. "No," said Clara. "I understand she was escaping. Your daughter had been kidnapped, Mr. Walker. That's all I know at this moment."

"I'll be on the next plane out of Atlanta. We were coming to Switzerland in a couple of days anyway."

A man's voice interrupted, overriding the woman's protests "This is Chris's uncle Lorenz Verli. We have already arranged for you to fly at six o'clock on Swissair. There will be two tickets waiting at the counter for you and your wife. You can make it, yes?"

"You bet, but my wife is coming over with a friend who booked the tickets for later in the week. Can I bring somebody else?"

"Depends who you want to spend six hours drinking with. We'll meet you at Zurich Airport. Have a good trip."

"Wait, Mr..."

Verli's tone was slightly amused. "You'd probably mispronounce it. Just Lorenz, will do."

"Your wife said my daughter was escaping. Escaping from who or what?"

"I will explain when you get here. Suffice it to say, I believe it was from Michael Slade, whom my nephew Chris tells me is related to you in some way."

"Yeah, he is in a way." Quade glanced at Isis who turned around and went into the bedroom. In a lower voice, he said. "He's Faun's half-brother, in fact. Crazy as hell. How's your nephew doing?"

A slight hesitation in Verli's voice cast the blame squarely on Michael Slade. "He will pull through, although the doctors tell me there is damage to his heart."

"Sorry. Chris is a good kid. Give him my best." They said goodbye, each with their own thoughts.

Quade finished drying off and went into the bedroom where Isis was already packing his clothes in a carry-on suitcase.

"Not too much, honey. I don't need a lot. I've got to get right back."

As he got dressed, she said nothing, but he could tell she was crying. When he finished dressing, he came over to her and took her in his arms.

But she pulled away and began mechanically refolding his clothes. "She'll hate me even more when she finds out. Is that why you didn't want me to go with you? Because it might upset her to see me over there?"

"No, it wasn't, and you know it, honey. You never have flown, even just up to Atlanta, much less over the Atlantic Ocean. That trip up to Atlanta was the farthest you've ever been except up to see…you know. It's best if you come with Kenya. Believe me, Sheldon will take your mind off anything. He'll probably end up flying the plane if you're not there. Can you just see Piglet as co-pilot?"

"Don't try to be funny with me, Quade. Why don't you say it? Say Michael, damn it! Say he's human garbage! Say he kidnapped his own sister! Say he tried to kill me. Say he's crazy!" She whirled around to face him, a person in agony, her face contorted in grief and rage. "But he's still my son!"

He tried to calm her down but even then he knew it was futile. When Isis was upset it was like a storm that had to abate within itself. "Shhh, you'll wake up Rudy. Big game tomorrow. You know he counts on you to be there for him. So stay here and see him play. I'll go see when I can bring our girl home. Everything will be okay, I promise." They both knew it wouldn't.

"You go to hell, Quade! I'm not going at all then. Go to Faun then. That's what you both want, isn't? She's always been Daddy's little girl, Faun has. You want her all to yourself, well, go ahead since it was my son who did that to her. My crazy bastard son."

Isis collapsed on the bed in convulsive sobs. He called Kenya and her warm voice answered immediately, no trace of sleepiness there. She sounded like a cup of hot chocolate on a cold day. Quade apologized for waking her up.

"Honey, you're talking to a night owl here. Nighttime is when I start howling at the moon. What's wrong? Any word on Faun?"

He told her briefly about the phone call from Zurich and Kenya said. "I'll be right over."

Moss called into Kenya' phone. "Yeah, I'm coming over, too." The big detective sounded jazzed, even happy. "Always wanted to see the Alps up close."

"How'd you know I was going to ask?"

"Kenya's going to stay with Isis until it's time to leave so Isis don't get cold feet and I want a piece of Michael Slade. Now get off the phone and let me get ready. We're outta here."

Quade got off the phone wondering if his line was tapped. He tried to kiss his wife goodbye but she just buried her face in the pillow. Her sobbing continued as he went downstairs to wait for Kenya on the porch. Looking up, he thought the early morning stars looked back without pity at the millions of human tragedies taking place on earth at that very instant.

Chapter 27

Faun spent two months in the hospital and another two in the Verli's home, recuperating from her injuries. In that time, Quade and Moss were joined by Isis, Kenya, Pearl, and Sheldon. Isis had immediately changed her mind after Quade had left, and surprised everybody by behaving as though she were a world traveler.

"I could have sworn she was part of the jet set, until the plane took off." Kenya looked around to see everyone waiting for the punchline. "Then I swear if the windows on that plane opened, she would have jumped out. As soon as the drinks cart came around, she ordered two brandies and that's the last word I heard from our girl until we landed."

"I made it though." Isis slid a look at her husband. "But I think I'll go home by boat."

Through her agent, Kenya had rented a luxury apartment close enough to Lake Zurich to walk. When she wasn't entertaining the Verlis with stories about her life on the road, Kenya was entertaining the night life of Zurich at a little bar the size of a phone booth where all the hip people hung out. Her act was reviewed by a well-known music critic as the next Lena Horne, then the offers to perform began streaming in to perform all over Europe. Most were legitimate.

Michael Slade was caught by police at the border where he was being chauffeured by Remi. He was still wearing the long blonde wig and clutching a bag containing Faun's hair. He was first hospitalized, but when the hospital's computers mysteriously crashed and he spit on a nurse, Slade was transferred to an asylum outside the city to await trial for kidnapping, conspiracy to commit murder, attempted murder, and human trafficking among lesser charges.

Bjorn's parents had come over also and, as soon as he was released from the hospital, planned to take him home to Mayo Clinic. Chris's mother Brigitta and sister Clara got together at the Verlis' flat. Like most of the real estate in Zurich, the flat was priced by its proximity to the lake and the view. Otherwise Mrs. Bjorn thought it resembled her hotel room.

"I don't see any trace of you at all here, Clara," Birgitta said to her sister. "We grew up on the farm with pictures and cats and plants all around."

"And frilly curtains and chintz slipcovers." They shared a laugh, but the moment was sobered when Clara grew silent, wiping the smile from her face. "And puppies and kids. Dad used to say it was like living in Kipling's The Jungle Book except there weren't any mongeese in Minnesota. No, there isn't anything I can relate to here." She peered around the flat as though seeing it for the first time as a metaphor for her marriage—sterile and devoid of passion. "Nothing." Abruptly rising to her feet, she found the smile again. "How about some coffee, Birgitta? Genuine Columbian Swiss Mocha. Then you must tell me all the news from home."

After a brief rundown of the gossip about friends and family, Mrs. Bjorn asked to see Faun. As Clara explained to Isis later. "I should have known that meant trouble. My sister has always been known for her bluntness, regardless of who she is hurting."

Standing just inside the doorway to the ornate bedroom, Mrs. Bjorn, a short, wiry woman with short, wiry hair, surveyed the girl on the bed.

"So you are the one my son gave up his promising career for." Mrs. Bjorn stood looking at Faun, her arm and leg still in casts. Her hair had grown back somewhat darker. All the anesthesia she had been given Isis had said. It was now two inches all over, giving her a Peter Pan look. "I hope you are never free of pain. It will be nothing compared to what our dear Chris has suffered. After all, it was your own brother who did all this to him. I hope to God they hang him."

So saying, Mrs. Bjorn turned and left the flat without uttering another word. Clara went down to the door until her cab came.

When she returned to the second floor, she peeked-in on Faun who she thought was sleeping and then went to clear up the coffee things.

Kenya and Pearl came back with all sorts of bags and bundles. They had been out shopping while Isis entertained Sheldon at the lake watching little boys sailing their toy boats.

"I believe I could get used to Switzerland." Kenya had bought one of each of a display of toy sailboats after Sheldon said he wanted one.

"You'd change your mind in the winter," Clara replied, marveling at American extravagance.

They tiptoed in to find Faun still asleep, snoring, her good arm hanging off the bed. As Isis went to adjust her daughter back on the bed, she noticed a pill bottle on the floor. The lid was gone and it was empty. It was Faun's prescription for pain medication. Isis knew what had happened immediately and she screamed to Kenya. "Call an ambulance! Faun's overdosed!"

Together they lifted Faun's inert body between them while Clara called the hospital, then Quade's number whose phone was out of range.

ↄↄↄↄↄ

Quade and Moss were headed out to the private asylum where Michael Slade had been moved. When they got there, after going through a series of interrogations and ID checks, they were ushered into an impressive office to see the director. Dr. Weiss was a tall, balding Swiss who greeted the two Americans with urbane condescension.

"You had no trouble finding us? Swiss roads can be a bit baffling to visitors."

"You try the roads around Memphis sometime, Doctor." Moss enjoyed the puzzled look on the director's face.

"Memphis? Surely you don't mean—"

"Egypt? No, Memphis, Tennessee, USA, sir. That's where I'm from. Now, he's from Georgia." Moss indicated Quade with a nod. "Georgia's roads are even more baffling than Tennessee's because the people there don't speak English."

Dr. Weiss gave a high-pitched dry laugh which said he didn't get the point but never mind. He detested the small talk Americans thought they had to make. It wasted his valuable time. "So you've come to see Mr. Slade, I take it?"

"This isn't a friendly visit, Doctor." His silence was making the director uncomfortable as if the big American with the scarred face was mentally x-raying the walls of the place. "We're police, law enforcement. I'm Chief

Walker and this is Detective Moss of the Memphis City Police. We're here to see Mr. Slade."

"I understand, but you see, Mr. Slade is a Swiss citizen. He is entitled to have legal representation whenever—"

"Is he here?" Moss leaned forward slightly. Since their combined weight and height could easily crush him, Dr. Weiss took a step backward behind his massive walnut desk.

"Of course." Weiss blinked rapidly behind thick spectacles. "At least, I think he is still here. Let me check."

"You think? Were you aware he was under arrest for murder, Doctor? That's a very serious charge, at least in the States. There's no thinking about it." Moss scooted forward to the edge of his leather chair like a quarterback on point for taking the hike. "So is he here or isn't he?"

"Hold it, man. Let him check, will you?" Quade put his hand on Moss' arm. "Calm down, big guy."

Dr. Weiss picked up a clipboard and held it as though he intended to defend himself with it in case things got ugly. He also pushed the alarm buzzer under his desk drawer. The office door swung open and two burly attendants rushed in.

"These gentlemen are leaving. Escort them to the door, please."

But Moss didn't budge. "He isn't here, is what you're telling me, right?"

Dr. Weiss spoke with new confidence, now that he had backup. "Mr. Slade checked out just shortly before you arrived. He posted bond, two million Swiss francs, I believe. His lawyer cited extenuating circumstances, his health being fragile. You see, given his physical condition, the judge just couldn't believe him capable of such actions."

Moss was developing an attitude that wasn't lost on the attendants. "Naturally, he isn't capable of killing somebody himself, but he can sure pay somebody else to do it. How could you let him go from here even if the judge set bail? Man is bat shit crazy. You know that, don't you, Doc? Bat shit crazy, and he's not finished killing people yet. Not while he's still breathing."

Weiss tried for sympathy from these two Neanderthals. "That may be so, but that will take many months to prove in court and Michael—Mr. Slade doesn't have long to live. Weeks, in fact. Days, even."

"Twenty-four hours is too long for that dude, if you ask me." Moss got out of his chair and the attendant looked ready to tackle him. "Come on, Quade. The inmates are running this asylum."

Quade was just getting warmed up after absorbing all the negative vibes Dr. Weiss was exuding. "Let me guess, since you are on a first name basis, this isn't the first time Slade has been here, is it, Dr. Weiss?"

Weiss hesitated just a millisecond. "Gentlemen, Michael Slade owns this hospital. That is to say his company Biopharma owns it. I dare say he can do what pleases him. As you Americans say, I just work here. Now, if you'll excuse me, I must make my rounds. I bid you *auf weidersehen.*"

ୠୠୠ

They were on the outskirts of Zurich when Moss got Kenya's phone call about Faun. Quade kept his eyes on the road, negotiating the speedway traffic.

Moss answered in his usual noncommittal voice "We'll be right there. Isis doing okay?"

"Depends what you mean by okay. She's hanging in there, that's about all." Kenya closed her eyes and turned away so that Isis couldn't hear. "You all hurry, ya hear? Fly!" She wiped away the tears that slipped between her lashes. "Oh, I need you, Abe." She rang off and sobbed against the wall.

Quade looked over at Moss who was looking straight ahead, phone still in his hand. "What's up? Anything wrong?"

Before he could bring himself to answer, Moss put his phone back in his pocket. "Nothing you can do anything about, bro. Nothing you can do anything about except maybe pray."

ღჳღჳ

Faun was in a coma for nearly a week while they flushed the medication from her body and kept her on a respirator. By the end of a week, she was breathing on her own again. She still hadn't opened her eyes.

Isis hadn't left her bedside and Kenya shuttled back and forth with clothes, chocolates, and food which she ended up eating herself. "You never know, when she wakes up she may want something sweet, and I made her some gumbo from my own recipe."

After a few brief visits, Moss felt like a fifth wheel, no comfort to the grieving mother or the unconscious girl. The only person he could do anything for was Kenya, and he did just about anything, including watching Sheldon run three nannies off. When he had enough of shrieking women running out the front door, their hair standing straight out, crying, "Kleine Schwarze!" Moss decided to put an end to it. He turned an appalled Sheldon over his knee and whacked his bottom ten times. By the tenth smack, he got a satisfactory howl and tears. Turning the now enraged culprit loose, he said. "If I catch you so much as even thinking you're not going to mind an adult,

I'll do that again, and I'm gonna keep on whaling on your butt until you're a nice kid to be around because right now, nobody can stand you."

Sheldon burst into tears. "Oh yes, somebody can!"

"Your mom don't count, if that's who you mean."

"That's all you know! Piglet can, that's who! And I want to go home. Now, ya hear me? Right now, this minute!"

Quade was equally awkward, akin to a wild animal finding itself in sudden captivity, prowling the sterile corridors of the hospital, as if he was looking for a way to escape from his own helplessness.

Finally, Moss got a call from Lorenz. "My friend in the American Embassy tells me he has a lead on Michael Slade's whereabouts. Appears Herr Slade is in Germany where he's seeking treatment for his heart."

Moss grunted in disgust. "Didn't know he had one. Go on."

The urbane Swiss got the joke on the up-tick. "I love the American sense of humor. Anyway, what is interesting is he has made reservations on a commercial airline flight for next week. From Zurich to Atlanta. Thought you would like to know."

"And your police are just going to let him leave the country, just like that. Man, if I were a criminal, let me live here in good ol' Switzerland."

"I admit it seems a little strange, even to me, and I was born here. But what can they do but let him go? He has posted bail, David Anderson said, and he must be allowed to seek treatment."

"Do you know the date and time of the flight?" Moss scribbled it down in a notebook and hung up.

When he heard the news, Quade said. "That's when the doctors said we could take Faun back to the States. On Wednesday. The hospital's already arranged the flight for us, but not if Michael's going to be on it. I wonder what his game is this time."

"I thought she was, you know, not ready yet." Moss tiptoed around the fact that Faun Walker was still. "What with the cast and everything."

"When she wakes up, they'll put in her in a walking cast. The sooner she starts walking the better." He grimaced, as if his old war wounds were kicking up again. "That way we'll know if there's any permanent damage."

"That's tough. But she's young and otherwise healthy, I bet she'll be fine." Moss felt the urge to slug somebody or break something. Instead, he just reached out and gave Quade's shoulder a punch. "I mean it, man."

"Yeah, with stuff they can fix. I'm worried about what they can't fix."

"Hey, you know what's gonna fix you and me up? Some of Saranjii's chicory coffee and pecan pie."

"And short stack and two sides." Quade grinned for the first time in a week. "I could handle that after the one boiled egg and toast that passes for breakfast around here."

"But first, we got to stop Michael from getting on that plane. Any plane. Anywhere. Cause he's fixing to take a whole lot of people with him when he goes out, I'll bet."

ℰↃℰↃ

In the hospital room, Isis was alone with Faun, trying to concentrate on reading a book when Bjorn walked in. He was thinner and taller than she remembered, but a smile flitted across his face when he saw her.

"Chris! We thought you had gone back to the States."

"No, don't get up. Mrs. West called my mother and told her about Faun."

"I can imagine what Kenya must have said." Isis closed her book and set it on the table beside her. "She wouldn't have held anything back."

"You're right about that, but my mother deserved it. Faun and I were both victims, and we're going to get on with our lives now that they've arrested the guilty ones." His eyes strayed to Faun on the bed. Her eyes were closed, but on hearing his voice, she had stirred briefly. "May I?"

Isis nodded and Bjorn walked to the bed, bending over the sleeping girl. He spoke in a low voice and stroked her fingers sticking through the cast. Then he kissed her lips.

As he turned to go, he knocked a book off her bedside table. He bent over to place it back and found Faun looking at him. There was no recognition in her tranquil blue eyes, but slowly she looked from him to her mother as if trying to make some connection.

"Mrs. Walker!" He didn't have to say her name again. Isis was beside Faun's bed, running her fingers across her forehead, caressing her daughter's cheek.

"You came back to us! You've been gone such a long time. Now we can all go home." Isis included Bjorn in her smile. "Including Prince Charming here."

Faun tried a smile and her lips formed the word "Klutz," but in her eyes was a look of recognition and they rested lovingly on Bjorn.

❧❧❧

When Quade told Isis Michael had escaped, that he didn't have long to live, he purposely avoided telling her what he suspected her son was planning. His escape was enough to cause her to shiver.

"It was as if someone had walked over my grave," she told Kenya later.

They were standing on Kenya's terrace overlooking one of the grandest views of the city in the twilight, yet neither one of them could break through the feeling of peril Michael's name inspired.

"We can't leave, then." Isis gazed at the towering mountains without seeing them. "Not until we're sure he's dead. Isn't that an awful thing to say that about my own son?"

Quade put his arm around her shoulder, pulling her to him. "But I have to go back, honey. I've already used up all my sick leave. I've got a job to do and people expect me to be there, on the ground enforcing the law. Besides, I hate to think what the hospital bill is going to be like. Luckily, Faun's got insurance, but it's probably just a drop in the bucket, given how everything is so expensive around here."

Isis lowered her gaze to include her husband's face against the lingering sunset. Her long fingers traced the scars on his face lovingly. He thought again how beautiful she was and what a miracle it was that, of all men, he had been the one to marry her.

"You're right, we have to go back. I have a good feeling about it. Let's keep to the departure date the hospital has made for us. That way, we'll know if Michael has anything planned."

"That's one helluva way to find out. Wait just a minute!" Quade stopped and stared at his wife. "Why do you think he's planning something?"

Isis, the beautiful and wise, only laughed. Her laughter floated out over the city like the cool mist coming down from the mountains. "Because he's my son, that's why."

ʘʓʘʓ

Across the Atlantic, the bulldozer growled as it tore

through the underbrush of the Thicket. Coveys of quail and nesting marsh birds flew up and the men hacking down stripling pines wished they'd brought their guns to the job.

"Look at all that good quail going to waste," one of the crew shouted. "Tomorrow I'm bringing my rifle. That ought to bring a few of 'em down."

"Aw, you'd probably just shoot the foreman in the butt, anyway," another worker said. "No matter, there's a no-hunting sign posted back there somewhere."

"Gonna take more than a bee-bee gun to take that big oak down." The man with the chain saw indicated The Mama Tree. "That's one big son-of-a-bitch, ain't it?"

"What's that shit hanging all over it?" One of the crew, taller than the rest, reached up and snatched a small bag down from one of the low hanging branches. A few of the men gathered around the huge oak, pulling down the prayer bags, tearing them open.

"Hey, this one's made of old timey feed sacking. Got something inside, looks like sand or ashes or some such shit. A tiny rock. A sea shell."

"What the hell? This one's got a bone."

"Probably some kind of voodoo spell," said the man with the chain saw. He cut a tentative bite out of the tree and looked up at a blank blue sky. "Funny, I felt a few drops of rain. Don't tell me rain is coming."

"You must be wetting your pants," came the reply from another other crew member. "It's clear as a bell up there. Not a cloud in the sky."

"Hey, look at this!" Another worker crouched below the tree where the bulldozer had turned up a furrow of red earth like a raw wound. With the point of his machete, he dug a green soapstone jar out of the dirt. The men gathered to look at the artifact, so clearly out of place in this jungle.

"Aw, it's probably made in China," someone scoffed.

"Maybe it's got meth in it. Open it, see, man."

The worker ran the blade of the machete around the seal of the green soapstone jar. Sniffing the contents to the delight of the crew, he made a face and emptied Holly's ashes on the ground. "Just a bunch of goddam dust! No meth, no weed, dammit!"

A sudden gust of wind spun the gray dust upward and carried it off among the other trees. "Anyway, my girlfriend can put some flowers in it when I get paid. Nothing like some roses to sweeten her up."

"It'd take more than roses to make my wife put out."

The crew laughed and got back to work, but ominous clouds began to gather overhead, blocking the sun. Within an hour, they heard thunder sounding like a preacher on Sunday morning as he promised hell and damnation to sinners.

The foreman came in his truck to tell them there had been a tornado spotted coming their way and to knock off work.

The next day the bulldozer wouldn't start and it rained all day. The creek flooded as if in solidarity with the rest of the Thicket and the area became impassable. The bulldozer sank in the mud and had to be towed out, but the tow truck also got stuck.

The Mama Tree still stood alone, majestic as ever, with a scar in her side where the chain saw bit deep but, eventually, it healed. Grass grew up around her roots again and a new crop of children were sown that fall. She was a survivor, the tree seemed to say, a lesson her human counterparts needed to learn.

అఅఅ

Kenya was just getting too much of a rush from club

owners around town to leave just yet. She told Moss as much when he asked her to go back with the Walkers in a few days. She just didn't tell him why. Kenya couldn't admit there was still the little unwanted scarfaced girl from Julia Springs in her that found attention hard to resist. Accolades to her were like drugs were to Holly.

"All right then, get yourself another babysitter because I'm outta here," Moss said with one eye on Sheldon.

As if on cue, the little boy yelled. "I want to go home and see Piglet and Uncle Freddy! Yes, yes, yes, yes! Take me home, Mama! Right now!"

"Okay, that's enough, kid," Moss said. "She's got the point. 'Member what I said." As if he was Piglet and had a turn-off switch, Sheldon spun around and marched away.

"You got him programmed or what?" Kenya was dressed to go out in her slinky sequined gown with the neckline open nearly to the waist.

"You heard what little man said. He's wants to go home. I do, too. You could get just as many bookings in Atlanta if you tried."

"Point is, I don't want to, okay?" She knew he wouldn't fall for the tough act anymore. So she rubbed up against him like a cat that wants to be stroked, purring in a way she counted on Moss not to resist. "Baby, baby, back home I'm just a club singer, a prop for the piano player, singing has-been songs. Over here, I'm kind of unique, you know what I mean? A little bit of dark chocolate among all this white stuff the Swiss *think* is chocolate. I want to keep all my sweet stuff for you."

If she was expecting him to buckle under her irresistible charm, Moss disappointed her. He knew she didn't want to have sex with him right now. It would mess up her hair and makeup. So the whole point was to get her way, which Kenya was an expert at doing. *Except not when her life was at stake*, he thought. *Nobody is an expert at that.*

"I got to go, Kenya. So stay here and be a star. Do your thing. Meanwhile, I still got a job, busting druggies and prossies like always. But I'll be waiting. There's no one else in my life, except my daughter."

It was agreed by all parties that Kenya, Sheldon, and Pearl would stay on until the end of summer. Pearl and Sheldon would go to boarding school—Pearl to learn French and Sheldon to learn discipline.

Kenya engaged a nanny named Frau Schulz. "If anybody can do it, the Swiss can. I've never seen such tight-ass people in my life. They make the Southern Baptists look positively loose as gooses."

"Don't knock the Baptists." Moss was packing and Kenya was unpacking just as fast. "They chastise as good as anybody."

In desperation, Kenya grabbed Moss's arm as he tried to close his half-packed suitcase. "Please don't go, baby, ya hear? What will I do without you here to come home to? To hold me close?"

"Then come home. Really home. Back to little po-dunk what's-it's-name and be happy with me and ol' Piglet and the twelve dwarfs in drag." He didn't dare put his arms around her. His hard-won resolve would just crumble.

Kenya stopped pleading with him and turned away, pretending nonchalance. "At the end of the summer, that's when I'll come home, when Sheldon and Pearl finish school, when I've had my run. Unless I get a better offer, then I might just stay."

Moss made a negative noise. "Or until the Swiss send the SWAT team after Sheldon to deport him."

"That's mean. I'm sure he'll do just fine."

"I'm simply telling it like it is. You really think the tight-ass Swiss are going to stand for his mouth? Better send him home with me, big, black daddy don't take no backtalk." The words were no sooner out of his mouth than Moss wanted to retract them. Fortunately, Kenya pointedly ignored the suggestion and the inference.

Moss breathed again, feeling like an underwater diver coming up to the surface again.

෴

Isis would travel home with Faun by cruise ship when Faun was stronger, and Quade and Moss would follow the hospital's plan, leaving the following Wednesday. Faun's and Isis's names would still remain on the airline passenger list, but their seats would be occupied by two security guards working for Lufthansa.

Michael Slade's name still hadn't appeared on the passenger list and the flight was full with the exception of two first class seats. The airline had been advised by the American Embassy that Michael Slade was deranged, and not, under any circumstances, to let him on board. However, under international rules, they had to allow wheelchair access to anyone that requested it. Wheelchair-bound passengers usually occupied the first row of seats in first class, next to the toilet, with extra leg room.

Quade and Moss watched that area of the plane seating online and it remained empty. No sign of Slade. Just before the flight boarded, an elderly wheel-chair bound passenger accompanied by her companion was boarded ahead of those waiting in line.

"Would you look at that? Just as cool as you please. One thing you have to give Slade credit for, he's a master of disguise." Moss jerked his head at the elderly woman, a signal to the two security guards to follow her down the ramp and hold her outside the plane until she and her companion could be thoroughly checked. "I don't think that's him, but she could be carrying something that he could use to bring the plane down. Let's go."

When they got to the bottom of the ramp, everybody was talking at once in what seemed like a re-enactment of the Tower of Babel. The focus of the confrontation was the elderly passenger in the wheelchair, who was yelling at the top of her lungs in German and waving her umbrella at the security guards as if she was challenging them to a duel.

Quade shook his head. "You were stationed here in Germany. Can you understand what they're going on about?"

Moss said. "I think the old lady is either going to sue the airlines or kill one of the guards, or maybe both. The lady in the green suit is saying she, the old lady, can't be a man because she, the lady, has to change her diaper and she can guarantee the old girl is a girl. Anyway, if that's Slade, he's doing a good imitation of one of those old timey dudes in tights trying to skewer somebody with that umbrella. The Slade I saw could barely raise a finger to push a button, much less swing his arm like a pro quarterback. Or yell that loud either."

The gate attendant came down the ramp midway. "Mr. Walker, a telephone call for you. You can take it at the gate."

The two men looked at each other. "You take it," Moss said. "I'll stay here, just in case. I wouldn't put anything past Slade. Besides, I need to polish up on my German."

Quade picked up the phone at the gate desk.

"Fool," a quavering, breathless voice said. "You stupid ignorant hick."

"Michael?"

"Yes, it's Michael and don't bother looking around. I'm not calling from anywhere near the airport. Just wanted to save you the trouble of bothering that poor old lady thinking I was her. I'm only thirty-seven and I won't get any older. I'll always be young. And so will my sister."

"Listen, Michael. Don't, don't hurt Faun any more. Or anybody, you hear me?"

There was an eerie laugh at the other end, ending in a screech like a rabbit whose life has been cut short by an owl. "Who are you warning, stupid rube? You can't stop me and you know it. You're absolutely helpless. So long, sucker!"

"Michael! *Michael!*" Quade was standing there yelling into an empty receiver when Moss walked up.

"Where to now?"

Quade shook his head. In his dark eyes, Moss saw the man he had pulled out of the burning wreckage of a Humvee. The same pain, the same quiet suffering, the same guilt at not saving others.

"Never mind." Moss nodded toward the concourse. "Let's go get a drink. They got bars every square foot of this airport. One thing I like about the Germans, they know how to drink."

"But we've got seats on that flight. They're going to board pretty soon."

"You're gonna go with Michael still on the loose?"

"It could have been a pre-recorded call or somebody pretending to be him. Anyway, I thought we were going home together. I've got to, Moss, or I might as well kiss my job goodbye."

Moss was unmoved. "Either that or your wife."

As if he had made up his mind long before that, Quade laid it on the line. "Look, Isis is Michael's mother. She knows him as well as anybody. He won't do anything to her. He gets too big a kick scaring the hell out of everybody else, though. That's just his way of letting people know he's still alive. Besides, he's too sick to live much longer. At least that's what Dr. Weiss said. And Chris is there. He won't let anything happen to Faun."

"Yeah, I noticed how that worked out back at the Alps."

As they were debating whether to stay or go, one of the security guards came back to the gate. He was holding a small, laptop tablet. "We found this in the old lady's bag that was attached to the back of the wheelchair. She hadn't put it through the security scanner at airport customs. Claims she forgot it was there. Says it belongs to her nephew. Want to take a look?"

Moss and Quade traded looks. Quade said, "Better let airport security bomb squad do the honors just in case. They'll have to okay it before she gets it back." Quade turned to Moss. "You going or staying?"

Moss sighed. "That woman don't need me except to carry her luggage and babysit. And keep her feet warm at night. Come on, I guess we can get a drink on the plane."

An hour into the flight one of the security guards whispered in Moss's ear. "There was an explosion at Zurich airport, in the security office. No one was in there at the time, so no one was hurt. They think it was a terrorist attack. All flights are grounded until further notice."

Quade looked half asleep until Moss shoved an elbow at his arm. "I'm getting another round."

"Make mine a ginger ale for me. I think my stomach's back at the airport."

"That ain't all we left back at the airport." Moss told him the news.

"Good old Mike. He almost faked us out. What's airport security always saying? Something like if a stranger tries to give you anything, report it."

"Yeah, it doesn't say anything about a nephew though. Looks like the security guards are making their move on the old lady now. Watch that one in the green suit. I noticed she's got calves like a man. I think I'll go to the restroom in first class." Moss got up and moved ahead of the plainclothesmen toward first class.

One of them told him to get back in his seat.

"But I got to pee and when you've gotta go, you've gotta go." Moss continued ahead of the two, pretending he was drunk to the amusement of the passengers. Another man was moving toward him from the first class section. Moss recognized another undercover guard.

"What's the trouble, sir?"

The woman in the green suit was looking around the side of her seat to see what the disturbance was. In the half light, her features looked distinctly masculine, her jaw rock hard with muscle. She had kept her alpine hat on, Moss noticed, bulling his way down the aisle, pushing the man aside who tried to block his way.

Moss was big and dark, a force to be reckoned with, and the security team decided to let him pass to the bathroom rather than risk a scuffle. As he drew level with the old lady and her companion, Moss suddenly lurched and tumbled drunkenly across their seats, pulling the hat off the woman's head as he went down. Her hair came with it, revealing a partially bald head of a man.

The passengers gasped as the pair grappled in the seat, falling into the aisle. Moss pinned the much smaller man to the floor. "Cuff him, somebody!" When the man under his knees kept up a string of curses in German, Moss slammed his head on the floor. The man went limp under him.

The old woman seemed to awake from her nap, and reached into her carry-on bag attached to the wheelchair to take out her umbrella. What happened next seemed to take place in slow motion as the guards rushed forward to handcuff the prisoner Moss had pinned to the floor.

As they gathered around Moss, Quade shot past them and did a flying tackle across the old lady's lap. There were two muffled barks of a silencer in rapid succession, a squeal like a rabbit pounced on by a hawk, and Quade's body slumped down, his big, scarred hands still gripped around the old woman's neck. The woman's head lolled at an odd angle, the gray wig askew, and the umbrella with a pistol attached to its handle clattered to the floor.

Both Michael Slade and Quade Walker were dead—Slade of a broken neck and Quade Walker shot through the heart.

Chapter 28

When the plane landed in New York, Moss stayed with his friend's body, which was taken by ambulance to a nearby hospital. He gave NYPD detectives the story of Michael Slade as best he could, leaving out the part about his birth.

Kenya, Sheldon, Isis, Faun, and Bjorn were on the next flight. Faun, like her brother, was in a wheelchair, her head lolling around as if she found it too heavy to hold up. When they all arrived at the hospital, Isis went to sit by Moss until they could visit the morgue. She found him with his head in his hands, his face wet with silent tears. In comparison, she seemed to be remarkably composed like a marble likeness of herself. She leaned her silken head on Moss's shoulder, her voice barely above a whisper.

"Don't," she whispered. "He would have wanted it this way, saving other peoples' lives, protecting us. You saved his life, so he just paid it forward. That was the way he was. He always said God meant to keep him here until he did something special. See? I bet he never told you about the time he tried to kill himself. That was what brought us together. That's what made me trust him enough to leave Lesbos and go out into the world. Because he was there to protect me, I didn't have to worry what people said about me. I didn't care. I had Quade. He was my strength, my wall to keep everything out, and I was his. We needed each other like you and Kenya do. Now my wall is gone and I've got to face the world by myself."

Moss shook his head. "I got to disagree there. Kenya doesn't need anybody. Just a babysitter and a butler. And a good manager. Kenya is her own damn wall."

"I'm here, aren't I?"

He raised his head and saw Kenya, standing there, holding Sheldon's hand. The child's eyes were very big as he looked around the waiting room of people who had come to claim people in the morgue. Then he went to sit beside Moss, peering up at his tear-stained face. "Are you crying? Mama says big boys don't cry."

"Well, your mama's wrong, little man. It's okay to cry when you've just lost a friend."

Not sure how to comfort a grown man, Sheldon took his hand in both of his small ones. "Like I lost Piglet?"

"Kind of. But Piglet's waiting for you at home, you'll see him when you get there. My friend won't be around anymore, see? He's reporting for duty someplace else."

"But where? Doesn't he see how sad that makes you? You ought to tell him to come back."

Moss looked at the little hands holding his. "Wish I could."

Hearing the gravel in Moss's voice, Kenya said. "Sheldon, hush. Don't ask so many questions."

Moss pulled the little boy up on his lap. "It's okay, Mama. We got to talk, me and little man here. Correction, my friend's going to be around every time you or I or Auntie Isis or your mama needs help."

Sheldon shook his head and rubbed his eyes. "But I thought that was what you were for. I'm confused."

A hospital social worker called across the waiting room. "Mrs. Walker, you can come with me."

Isis stood up, took a deep breath, and then looked at Moss.

He held Sheldon close to his chest as if he needed the child's comforting. "I've said goodbye on the plane. Want me to come with you?"

Isis took a deep breath as if she were going to jump into a river. "No, I'll do it alone. I've got to begin sometime."

He watched her walk away. "He always said she was the most beautiful woman he ever saw. I agree."

Kenya nodded, sending tears cascading down to collect in the corners of her mouth. "Come on, Sheldon. Let's get you some dinner. Or breakfast. Oh, I don't even know where I'm at." She tried to smile and tasted salt.

Sheldon slid down from Moss's lap. "I do, Mama. Come on, I'll take you there. We passed the coffee shop as we came in."

Isis arranged for two funerals, one for her husband, another for her son. Quade's body was to be viewed at the funeral home and then cremated in a Native American ceremony afterward. His ashes were scattered in the Thicket.

Michael Slade would be interred at a private ceremony at Lesbos, his grandmother Lois presiding. Isis surprised everybody by calmly going about arranging for her son and her husband to be buried. Too calmly, Kenya observed to Moss, who shrugged off the implication that there was something wrong with that.

"That's how he would want it. If she was a mess, he couldn't leave in peace. She knows that. It's like she was almost expecting him to go that way." They were in Kenya's king-sized bed, sharing a bowl of popcorn and watching TV. "He just was paying it forward, she said."

"Like soldiers wives, yeah?"

"Kinda like that, yeah."

They munched in silence.

"Would you expect me to be like that? Like a marble statue?"

Moss shook with silent laughter. "Girl, you ain't no statue that's for sure. More like one of those geysers in Yellowstone Park. What do they call it, Old Faithful?"

She hit him with a pillow and he swung it back at her. The phone rang and the voice mail said. "Miss West, this is Anita Blackstone. You don't know me, but I own Anita's African Styles in Atlanta. I do your sister's—I take it Toya's your sister—hair and, after she left yesterday, I found her little baby in his car seat in my dressing room. I tried calling her but her phone is turned off. The baby's okay, but I don't want to call DFACS because if I do, she won't get her baby back. I know that for sure. She's on drugs, I guess you know."

"Oh, my god!" Kenya extracted herself from Moss's arms and picked up the phone. "I'll be right there!"

Moss looked at her, flailing in the over-packed closet for something to wear. "I suppose you want me to babysit?"

Kenya turned around, three hangers pressed to her chest to cover her nakedness in a sudden fit of modesty. "Say what? No, I expect you to come with me like any decent husband would do instead of lying there like a big bump on a log! And pack Sheldon up in a blanket. He's got a new baby brother. Tell him he'll have to like it or else! Now, which dress should I wear, the red one or polka dots?"

"Well, I like red—" Moss suddenly choked on popcorn. "Wait, you just said husband!"

Kenya turned back to her closet with a smile. "Fine, I'll wear the polka dot one. I'm glad you finally made a choice."

೧೦೮೧

Cleared of all charges, Bjorn went back to finish his doctorate at the state university and Faun went with him, not as a student—she seemed to have given up all ambition for the moment—but because she couldn't bear to be parted from him. Bjorn knew that he was temporarily a stand-in for her father as her protector, and he flourished in the role.

On the other hand, he knew that one day, when all her wounds were healed, physical and mental, Faun wouldn't need protecting anymore. She would be her take-charge self again, picking up her research where it had been interrupted, pursuing the patent for her mobile application for genomic testing. For the interim, she was content to take a few classes on line and wait for him to come home, keeping the door locked and bolted until she heard his knock.

As Michael Slade's empire unraveled, it created a seismic wave in the international business community. Under the international banking regulators' scrutiny, many of his scientific ventures came under fire.

The National Institute of Health in Washington, DC found faulty scientific data from questionable experiments, many on human subjects without their consent. As international scientists probed deeper, it came to light that patients in many of his hospitals had had tissue biopsies or organs unnecessarily removed and used in Slade's laboratories for research without their knowledge.

It appeared that Michael Slade had devoted millions of dollars to finding, not a cure for ALS, but merely a protocol that would prolong his own life.

In a curious sort of reverse body-snatching, he had directed all hospitals in his network to admit patients with ALS free of charge, whether they had insurance or not. Usually, their insurance had run out and their families were happy to shift the burden of care to the hospital. Buried deep in the paperwork, however, few if any noticed a doublespeak sentence that included the patient's agreement to experimental treatment. The latter included surgery to biopsy tissue from various parts of the brain.

Slade's final gesture of charity also included dying paupers, the indigent, and refugees. They turned out to be a control group for ASL patients as their burials were at public expense and no expensive autopsies were performed.

Records and assets were immediately frozen, medical staffs bailed as one by one, Biopharma owned hospitals in four different countries were shut down. The ripple effect caused ancillary businesses such as All-4-A-Dollar stores to close down as well.

In the Thicket, the bulldozer sank deeper into the boggy marsh, looming just above the hole it had dug for itself, like a prehistoric beast caught in a tar pit. In the playful summer breeze, the prayer bags and medicine bundles danced joyfully from The Mama Tree's branches. It was as if the hands that hung them there had formed an invisible barricade around their beloved tree, preserving it for another generation.

Chapter 29

In the town of Julia Springs, Grover Moss settled down to such a level of domesticity that his mother came down from Memphis to see for herself.

At first inspection, Celia Moss told friends back in Memphis that Magnolia Alley looked more like a boarding house than a home. In addition to baby Jonathon, there was Freddy, Sheldon, and Ashley Pearl who had come back from boarding school in Switzerland with a skiing instructor named Nicki in tow.

Then Kenya found out she was three months pregnant, nearly blowing Moss out of the ballpark and scandalizing Mrs. Moss who demanded her son marry the mother-to-be without delay.

The ceremony took place at Glory Road Church in September, outdoors because of the overflow of guests. It was Kenya's idea to let Isis plan the entire thing.

"Give's her something to do to take her mind off her grief and for the town to see her as something else besides the wife of Chief Walker," she told Moss.

Freddy was best man, Ashley AKA Pearl and Faun were bridesmaids, and Sheldon was the ring-bearer. He wanted to bring Piglet along but Isis firmly drew the line, allowing Piglet only to serve drinks at the reception.

"That ought to clear out the faint-hearted," Moss said. "To see this three-foot high waiter on wheels carrying a tray full of rum punch around. On the other hand, the hardline drinkers might head for the good stuff at the bar."

The reception was held at the city park since the whole town was invited. Saranjii's Place catered the Low Country Boil with two kinds of wedding cake and everyone said it was the best wedding they had ever been to.

To prove it, they filled the to-go boxes to the max with everything on the buffet table.

"They always say it was the best wedding they'd ever been to." Kenya kicked off her satin heels to dance with her groom. "It's considered bad manners not to, even if the whole thing was a disaster."

"I thought when Sheldon didn't want to give up the ring, disaster was on the way. But somehow Freddy talked him into taking it off and giving the ring to him. Wonder what he promised him?"

"That he could dress Piglet up as a ghost tonight, put his Halloween mask on him, and scare your mother into going back to Memphis. She made him take a bath this morning and scrubbed behind his ears is why he's got it in for her." Kenya smiled up at him as he took her in his arms. "I told Freddy to get her a motel room."

"The old girl'd probably just tell her church circle she exorcised a demon." Moss mirrored her smile the way he mirrored her moods. Everything about this woman echoed in him like the sound of laughter in an empty cave. "Whadda you say let's get this party started, Mrs. Moss."

They took a turn around the dance floor, which by day was a basketball court. Isis and the people from Lesbos had transformed it into a fairy tale pavilion with col-

ored lanterns lighting up the city park and candles floating in the public pool.

"I never thought I could be this happy," he said,
beckoning to the crowd to join them. "Kinda scares me,
you know what I mean?"

Kenya made a face as if he had stepped on her toe.
"No, you're not, you're bored. Admit it."

"A little, but in a good way bored. It's nice for a
change. Beats busting druggies." He tried to shut her up
with a big grin. It didn't work.

"I've been thinking."

"Oh, no." Moss twirled his bride around, showing off
her blue garter. "Couldn't you just give it a rest? This is
our wedding, for Pete's sake."

Kenya's topaz eyes were already miles away, mirror-
ing the candles in the pool. "No, really. I've been thinking. Quade's job comes up for a run-off election next
month and I think you'd make an excellent police chief.
Isis says so, too. She says Quade would want it that way.
What do you say? That'll keep you busy and out of my
hair."

"Out of your hair? And what will you be doing, Mrs.
Moss, besides looking after little Moss, Sheldon, and
Jonathon."

"I've already picked out a name for the baby, Abraham Junior, and I'm getting ready to make Magnolia Alley into a recording studio. My own record company. My
own label. It's going to be called Slo Ride Productions."
She looked up at him with her naughty smile.

"Does that means what I think it means?" Moss
sighed and shifted down to a slow dance. "I guess being
the chief of police of a one-horse town is better than being Mr. Chantal West and changing dirty diapers. Besides, I've already turned in my application."

"You bastard." But instead of fire, there were only

little flames of affection in her eyes. With a little giggle, Kenya snuggled close to his chest. "Wait till I get you home."

"That's exactly what I'm waiting for. But just so Piglet doesn't interrupt us, I've booked a hotel room in Macon. The bridal suite, as a matter of fact."

"I want to make one stop along the way, though."

"I figured you'd want to change out of that wedding dress, no matter how beautiful you look, R&B princess."

"No, I want to wear it. You'll see why. Just let's go, okay?" The urgency in her eyes told him not to argue.

Kenya sprinted for the car, rice raining down her back, screaming in delight. Moss got behind the wheel of her Cadillac and they drove away, tin cans trailing behind them. Outside of town, Moss got out to cut the tin can trailers loose, and Kenya slipped behind the wheel, still in her veil.

"I've got to go see The Mama Tree," she said. "To let Aya and Holly see me dressed up like a bride. And you, naturally. And to bless our marriage."

"If it's that important to you," he said with a sigh, "then let's go."

They parked in The jumping-off place, now renamed Tanner's Point, the way towns have of renaming things after prominent people, confusing the locals who still call by its old name.

Moss watched as Kenya put on her satin pumps. "You're going to get those shoes all muddy." He knew by the distant way she looked at him, she was under the spell of the Thicket already.

"You sound like your mother," his bride said. He could already see the cat fights looming.

"Sorry."

He let her lead the way into the living, breathing green entity, knowing he should be in front, but also knowing she had grown up here. He remembered that night outside Lesbos where he was wandering lost, nearly falling in to the murky looking water of the creek, afraid of stepping on alligators and snakes until he was rescued by the captain of the Amazonian guard, the delicious Hazel.

Kenya looked around at him as though reading his mind. "Don't worry. Miss Snakebutt Hazel is playing right guard on the Belgian All Stars. And she's got about twenty little Belgian boyfriends."

"Only twenty?"

"Don't be funny."

They passed Lesbos which looked more than ever like an apartment complex than a commune. On down along the creek where Kenya began to sing to the alligators coughing on the banks. "Baby, hold on to me. The future's not ours to see…"

Finally they got to The Mama Tree, and there, Kenya let go of his hand. He watched her go hang a little white satin bag on one of its branches, standing there a long time. Through the chorus of frogs and crickets, Moss heard a sibilant whisper as though his wife was singing the words of a childish song. He no longer felt like a fool, standing there in his rented tux, ooze settling into his patent leather shoes. *The place has a definite spell,* he thought. *As though thousands of voices were offering up prayers to the stars above and, in return, the stars were raining down blessings. My church-going Baptist mother would call it ancestor talk, the same way her mother had referred to the sibilant whispers in the trees.*

Presently, Kenya came back to stand beside him. Taking his hand in hers, she raised them to the night sky. "Aya and Holly and all the rest who have gone before, here stands my husband and I, asking you to bless our marriage and our baby. Holly, we have avenged your death and you can rest in peace, knowing that the people responsible have been brought to justice. Aya—"

The spell was shattered by the sound of Kenya's phone ringing in the beaded purse dangling from her wrist. It was the opening bars of "Blueberry Hill," Holly's ringtone.

"Don't answer. It's probably Sheldon wondering where you are. Go on with what you were saying, honey."

"No, it's Holly. I know by her ring tone." Kenya fumbled in her purse' Taking out her phone, she said, "Holly? Is that you?" There was a long silence. "Hello? Who's calling?"

After another long pause, a man's voice answered, "Sorry, wrong number."

About the Author

Even as a child, Trisha O'Keefe was impressed by the inherent power of alternative medicines. Indigenous healing practices are an ongoing theme in her novels. As a native Southerner, O'Keefe claims to have "a lot of red dirt" flowing in her veins. Growing up, she spent summers on her uncle's farm in South Georgia, "mainly getting into trouble." That trend has continued throughout her life. After traveling abroad for fourteen years, running into revolutions or governmental coups nearly everywhere she went—even Britain was in the midst of a labor strike when she moved there—she returned to the States. She is the daughter of Jimmy Jones, a well-known journalist for the *Atlanta Constitution* under Editor Ralph Magill. One of her earliest memories was the sound of a typewriter rattling away in the middle of the night. You would think that would have cured her from ever putting two words together, let alone a book. Still, at age six, she co-wrote *Spot, The Dog* with her sister, followed a long time later by *Hanahatchee, Poseidon's Eye*, and *Love Song of the Chinaberry Man*. Two more novels, *The Magi's Well,* and *The Mama Tree* will be published in 2016. "I guess some things you can't cure," O'Keefe says. "You just have to go where they take you."